THE
AWAKENING

The
Awakening

Dorine White

Skyrocket Press

ISBN: 0692296077
ISBN 13: 9780692296073
Library of Congress Control Number: 2014916927
CreateSpace Independent Publishing Platform
North Charleston, South Carolina

Skyrocket Press
Saugus, California

For my family

KYLER

Something was wrong. The short hairs on the back of Kyler's neck stood up, straight and tall. He glanced toward the dense forest that bordered his aunt Martha's property. Large evergreens crowded every inch of land not tilled for farming. For some reason the familiar-looking trees loomed dark and foreboding, and he couldn't shake the feeling that he was being watched. He narrowed his eyes, looking for the source of his troubles, but nothing surfaced. With a shake of his head, he returned to weeding the garden, taking comfort in the familiar yet annoying task.

His first chore of the morning, by his aunt's decree, was to take care of the herb garden. He'd rather be sleeping—what teenager wouldn't? Looking at the kiwort plant in front of him, he made note that most of the leaves were spotless. There was still time to save it, if he could find the bug eating its leaves. If he didn't, his aunt would know. She was freaky that way. He looked at the forest one more time, crossing his arms over his chest and staring defiantly at the tree line. Then he bent over the plant.

Under the bottom leaf, he spotted a caterpillar, its fuzzy little body inching its way toward a morning feast. Kyler pinched the culprit between his thumb and index finger and popped it. Green slime oozed down his fingers, slick and gooey. He wiped his fingers down the front of his shirt, and a greenish-yellow smudge joined other stains of dirt and grime.

Rays of sunlight filtered through the sky, dancing off Kyler's sandy-blond hair and hitting the garden with welcome light. His blue eyes squinted as he glanced up into the brightness. He flexed his arm muscles, feeling tendons stretch and skin pull. Farmwork was dull, but it had its advantages. He was well built for his age, and he could tell by the way the girls in the village eyed him that they felt so, too.

As he moved on to the next plant, he felt that odd sensation again, as if something was watching him, and not in a friendly way. Goose bumps broke out on his arms, bumpy and rough. He whipped around to surprise whatever was watching, ready to pounce, but again he saw nothing. He decided to finish his work, and fast.

"Here's your water. Hope you like it." Martha insisted Kyler talk to the plants as he took care of them. She believed it helped them grow, though he thought it was odd. But at the moment, he was talking loudly, thinking to scare off whatever was near. If it was an animal, the sound of a human voice should chase it off.

He cast his thoughts forward into his daytime schedule. After the garden came lessons. At least he got to sit down for a while. Martha had insisted he know how to read and write. In fact, for his sixth birthday his aunt had given him a leather-bound notebook with a brass clasp. She'd told him it was for writing down his thoughts and, of course, the names of all the plants she wanted him to memorize. He'd used it as a door-stop until she caught him. Now, he carried it in his side pouch, ready for any spur-of-the-moment Aunty quizzes.

Kyler moved on to the last plant in the row. It was an ugly shrub with gnarled branches and dark green leaves with black specks. *Splash!* Kyler dumped the rest of the water over its roots.

"Done."

He walked away slowly, not showing any fear. He even paused, brushing off a speck of dirt from his pants. After resuming his casual stride, a large shadow passed overhead, blocking out the sun. Kyler stopped and then peeked at the sky through his fingers. A gigantic bird soared among the clouds. Its proportions seemed all wrong, but Kyler couldn't tell exactly what bothered him, other than that it was the largest bird he'd ever seen. It circled the farm twice before flying off. Kyler shook his shoulders and then strode for home, trying to project an outward calmness to anyone who might see him.

KYLER

The black ink dripped from the end of his pen into a little dark pool on the paper.

"Careful," Aunt Martha's voice floated in from the kitchen.

Man!

"If you make one mistake, people will think you wrote *fish* instead of *kettle*. It can screw up the whole meaning of things." A short woman entered the room, wiping dusty hands on her apron. Her patchwork dress of bright reds and brilliant blues billowed out around her like a tent. She had a round face and cherry cheeks. No one could miss the family resemblance in her and Kyler's eyes; however, where he was lean and muscular, she was plump and stocky. Her smile lit up any room she entered.

Aunt Martha walked up and put a chunky hand on his shoulder, squeezing gently. Her eyes scanned his work, missing little.

"You did a pretty decent job, considering the big blot of ink in the middle of the page."

Kyler looked up at his aunt. "These lessons should have stopped years ago. Boys my age are apprentices. Some fifteen-year-olds are already engaged. I don't see what good it will do me to learn all these words. You're the only person I know who can read."

"Kyler Birkwood!" Martha gestured around the room. The den was filled with curiosities and a monolithic bookcase filled with old books. A meager fire sputtered in the den's fireplace across from where Kyler sat. Around his lesson table were books piled in little towers. "What would you do?" asked Aunt Martha. "Live here with all these treasures around you and not even know what they said?"

Kyler looked around the room at Martha's beloved books. A threadbare oval rug adorned the middle of the floor, covered with parchments and manuscripts. Martha's overstuffed comfy chair sat near enough to the fire that she could stay up late reading while keeping her toes warm. What Kyler wouldn't give to be surrounded by girls instead of books!

Across the way, two far doors stood open. One led to the kitchen, where Kyler could smell the mouthwatering results of Martha's baking. The other opened into a hallway leading to their sleeping rooms.

"What good will they do me? A farmer doesn't need to know how to read."

Aunt Martha snorted.

"Words are more than just images on a page. They can have a life all their own."

"You keep telling me that, but they haven't helped me yet!"

Martha walked across the room to the bookcase, her apron bow swinging as she went. Pointing a stubby finger along a row of books, she unconsciously stuck out the tip of her tongue as she concentrated. She stopped at one of Kyler's readers from several years ago.

Her fingernail scraped its spine before she finally pulled the book out and walked over to him. It landed with a plunk on the table, and a puff of air floated his writing paper to the floor. Martha licked her fingers and started turning pages. When she found what she was looking for, she turned the reader and pushed it toward Kyler.

"You know more that you think." Her finger pointed to a word at the center of the page. "Read it."

"*Fire.*"

"Right. Now picture the word in your head?" Kyler rolled his eyes. Aunt Martha knocked him in the back of the head. "Close your eyes."

He sighed but closed his eyes. The lovely image of Julia flashed before him. She was hot. A smile tickled the corners of his lips.

"Are you concentrating? Can you feel its heat?"

Kyler refocused his thoughts. Soon sweat began breaking out in little droplets on his forehead, and heat began radiating from his head.

"Now, picture the word *fire* in your head and say the word."

"Fire," breathed out Kyler from between parched lips. Suddenly the room grew warmer. Startled, his eyes flew open and he looked around the room, but everything appeared the same.

"Dude! You had me going there for a minute. Nice try, Aunt Martha." Kyler stood up and kissed her on the cheek as he headed off toward his bedroom. "I'm going to lie down. I feel really tired. All this studying, I guess."

"Right, dear. You just go and lie down awhile." She laughed. "Reading can really fry your brain!"

Almost to the doorway, Kyler paused to glance back at his aunt.

"I forgot to mention that there was something out in the woods today. I think it was a large bird, but it seemed awfully strange."

"Did you get a good look at it?"

"No, I just saw its shadow as it flew toward the forest, but it felt wrong."

"I'm sure there's nothing to worry about, but I'll ask around next time I head to town."

He knew he'd placed his information in capable hands and went off to take a nap. *Strange*, he thought. He was never this tired so early in the morning, and he felt surprised that Martha hadn't scolded him.

KYLER

Crisp leaves broke under his toes as Kyler strode through the dense forest. Everything felt peaceful as the afternoon sunlight filtered through the trees, and the air smelled of damp earth. His thoughts turned toward the village dance taking place later that evening. He planned on dancing with Julia.

He hurried along, making his own path through the forest, cutting through the growth with ease. In his hand he held the wooden walking stick that Aunt Martha always had him carry on their walks. At first he'd protested, but he had soon figured out that when she said she wanted to take a walk, she meant a *long* walk. Now, the staff felt comfortable in his hand. Its smooth surface reassured him as he gripped the well-worn wood. He didn't even need to think about catching himself from a misstep. He naturally corrected his balance with the placement of his staff.

Kyler could hear from the slowing of Martha's steps that she was almost ready to call it a day. His intelligent blue eyes scanned the area ahead, looking for anything he didn't recognize. He sniffed the air. It was slightly cooler and mustier here. Maybe there was water nearby? He pushed on past the bush in front of him, just as he heard Martha's footsteps stop altogether. She hadn't said anything yet, so he went on ahead.

As he moved around a tall tree, his left foot slipped out from under him and he went down into a wet, sucking mud puddle. He'd find nothing interesting there. But mud meant water, and water meant animals. He strained his ears, listening for movement. Nothing.

"Kyler?" his aunt's voice called.

"Over here, Martha! I took a bit of a dive." Using his staff for leverage, he pushed himself up off the ground with another sucking sound. Mud fell off of his pants and splattered onto the ground, heavy and wet. He wiped off his forehead with a little piece of shirt that had escaped the mud bath. As he leaned over to pick up his side pouch and notebook, he noticed something on the other side of the muddy depression.

"Hey, Martha!" he yelled. "Come look at this."

After sidestepping the puddle, Kyler walked around to the other side to get a closer look.

"Don't touch it! I'm almost there."

"No worries. It's just some prints in the mud." Kyler took a closer look at the tracks, his mind curious because he could not identify them. They looked like those of a large animal, but each footprint revealed only three marks, like the talons of bird. His aunt's shadow enveloped him.

"I think it's something new," he said.

"Move over and let me get a look." Martha did her best to assume a squatting position at his side.

A heavy silence filled the air, and then Martha suddenly stood up, turned, and walked away.

"It's time for dinner. Let's hurry home."

"What about the tracks? Weird, huh?"

"I'm not sure. I need to look in my books. Now, hurry up. It's getting dark."

"What?"

She continued on her way, but Kyler could sense something wasn't right.

He didn't let the issue drop. "What kind of tracks were those?"

Martha didn't answer, nor did she slow her pace. Kyler couldn't get a word out of her.

After dinner he was in his room getting ready for the dance. He'd just wound his belt around his waist when Aunt Martha stepped into the room.

"Where do you think you're going?"

Kyler cocked his right eyebrow. "The dance."

"Oh. Sorry. No can do. You need to stay home with me."

"What?" Kyler spread his arms wide in anger. "You've known about it for the last few weeks."

"Kyler. I rarely put my foot down. But this time I need you to trust me. There's something going on, and until I find out what it is, you're staying close to home."

"Give me a break. I'm not a kid, and I can take care of myself," he said, scowling.

Emotions played out over Martha's face. Finally she bowed her head. "You're right. You're old enough to decide for yourself, but you go straight there and come straight back. No detours."

"Agreed." He stuck a sprig of parsley in his mouth and gave Martha a hug. "Stop worrying so much. I'll be fine."

MARTHA

The first hour after Kyler left for the village dance, Martha walked in circles around the living room. When she realized she was getting nowhere, she stopped and focused.

Why can't I shake the feeling that something is wrong?

She walked over to the bookshelf and began scanning titles. Her book collection was very rare. So rare, that if old friends knew, they'd raid her house and take every last work. Kyler was right about no one else in the town having books, but Martha's family wasn't originally from this area. Though that was all Kyler had ever known about them.

She sighed, the pressure of secrets and of ages past weighing on her shoulders.

"He's old enough to know," she told the flames in the fireplace. "But I wanted his father to tell him. My stupid brother really made a mess of things."

She thought about her younger brother and his wild, prankster ways. He'd played the worst jokes on her when they were little, and he'd gotten away with it, too.

"Where are you now, dear brother?"

Kyler's parents had been scheduled to return from one of their expeditions more than two years ago. He was old enough to travel with them now, or to be sent to school. Martha would miss him, but he was getting too old for her to watch. His stance on going to the dance was a sure sign of his growing independence; however, the more time that passed without Kyler's parents' showing, the more worried Martha grew. It wasn't unusual for them to be gone for years at a time, off trekking in the wild, but she knew her brother had wanted to be around for Kyler's thirteenth birthday.

The feeling of unease returned, and Martha turned to her pile of books. The tracks Kyler had found in the woods had set off warning bells in her head, but she didn't know why. It was time for some research.

KYLER

The next few days passed oddly. Ever since they had come home from their long walk, Martha had been digging through her books. She hadn't even reminded him to do his chores. He'd done them anyway, but no more than necessary.

He dropped his spoonful of soggy stew back into his bowl, sloshing broth over the sides.

I wonder if Julia can cook?

Kyler cleaned up his meager meal and washed down the kitchen table. The room seemed empty without Martha puttering around. The normally cheerful fire was out, and dishes were piled up in the sink. *I did my part,* thought Kyler. *I cleared the table. I'm sure Aunt Martha will get to the dishes soon.* He swatted at a fly buzzing around and then watched it land on his latest addition to the kitchen sink. The unpleasant smell of rotten food and mold filled the air. Time to go.

In the living room, everything was chaos; everywhere he looked, open books lay askew. Kyler's aunt had her nose dug deep into a dusty old bundle, and from its yellowed pages, Kyler guessed it was hundreds of years old.

"I'm off to bed."

Martha didn't even bother looking up as she waved him off.

With a shrug, Kyler walked into his room. Outside he could hear the wind kicking up and the quiet tapping of rain on the roof. He added a few logs to the fire before climbing into bed. Soon, the rain picked up its tempo and the wind howled. He could hear it striving to pass through his shuttered window. A sharp whistling began when it finally achieved its goal. The eerie sound echoed through the room, causing Kyler to pull his covers up higher and snuggle down deep. A moment later he was asleep.

BANG!

Kyler shot straight up in bed, blinking away a sudden flash of light. His heart thudded like crazy.

BANG!

The walls trembled and a picture fell down with a crash. *It's just a storm*, he thought. *We've been through plenty of those.*

HOWL!

Kyler sprang out of bed with a lurch. That was not the wind! He pulled his blanket off the bed and wrapped its warmth around him. He slowly tiptoed out of his room, looking for Aunt Martha.

As he approached the den, Kyler slowed. He could hear noises coming from the room beyond: voices, and more than one. He peeked his head around the corner, but then jumped back.

In the living room, Martha crouched over a ferocious wolf. Blood dripped from its fangs, and its claws dug into her thigh as it kneeled in front of her. After taking a deep breath, Kyler grabbed his staff from the wall and leapt into the room.

"Aha!"

Martha looked up with surprise. "Put that thing away and go get me some towels!"

Huh? Adrenaline still racing through his veins, Kyler rocked on the balls of his feet, ready to charge.

"Kyler. Towels."

He took a moment to breathe before putting down his staff and then he turned toward the kitchen. Upon returning, he watched as Martha cradled the beast's snout in her hands, and then craned its neck so she could look into its eyes.

"I've got the towels," he stammered. The iron-rich scent of blood filled his nose, and looking closely at the wolf he could see chunks of loose fur and long gashes tearing through its side. The wolf was seriously injured and its pain-filled howl cut through the air as Martha tried to use the pressure of a towel to stop the flow of blood.

"Go back into the kitchen and get my bag of herbs from under the sink."

Kyler shrugged as his mind reeled. She really seemed to care what happened to this wolf. He turned around and headed back to the kitchen.

Now that he'd collected himself, he was almost bowled over by the stench of the dirty dishes that hit him. He pushed aside the curtain under the sink to find a well-worn black bag. It was full of Martha's dried herbs. She never knew when she would be needed as a midwife or at someone's sickbed, so the bag was always ready. To Kyler the bag always smelled of oregano. Usually he enjoyed the smell, but today the reek of the dishes overwhelmed the fragrance. He grabbed the bag and hurried back to the den.

The wolf didn't look as frightening now, lying there injured, curled into a ball. Kyler noticed the way Martha carefully wiped away the blood, cleaning the fur, leaving a clear area to be treated with the herbs. He placed the bag at her side and then took a step back.

Martha crushed some herbs in her mortar, pounding the mix into a poultice. Gently she applied the medicine to the wolf's tattered body. Each time her fingers smoothed the concoction onto its wounds, the wolf tensed in agony, its eyes squeezing shut. Kyler expected another piercing howl, but instead the wolf accepted its treatment with only a whimper.

When the beast was covered in herbs, Martha went to get some hot water from the fireplace, and placed it in a saucer. She added some herbs from her bag and made a quick tea. Holding the saucer under the wolf's nose, she tried to get it to drink.

"You've got to drink this. It will ease the pain," Martha begged.

Talking to wolves. Talking to plants. What will she talk to next? wondered Kyler.

The wolf began to lap up the tea, its coarse pink tongue whipping in and out of its mouth. Within seconds the creature had visibly relaxed, and a shudder ran through its body.

"Thank you."

What was that?

"Aunt Martha, did…did the wolf talk?"

Martha nodded as she placed the saucer of tea onto the floor. She then rested the wolf's head on a rolled-up towel and softly stood. The animal had fallen into a deep slumber, its breathing heavy and strong. Martha headed for the bed-rooms, motioning for Kyler to follow.

"We'll let him sleep awhile," she whispered when they'd reached Kyler's room. "His head is so full of pain, we probably couldn't make heads or tails of anything he told us." Martha settled herself onto the foot of Kyler's bed and patted the empty space in front of her. "You should sleep, too. The storm will leave behind lots of surprises."

In all the excitement, he'd forgotten about the storm. There would definitely be a lot of fallen branches and debris to clean up in the morning. Last summer's big storm had taken the chicken coop and tossed it into Mr. Salmen's field. It had taken weeks to find all the chickens.

"B-but," Kyler stuttered. "I swear I heard it say thank you."

"You did, dear. We'll discuss it all in the morning. For now get some sleep. Walter should be ready to talk after a good breakfast."

"Walter? Who's Walter?"

"The wolf, dear. His name is Walter. He's an old friend. We went to school together."

Is she fooling me?

"Go to sleep. It will all be clear in the morning." She walked out of the little room. "I hope," he heard her mutter under her breath.

"Did you say something?" Kyler asked. She didn't answer.

Who can sleep on a night like this? Nevertheless, it wasn't very long before his eyes drooped shut.

KYLER

By the time Kyler arose the next day, the sun was high in the sky. He yawned. A remembrance of something tickled his brain, wanting to surface. There was something he needed to think about. He rubbed the sand out of his eyes as his mind slowly focused. A dream? No, not a dream. A wolf.

He ran from his room, hopping on one foot and then another as he pushed his feet into his shoes. The floor was always cold until the heat built up and warmed the house in the late afternoon. He ran into the den as awareness flooded through him. There, in the middle of the oval rug, lay a large black wolf. It had streaks of gray throughout its coat. At least it looked gray. It was hard to tell with all the dried poultices on it. The wolf raised its head at Kyler's entrance. Intelligent eyes looked out through an animal's face.

Martha's footsteps sounded in the kitchen, and then a vision of blue entered the room carrying a tray for afternoon tea. Martha looked like her old self again. She'd obviously done the dishes, because he hadn't left a single clean bowl or cup on the shelf. She smiled at him as she went over to the wolf. After placing a saucer in front of the hairy animal, she then sat down in her comfy chair.

"He's very much improved today," Martha said between sips of tea. "If he'd gotten here any later, I don't think I could have saved him."

Kyler looked from his aunt to the wolf and then back again. It had definitely not been a dream last night. "You said his name was Walter."

"That's right."

"This is so weird."

"Well, let me start at the beginning. There are so many things to tell you." She glanced at the wolf. "Walter, join in whenever you want."

The wolf blinked.

"When I was just a girl..." Stopping, she shot a look at Kyler. "Don't even ask how long ago! Anyway, I went to school. It wasn't just a normal school like they have in some of the big cities. It was a school for, shall we say, gifted and privileged children. My second year there, I made a wonderful friend named Walter."

"The wolf?" interrupted Kyler.

"Yes, but he wasn't always a wolf." Martha smiled at Walter. "He was a very kindhearted boy who protected the newer students from bullies. He had short black hair and stunning green eyes. If he wasn't in class, you'd find him in the forest with the animals. He had a way with shy creatures, whether animal or human."

Walter nodded his head and then spoke up. "One day I took a nap in the sun and had this strange dream. I envisioned my body slowly lengthening, my nails growing sharp, and I even sprouted fur. When I woke up, I found it hadn't been a dream at all. I had really turned into a wolf." Walter grinned at Kyler. "Turns out I was a shape-shifter. I'd just taken a little longer than most to find my true talent."

What? thought Kyler. *A shape-shifter?*

Martha picked up the story. "As the years at school went on, he spent less time as a human and more time in the shape of a wolf. The teachers warned him to be careful."

"There's one problem with shape-shifting. If you keep the shape of an animal too long, you lose the ability to return to human form," said Walter.

Aunt Martha shook her head, remembering. "One day I heard that Walter had permanently transformed and had been expelled from school! It was awful. The teachers had warned him about it so many times."

Walter went on. "I'd done it on purpose. I felt so much more alive as a wolf. All of my senses were heightened, and I much preferred spending my time in the forest."

Martha patted Walter's head. "He visited me throughout the years. Weren't you running a wildlife preserve?"

"Naturally," Walter said as he shifted into a more comfortable position. Kyler still could not believe he was hearing words come out of a wolf's mouth. Walter looked at him knowingly. "It takes a little getting used to."

"But who attacked you, Walter? I've never seen an animal come against you," asked Martha.

"That's what got me into this mess. I was so confident in myself I didn't think to take precautions."

"What happened?" asked Kyler.

The wolf licked his lips, and slobber collected at the side of his jowls.

"Just over a week ago, animals began swarming into my valley. At first I thought it was some freak migration, but with a little investigation things took on a whole new picture. I followed their trails. After several days I started to find animal carcasses.

"We'll, I wasn't about to stand for it. I've had peace in my valley for over twenty-five years! I set out immediately to stop whatever had scared and killed these creatures. In my pride I thought I could deal with whatever was out there." The wolf shook his head. "I was wrong."

Walter's body trembled. "I continued searching and found a large nesting area. Bones were scattered on the ground around and inside the nest. I started to creep up on it. I could smell nothing alive around me, so I wasn't concerned. Some of the bones looked odd to me. I stepped on one and it scratched my side. I looked down to see a human hand jutting out from a bush. It was picked clean except for the fingernails!"

Kyler dropped into the chair next to his lesson table.

"I wondered what animal could have done this. What would hunt both man and beast? As I got closer to the nest, a breeze floated by, and I could hear a flapping sound. A new, rotten stench rose up. Seconds later I was hit from above. Claws raked into my sides. I put up a pretty good struggle. Even so, I was ready to say my prayers when the flying beast suddenly tilted its head, as if listening to something far off. A second later it flew away, leaving me a mangled mess. It probably planned to finish me off when it came back, but I wasn't about to wait around. I'd wandered far from my valley, so I headed straight for Martha's. It was slow going. Many animals had to help me along the way."

"I'm glad you thought of me, Walter," said Martha. "Any idea what it was that attacked you?"

"As I inched my way here, my brain ran over and over the details of the fight. At first I thought it was a flying lion, but then again it had three frighteningly long talons on each foot, not paws."

"Did you say three claws?" Kyler quickly looked over at his aunt. Her face had grown quite pale.

"Yes, three sharp flesh-tearing talons. It took me a while to figure it out, but I remembered a story I'd heard as a child. It was about a flying creature with the body of a lion, sharp claws, and a beak. It was the companion of Mordrake the monster. Stories say it fought by his side in battle and craved the taste of fresh blood, human or otherwise."

Aunt Martha's head shook up and down. "I was afraid you were going to say that. I've been digging through all my books and have only once seen a reference to a three-taloned beast. It was in an old bedtime story."

"What was it?" asked Kyler.

Aunt Martha's voice and Walter's sounded at the same time.

"The Griffin."

MARTHA

T he next morning, Martha stood in the doorway of Kyler's room waiting for him to awake. As the sun broke through the window and cast a bright beam onto her nephew's closed eyes, he finally sat up and stretched.

"No chores today," she said and then dropped two satchels on the floor. Both were filled with clothes. "Hurry up and get dressed. I've got breakfast in the kitchen."

She was packing herbs into her medicine bag when he shuffled in for food. She shared a smile with Walter as he lounged near the oven pit, soaking in the heat. Kyler pushed more satchels out of the way as he filled his plate with sausages and eggs.

"What's happening?" Kyler questioned. "Where are we going?"

Martha stopped what she was doing and looked at him. "Walter and I are going on a trip. You are going to school."

"School?"

Martha nodded her head.

"Something has come up and I need to go check on it. You'll be safe at the school with another one of my old friends. It's the school I was telling you about yesterday. Your father went there, too, you know."

"My...father..." stammered Kyler. "I didn't know that."

"Think of it as a chance for a little investigative research. Your father was a pretty popular fellow. There's probably information about him somewhere at the school for you to find."

She was baiting him, but she knew the chance to find out about his father would be too much for him to pass up. When he was five, his parents had decided to explore the world without him. They'd popped in every now and then, bringing treats and souvenirs. When he was eight they had come to visit and told him marvelous stories of their adventures. They'd seen ice giants in the North and discovered a race of gnome-like creatures to the west. Martha knew that Kyler thought they were made-up stories, but now, maybe he would see the truth.

"Okay. It can't be all that bad. How long will I have to stay there?"

"Trust me. It will be as quick as I can make it." Martha smiled.

"When do we leave? Do I have time to tell Julia good-bye?"

"Sorry, no. We leave right after breakfast. I've already packed your bags."

"But..."

Martha didn't give Kyler time to finish his sentence before she headed out of the room.

The party of three set out two hours later. Martha shuffled behind, leading their old donkey, Sam, their travel gear strapped tightly to the animal's sides. The donkey's back swayed and was bowed heavily from years of labor. Kyler walked ahead with his side pouch thumping against his hip. He gripped his staff tightly, and Martha knew he was angry about their abrupt departure. She'd made sure he brought his notebook and plenty of socks. Walter loped casually back and forth between Kyler and Martha, scouting ahead and keeping them company.

It was a pleasant morning, sunny and bright. The previous night's storm had cleared the air, and the scent of pine filled Martha's lungs. Birds chirped in the trees and there was a light breeze ruffling her hair. It was a good day to start off on a new journey.

They traveled for days before reaching the school. Kyler had stopped complaining after the first day. She was proud of him. At night when they sat around the campfire, she'd seen how bad his blisters looked. As they neared the city, she could see the excitement growing on his face. It was strange. She'd grown up here, so it was like coming home, but for Kyler it was the unknown. First they passed several small cottages and ample farmland. A bit closer to the city, they passed shops and several craftsmen. There was even a trader's market. Colorful banners swayed in the breeze, announcing different shops. As they came around a bend in the road, Martha watched Kyler's eyes as he finally beheld the school.

Before them, the road led upward toward a plateau and the school. Upon the green grass stood several stone buildings. Even though they were all connected, they appeared to have been built in a haphazard fashion, each appearing different in age and architecture. More had been added since Martha's time as a student. Some rose tall and majestic; others were squat and long. The area around the school was beautiful.

Large evergreen trees faded off into the horizon, and a lake surrounded by more trees poked out from behind the school's stables. Off to the side was a large field where horses munched on green grasses.

A large circular area was roped off nearer to the school in which several boys fought with swords, battling one another under a teacher's watchful eye. Martha could hear the metal clangs echoing on the air. Students walked between the stone buildings while a few taller people wearing black robes talked among one another. Martha couldn't help but smile. She'd left for a good reason, but the scene was so nostalgic.

Martha continued on down the path and stopped in front of the largest building, its door hanging open like a huge mouth. Through the darkness, a tall man in a black robe emerged. He had a thin build, like that of a scarecrow, and a tidy brown beard. His eyes were dark and deep set. Martha smiled in glee.

"Ernie!" she yelled. Having reached him in fewer than two steps, she was now giving him a big hug. Walter hung back, waiting to be noticed, until with a whoop the tall man jumped his way.

"Walter, you old goat! It's so good to see you."

"You, too, Ernie. I take it you got the pigeon's note?" said Walter.

Ernie smiled. "Just this morning. I've barely had time to get a room ready for the boy."

Martha pushed Kyler forward. "Thank you. I owe you one. He's a good boy. I think he may surprise you."

"Any relation of yours is always welcome. We'll take good care of him." He took Martha aside and continued, "If what you wrote is true, haste is necessary. If you can bring back evidence that Mordrake and the Griffin are awake, we can bring it before the council of mages. I doubt they'll believe you otherwise. To everyone today the story of Mordrake the monster is just a fable."

"I know. But I sense something is happening." Martha looked toward Kyler. "Take good care of my boy."

"Take care of yourselves, too. I want both you and Walter to come back safely," said Ernie. "Don't take any chances."

With a quick hug and a kiss good-bye to Kyler, Martha turned away and headed back down the path. Walter followed quickly behind.

KYLER

Upon taking a deep breath, Kyler followed Ernie into the main building. He had nowhere else to go anyway. Quiet fell heavily upon his shoulders as he stepped into the huge room. Paintings lined the walls, rich carpets covered the floor, and gilded furniture completed the decor. Kyler stared. From the outside, the school had looked pretty ramshackle. Now, it was like entering another realm.

"Breathtaking, isn't it?" Ernie commented. "This is our main hall. You can get to any room you want by passing through a doorway. Just think about the room you want as you step through, and you'll end up where you should." He winked. "At least we haven't lost anyone yet."

Kyler opened and closed his mouth like a fish, but no words came out. He'd never imagined such wealth. Then Kyler processed what Ernie had just described.

"Isn't that magic?" Kyler whispered.

"You'll find a lot of things here are magic. Didn't your aunt tell you? This is the Conservatory of Magic." Ernie looked at

Kyler with an interesting expression. "You had no idea, did you?"

"No," Kyler answered. "She just told me this is the school where she and my dad went."

"That's true enough," said the tall guide. "Both of them were fine mages. We also have many students who are not magical, but are noble born"

"Martha knows her herbs and stuff, but magic...come on."

"Your aunt is very gifted. She graduated first in her class. She was even on the council of mages until she got fed up with all the bickering and retired to the country."

"Really? I mean, there's Walter and everything, but I just can't see Aunt Martha doing magic."

"I'll tell you all about it another time," said Ernie. He turned and began walking toward a far doorway. "Right now we need to get you settled in your room. Then there are placement tests, but considering your family heritage, I'll be excited to see what you're capable of."

Kyler followed Ernie through the doorway and stepped into a long hallway lined with doors. He looked back the way he he'd come. The doorway shimmered with a hazy gray aura.

"This is the dorm area," Ernie explained. "You just need to follow the doors until you find one with your name on it." The two walked a little ways, listening to laughter and instrumental music coming from behind many of the doors.

Each door was different. The first one he passed was pink with bright yellow flowers. The next had live grasshoppers swarming in waves back and forth across the wood. It boggled his brain. Every ten doors or so was a student alcove filled with sofas and comfortable chairs. The walls were painted a coffee-colored yellow, and large stained glass candelabras hung from the ceilings.

Students lounged about with their stocking feet hanging over the sofas and homework in messy little piles around them. Some students sat cross-legged on the floor in small study groups. All of them ignored Kyler as he passed, but he couldn't help but admire some of the girls.

Farther down the hall, the door decorations grew more amazing. From one door covered in grass Kyler could hear crickets chirping and see dandelions sprouting out in little patches. Even more intriguing was a door with a moose head mounted on it. It was impossible to tell where the wood ended and the moose began. They merged into one as the knots of the wood turned into the hair patterns of the moose. *Amazing!*

As Kyler walked by the door, the moose head swung to face him, its big brown eyes staring at him intently. "No one's home. Go away."

Kyler tripped backward. Ernie only grinned. After a few more wondrous doors, they arrived at a door of plain undecorated brown wood with the name Kyler painted in black along the top of the frame.

"Here we are," Ernie said as he pushed open the door. "Home sweet home."

Kyler hesitantly stepped into his new living abode. White walls stared back at him, stark and empty. To his left a lumpy mattress rested on a rusty bed frame. A pillow, two folded sheets, and a brown blanket were stacked neatly on top. A desk and chair that had obviously seen better days sat in one corner and an old beaten wardrobe in the other. Completing the ensemble was the shabby rope rug that lay in the middle of the floor, its colors faded and dull. The only thing not drab about the place was the sunlight pouring in from the sole window.

"Don't worry about it." Ernie patted him on the shoulders. "You'll find the room takes a while to get to know you. Once it's got you pegged, you'll be surprised at what turns up. We just start you off with a blank slate."

Kyler was not convinced. *How can a room get to know me?*

"Thank you, Ernie," he said. "I'm sure I'll be fine."

"Time for your first lesson. All teachers here are to be addressed as either 'master' or 'madam.' So call me Master Ernie. I'll let you unpack. You'll find your bags already in the wardrobe." He turned to walk out, but glancing back he said, "You see, it's getting to know you already." Then he headed out.

Kyler looked around the room. *What did he mean?* Then he saw it. On the windowsill, where nothing had stood before, sat a potted plant. And not just any plant, the minty aroma of a starplant filled the air. He smiled as he seated himself on the bed.

After unpacking his few possessions, he decided to go exploring, and took off down the hallway. *Let's see...where to? What about food?* Kyler thought about a kitchen as he went through the main hall doorway, and stepped into a room bustling with activity. The scent of fresh baked bread filled the air, reminding him of his aunt Martha. Light streamed in from many vertical windows, bathing the room in a cheery glow. Across the way, a large hearth covered almost the entire back wall. Pots of all shapes and sizes hung from the rafters, and baskets filled with grain dotted the floor. Kyler heard the sound of pounding and chopping over the squabble of chickens. He could guess what was for dinner that night.

A large woman in an apron called out, "Darcy! We need more firewood! We've got to get the oven blazing!"

Within seconds a girl entered the kitchen from a side door, struggling with an armload of split logs. Her face was smudged with dirt, and sweat circles were visible under her arms.

After brushing a stray tendril of auburn hair behind her ear she spoke, "I just finished this pile." She dropped the load in front of the hearth. "I'll have another done before evening lessons."

I wonder who she is? Kyler admired her glistening red hair, until the girl snorted and headed back outside.

It was time to explore somewhere else, so he stepped back through the doorway, thinking about books. When he emerged, he was in the most wonderful room he could ever imagine. Despite all his griping, he loved books, and here were shelves and shelves of them.

"May I help you? Is there a topic you're interested in?" said a little old lady with spectacles from behind a pile of volumes. She seemed friendly, but her hair was tied back into a bun, giving her a severe appearance. "I said, may I help you?"

Kyler sputtered, "Um…Herbs, I'd like a book on herbs." *Man*, he asked himself, *why'd I choose that?*

"That wasn't so hard, was it?" The librarian walked away, talking to herself. She returned a few minutes later with a book covered with plant pictures. "This is the herbal index. Just find what herb you're interested in, and it will tell you what books we have here in the library and what shelf to find them on."

He took the book and opened its pages. A basil leaf shined up at him. He immediately recognized the plant, but he couldn't understand the symbols next to it. They looked nothing like what Martha had taught him. Confused, he turned to the middle of the book. There was a picture of a mandrake root. The symbols next to the picture again made no sense. He shut the book in frustration. What good was a book if he couldn't read it? *Dude…*He recalled a certain lecture from his aunt on that very subject. He placed the book on a nearby table and walked back through the door. He forgot to think of anything as he went through. There was a moment of darkness, and then he stepped out into the dormitory hallway. *I guess there's a fail-safe,* he thought.

He walked slowly until he found his door. It wasn't hard to miss. Its plainness stuck out like a sore thumb. Inside the room a piece of paper floated in the air above his desk, a note from Master Ernie. With a stretch, he grabbed the paper from the air. It said he needed to report to the headmaster's office—not that he knew where that was. When he'd finished reading the note, it floated out of his hand and landed on the desk, right next to a new potted plant that smelled of jasmine.

KYLER

Kyler stepped into a large room cast in shadow. There were no windows, and besides a few candles, most of the light came from the flickering waves of fire in the hearth. Rows and rows of books lined the walls. He faced a large desk, behind which sat three teachers in their black robes. He recognized Master Ernie on the right. He glanced at the robed figure in the middle. The man was very old, one-foot-in-the-grave old. He had a long white beard and a wrinkled face like a dried apple. Gnarly fingers poked out from under his cuffs, and he exuded a sense of power.

Kyler shifted his attention to the woman on the left. She had a crooked nose and two double chins. She wore the hood of her cloak low over her brow, casting a shadow on her forehead. Her long brown hair flowed from either side of the hood and ended halfway down her front. Kyler didn't know what to do, so he just stood there.

Phlegm crackled as the old man cleared his throat.

"Welcome, Kyler. Master Ernie has recommended you to our school."

Ernie smiled at Kyler, and a little of the tension left the room.

The old man continued, "I am Headmaster Lex. You already know Master Ernie, and this is Madam Maxine. She is in charge of new students and placement. It will be her job to make sure you find a place at our humble school.

"You will not see Master Ernie much. He is in charge of advanced students." Master Lex leaned back and gestured toward Madam Maxine. "Would you please explain placement to him?"

"My pleasure. It's very simple," she began. "First, we'll give you some passages to read and ask you some questions. Your reading skill and comprehension will be judged for placement in general classes. Second, we will ask you to complete a task for us. How you attempt to solve the task will give us clues about your magic potential, if you have any." Madam Maxine rose and crossed the room toward Kyler. She handed him a single sheet of parchment. "Please read this excerpt aloud."

Kyler looked down at the paper in his hands. His confidence left him in a rush as he recognized the same symbols he'd seen in the library book. Little beads of sweat broke out on his forehead. They expected him to know this stuff, so why didn't he? *What's Aunt Martha been teaching me?* He tried to decipher the writing by squinting. Maybe this is a test. Maybe there's a hidden message. He turned the paper to the side. It looked even worse from that angle. He turned it over and held it up to the light. He recognized nothing. Madam Maxine cleared her throat.

"We haven't all day."

He had to say something. "I'm sorry, but I can't find the hidden message."

Master Ernie shifted uncomfortably in his seat.

"There is no hidden message," Madam Maxine replied. "It's a passage written in basic common. Are you telling me you can't read one word from that paper?"

Pride welled up inside Kyler. He wanted to explain that he knew how to read. That his aunt had begun teaching him to read and write when he was six years old. He wanted to slam the paper down on the desk. He wanted...but the proof was right in front of his eyes. He couldn't read a word.

"Yes, Madam Maxine. I can't read this paper."

"Well now, that's going to cause us all sorts of problems." Madam Maxine looked over at Master Ernie and gave him a disapproving look. She stacked all the papers before her into a neat pile. "I guess we won't need the rest."

"Isn't there something else I could try reading?" Kyler begged.

Madam Maxine shook her head in the negative. "That was a level one primer. Students four years behind you are learning it." She looked at the old man. "I think I'm done with my part. We'll have to place him with the first-year students. He'll be the oldest in the class, but there's nothing we can do about it. I can't place him into any other classes until he learns the basics."

Master Lex nodded his head in agreement. "I don't think there's any point continuing on with the placement. Even if he has some magical potential, we can't train him to use it until he can read his textbooks."

Kyler felt dejected. How was he to make friends when placed into a class with youngins? All the other students his age would make fun of him. He had to try something.

"Please let me take the magic test," he begged. "Just let me try."

Madam Maxine puckered her lips to say no, but Master Ernie spoke first. "Why not? I can't see the harm in it."

Her seat creaked as Madam Maxine sat farther back in her chair, her eyes speaking volumes. Kyler could tell she thought this was a waste of time and wanted to be back with her class, teaching students with potential.

Master Ernie stood up and walked toward Kyler. He placed a candle into his hand.

"Now light it."

Kyler looked at Master Ernie's hand. There were no matches in his palm. *How am I supposed to light a candle without matches? Wait, they said "magic." But I don't know any magic, do I?* He focused on the candle.

He remembered his aunt's lesson where he pictured the word *fire* while silently speaking it within, but the wick stayed clear. Nothing happened. With a sigh he handed the candle back to Master Ernie. He hung his head in defeat and turned to leave the room.

"Don't worry, Kyler. We'll have you up to speed in no time." Master Ernie tried to sound cheerful, but it didn't help. "I'll come by your room later with your class schedule."

Kyler exited the room, but paused in the hallway, the instinct to fight still in the forefront of his mind. He was about to step back into the office when he heard Master Ernie speak.

"I don't understand it. Martha's nephew should be bursting with potential. Though it's too early for him to actually light the candle, we should have noticed some flicker of power around the wick."

"Maybe her retirement from magic included the teaching of magic, too." Maxine suggested. "You never know what another person is thinking. Who in their right mind would quit the council of mages?"

The old man's quiet snores found Kyler's ears, and he heard both Master Ernie and Madam Maxine sigh. That was his clue to leave, so he ducked through another doorway and thought of his dorm room.

WALTER

The road sloped down toward the fishing port at an awkward angle. Walter loped over patches of dirt and rubble, while looking at the view before him. The dwellings he approached could scarcely be called homes. They were hovels pasted together with sticks and mud. Many leaned against trees for support, while others stood on their own with piecemeal stone chimneys to support their weight.

Children ran around with dirty faces and bare feet. Some of the women stopped working as Walter passed through. The hunger in their eyes betrayed greedy thoughts, but no one had enough courage to chase after a wolf.

Glad to leave the smelly hovels and hungry eyes behind, Walter raced over cobbled paths. The closer he drew to the port, the more the smell of salt water filled his nose. He drank in the damp air with a pleased snort. The port was still at least a mile ahead, but from his vantage point he could see the water's edge. Large vessels of all kinds lined the banks. His keen hearing picked up the hollers of men as they off-loaded barrels and crates.

As far as his eyes could see, homes were crammed together like puzzle pieces. They rose between twisted streets and alleys, making the city into a maze. Walter wasn't sure the salty air could cover the stench of a human population so tightly packed into a city. Closer to the docks, large warehouses sprang up like gophers from holes. He stopped on the path, waiting for Martha to catch up with him. A wolf alone was a sure way to get captured by traders. He needed her presence as his master to use as a disguise.

"I see you finally decided to stop." Martha's voice floated up from the path behind him. "I was afraid you'd run all the way down to the port."

While turning his head, he cocked an eyebrow in her direction. "What? And miss a grand entrance with you?"

Reaching his side Martha scratched his thick head. "I think someone's a little full of himself!"

"You know the plan won't work without you holding me by a leash."

The plan was to listen to the gossip of the village. Martha figured that with all the comings and goings of a fishing port there were bound to be rumors and real information floating around. Their job was to separate the junk from the treasure. Key phrases like "large flying monster" or "missing villagers" would be tip-offs. With Martha holding his collar, he would appear to be no more than a tame pet. They'd be able to eavesdrop on all sorts of conversations.

"Let's head straight for the dock," suggested Martha. "There's nothing like a drunk sailor for telling stories."

As dusk approached they settled on a tavern were several sailors loitered. The aged sign hanging from above the door proclaimed it "The Rusty Wench." Walter sniffed the air. The stale scent of beer clung to his nostrils and mixed with the earthy scent of unwashed bodies. A sneeze burst through his snout, spraying spittle upon the sailor in front of him. The sailor turned with a crude remark, but seeing Walter, his mouth snapped shut. Martha patted the wolf's head like that of a good little pet and pushed through the door into the bar.

It was unbelievably noisy. Brawny men sang drunken songs at the top of their lungs, and barmaids squealed as old men tried to pinch them in passing. Each table's conversation seemed louder than the next's. Martha made her way to an empty table near the corner of the room, and then she signaled for Walter to take up a position at her side. She plopped down onto a greasy chair.

A barmaid squeezed her way trough the din toward them. Giving Walter a wide berth, she asked, "What will it be? We've got ale, mutton stew, and more ale. Your choice."

After clearing her throat, Martha replied, "Well I guess I'll have the ale then, and bring a large bowl of stew for my dog."

The server looked Martha squarely in the eye and said, "We don't serve animals. And that ain't no dog!"

Martha tsked, slipped her hand into a side pouch hidden deep beneath her folded skirt, and pulled out a half crown. She placed it on the table, where the light of the fire bounced off its polished surface. "I said it's a dog, and it needs a bowl of stew."

The server deftly slipped the gold piece into her apron and treated Walter with a wide smile. "And what a fine dog he is. I'll be right back with your order."

Martha and Walter had stayed at their table eating and drinking for almost an hour before Walter's ears perked up at a conversation being held two tables over. He'd made out a low baritone telling the story of his escape from a village far to the east. By thumping Martha with his tail, he directed her attention toward the other table. She muttered a few words of power to herself, and Walter was soon able to hear the far conversation in perfect detail.

The baritone continued, "I tell you it was Orcs! I don't care if you believe me or not! I seen 'em with me own eyes. They attacked the miller's house right in front of me. I was heading over that morning with a wagonload of grain. One of my horses picked up a pebble, and I had to stop and scrape it out of her shoe. And it's a good thing I did, too! If I'd been on time I would've been Orc bait."

The drunken man's eyes widened in remembrance. "I had just rounded the corner to the mill when I heard a blood-curdling scream. The miller's wife came running out of the house with her arms waving in the air. Not a second later, the ugliest creature I ever saw came chasing after her! It took me a while to realize it was an Orc. Me ol' mother used to have a picture book she'd show me sometimes when I was a kid. The ugly old creature looked exactly like the Orcs in her book. It chased the miller's wife into the next field. I quickly unhitched my mare from the wagon and took off toward home. I warned everyone I passed, but they thought I was crazy." The man tipped back in his chair, balancing on two wobbly legs. He gulped down a large mouthful of ale before bringing all four chair legs back to the floor. "They weren't laughing an hour later. When I fled I turned back to see smoke rising in the distance and heard screams floating on the air."

The other men at the table looked on in wonder. They couldn't figure out whether to believe this man or not. Walter knew Orcs hadn't been seen in centuries.

While Walter paid careful attention to the story unfolding before him, he also kept his other senses on alert. In the far corner of the bar, where the light of the fire didn't quite seem to reach, a man sat nursing a mug of ale. His eyes peered intently out from under the hood of his traveling cloak. He signaled a serving lady over to his table, and pointing to Martha, he directed the girl to serve her ale on his tab. Walter thought Martha had an admirer, and focused back on the baritone's conversation.

Soon, Walter sensed the return of the serving girl from the vibrations of her footsteps upon the floor. She placed a new mug in front of Martha. Intent on listening to the conversation a few tables over, Martha didn't pause to think as she picked up the mug and took a sip.

KYLER

The sounds of nighttime filled Kyler's ears as he headed toward the school garden. He thought about the previous two weeks at school as the bugs lazily flew around him. The garden was the only place that felt like home. A full day of classes tired him out. It was nothing like farmwork. He was the oldest kid in his reading class and obediently sat with younger students around a table as the teacher flipped through her letter cards. Making things worse were the numerous storybook pictures that covered the walls, making him feel like a child. He was determined to move ahead, but struggled to learn all that was placed in front of him.

The other boys in the dorm pranked him. He could hear their comments as he passed them in the halls. He knew what they were saying, comments about how even the youngest children could read basic common, or how he was a charity case or really addled in the brain. It took all his restraint not to punch their lights out. Luckily the girls ignored the boys in the school, and Kyler often caught the ladies giving him the eye. Even so, he escaped each night into the garden, where the smell of herbs and plants relaxed him.

If it weren't for the gossip, he might actually enjoy his classes. He'd discovered a new love of learning. The new way he learned to read was different than what his aunt had taught him. He could only figure she had taught him to read and write in another language. He'd asked a couple of other students if anybody spoke a different language, but was told no, "everyone speaks basic common." So, he persevered and decided to learn as much as he could.

He sat down on a cold stone bench within the garden. He took his notebook out of his side pouch and opened it to a blank page. There were tons of plants here, including species of herbs he'd never seen before. He drew their pictures with precision and then wrote down as much description as possible. The notebook never seemed to run out of pages. *Magic?* he wondered.

The peace of the garden began to wash over him, and he let his eyes begin to droop. He missed his aunt. He hadn't realized how much he would miss her until she was gone. While taking a deep breath, he let his thoughts go.

A sudden chopping noise cut through his peace. The noise was a new one, so he decided to investigate. He walked along the outside garden path heading toward the kitchen area. Rosebushes lined the way, their red flowers in full bloom. As he drew closer, the noise grew louder until finally, rounding a bend, he was greeted by an unlikely scene. A girl with auburn hair twisted up onto her head was chopping wood. He watched her place a log on top of a stump and with a hardy swing split the wood with her axe. Kyler recognized the girl from his first day at school as the kitchen servant he'd seen helping out.

It seemed a little odd to him that the school would have a girl chop its wood. *Wouldn't one of the servant boys find it easier? Maybe she's being punished for something.* He watched again as she swung the mighty axe. He actually saw her arm muscles flex as the axe made contact with the wood.

"Excuse me," Kyler attempted. "Can I help you with that?"

"Why would I want you to do that?" the redhead answered, looking a little put out by the interruption. "This is my free time! Go find yourself something else to do."

"I just thought you could use a little help."

"Why? Because I'm a girl? Because this is a boy's job?"

"I'm sorry, I didn't mean to offend you," he apologized. "I just couldn't figure out why they'd have one of the servant girls chopping wood when there are so many field hands available?"

Kyler saw her face turn the same color as her hair. Her back straightened and her eyes narrowed in on him.

"Servant girl!" she yelled. "Servant girl! I'll show you a servant girl!" And with a grunt of indignation she sent the axe flying in his direction.

Kyler tensed, but decided not to move; the girl's throw was off. He realized she'd meant to aim badly when the axe sunk deeply into the tree a good six feet away. He'd had enough. Girls were hard enough to understand. Girls who threw axes should be avoided at all costs!

As he left, he heard the redhead retrieve her axe.

"Stupid boys!" she hissed.

Back in the garden, Kyler sat on another bench while trying to forget about the girl. He focused on studying a new flower, wondering what it could be. As he thought about the plant, he felt another person's presence coming down the path. He looked up to see a teacher he'd not met. The man was middle-aged and wore spectacles that hung from a chain around his neck. His hair was thinning, and his ears stuck out like butterfly wings. The oddest things were his bright purple fingers; they reminded Kyler of beets. As he walked closer, Kyler shut his notebook.

"I've been meaning to come out and talk to you for a while," voiced the unknown teacher, "but one thing or another has always stopped me. I'm glad you're still here."

Kyler cleared his throat. "Did I do something wrong? I thought the garden was open to everyone."

The teacher chuckled. "No, no, you're fine. I just happened to notice you in the garden a lot."

"It reminds me of my aunt's garden" answered Kyler.

"I see." The teacher seemed very happy. He walked over to a plant in the garden and pointed to it.

"Do you know what this is called?"

Kyler was relieved that the teacher had picked one he knew.

"That's a willow bush."

"Very good," the man replied. "Do you know what it's used for?"

"Well, my aunt used to grind its leaves up and place them in a tea. She gave it to moms after they'd given birth. She said it helped them feel happier."

"Yes. That's right." He said. "It's a mood stabilizer. It helps with depression." The man moved over to another plant. "What about this one?"

Luck was with Kyler. "That's a lovelace. I've heard it's used in love potions."

Chuckling, the teacher nodded and then asked, "Do you know who I am?"

"No, but I know you're a teacher."

"Well, yes, but that's obvious. I'm Master Avery. I'm in charge of potion making. Why haven't I seen you in class before? You look old enough. How old are you?"

"I'm fifteen."

"Well, you're definitely old enough. Why aren't you in my class?"

"I…" Kyler was almost too embarrassed to reply. "I can't read, so they won't let me in any higher classes. I'm learning fast though!"

"Well, I don't see why they didn't ask me first. It is my class," the exasperated teacher replied. "Show up on Tuesdays at nine a.m. Just think potions class, and you'll pop right in."

"Will they let me?"

"You don't worry about that. I'll have a talk with Madam Maxine. A boy as knowledgeable as you about plants, and not in my potions class? That's just ridiculous! Besides, you don't need to read a textbook to learn potions. You just need to know how to measure and stir."

"Thank you," said Kyler. "I'll be there right on time."

"See that you are," the teacher said, turning away. "Nine a.m. sharp."

Kyler could not believe his good luck. Someone had recognized his potential.

DARCY

"**D**arcy! Darcy! Cook wants more wood."

"More, more, more," Darcy muttered to herself, but her thoughts drifted back to the young man who'd interrupted her minutes ago. She'd seen him around the school, but he wasn't in any of her classes. Good thing, too, because after what he'd said, she'd probably punch him in the face the next time she saw him.

With a twist, she reclipped her hair and hefted the axe onto her shoulder. Just because she was a sixteen-year-old girl made no difference. She was as good as any boy. Her long auburn hair was her only vain attribute. She couldn't bear to cut it. Clothes didn't matter a smidge. At the moment she wore a loose-fitting white blouse with brown baggy pants. Perhaps not the most popular fashion, but she loathed wearing dresses. A smile grew on her face as she reached up over her head and stretched. Chopping wood was definitely paying off. Others might think she was crazy, but she knew exactly what she was doing.

She knew what her older brother Leroy thought, too. He was two years her elder and went to school here also. Whenever he saw her heading off to chop wood, he'd give her a disapproving stare or tell her that it wasn't her place. Her place! *Ugh!* Many students at the school knew she came from the royal family, but she'd convinced them in the first week of school never to call her "princess." The one boy who did, well, his nose never looked the same. The other students didn't even bring it up anymore, and she never mentioned it.

Leroy had nothing to worry about. He could do whatever he wanted because he was a boy. The first time she tried to attend sword-fighting class, the boys had laughed her right off the field. The teacher didn't even let her try to show him her skills, but she'd show all of them. Little did Leroy know why she chopped wood.

A plan had evolved in her mind after that first sword class, and she'd sought out a classmate named John to help her. He had a bad habit of wiping his nose with the back of his hand and complaining about his allergies. She'd convinced him to help her out. John hated fighting, and the chance to skip sword class and hang out in his room suited him perfectly. No one needed to know the kid in the padded gear and helmet was not John, but really a longhaired, fiery girl! She even added a couple of snuffles and sneezes for effect. They wouldn't start fighting without safety gear until next year, and she figured they'd have to accept her by then. She split her last log with an angry thunk. Free time was almost over, and she needed to wash up and head to her next class.

WALTER

Walter nudged Martha's foot with his nose. He noticed she'd begun to drift off at the table. Opening her eyes a crack, she looked down at him. "I guess I can't hold the ale like I used to."

With a woof of agreement, Walter pushed her to her feet.

"Let's find a place to sleep. I feel like I could doze for a hundred years."

While following Martha out of the tavern, he began to notice her footsteps weren't quite even. He laughed to himself, knowing he'd tease her about it in the morning. They walked toward a stable full of horses. Martha looked around and then stumbled over to an empty stall and slumped down onto a pile of hay. Alarmed, Walter went over to her. This was definitely not the place to spend the night. He grew worried when his licks upon her face did nothing to awaken her. Suddenly a large burp erupted from her mouth. Jumping back out of the stall, Walter tried to keep from gagging. The burp's stench filled his nostrils and threatened to overcome him. A few breaths of clean air, and soon he felt well enough to think. A strange thought occurred to him. Something about Martha didn't seem right. She'd only drunk two cups of ale. She shouldn't be this wasted. And what was that sweet smell that still clung to the fur around his nose? He approached Martha cautiously, sniffing for the sweetness. The odor was stronger as he approached her face. Her smelly breath reminded him of something. He just couldn't place his paw on it.

Then it hit him like a ton of bricks. *Poison!* He smelled poison on Martha's breath. A snarl issued from deep within his throat as he began backing out of the stall. A sleeping poison. Who would do that? Then he remembered the hooded man in the bar sending Martha a drink.

No sooner had the thought crossed his mind than a heavy object fell upon him. With anger he flailed about in a net. Two men approached him warily. If they came just a little bit closer, Walter knew he'd be able to reach them with his claws.

Suddenly the men stopped. The large one pulled a tube from his pocket and placing it to his lips, aimed right at Walter. A sharp sting erupted behind his left hind leg. Walter snarled in anger as he tried to break free of the net, but something was wrong. His vision grew blurry and his legs wobbled as he stood. His last thought before darkness claimed him was about Martha's safety.

The next thing he knew, the smell of salt water filled his nostrils. He struggled to open his eyes, but they seemed crusted shut. His body rocked to and fro in sickening swirls. He opened his mouth to speak but found his tongue so dry, it hung limply behind his teeth. Finally blinking open his eyes, he was aghast to find himself inside a cage. Memory began coming back in slow pieces. He remembered two men with a net and Martha. Martha had been poisoned! He struggled to stand as adrenaline pumped through him.

"Don't try to stand right away. It usually takes a few minutes to get your bearings," a voiced announced from behind him.

Turning around in the cage, he found himself facing a large fox.

"The drug they used to knock you out takes its time wearing off, and from the size of you, they probably gave you a huge dose."

Rolling his tongue around his mouth, Walter tried to pick up some moisture. With a raspy voice, he struggled, "What happened?"

"The traders got you. Just like they got the rest of us."

Walter raised himself enough to follow the fox's gestures. He appeared to be in a large room. Everywhere he looked there were various cages and crates. Animals of all kinds looked at him forlornly. He made out a swath of light peeking down through the ceiling from a door above and stairs leading down to his level. He could see shapes hanging from the rafters near the stairs that swayed as the floor rocked. He put one and one together and realized he must be aboard a boat.

"What will they do with us?" Walter asked.

"That depends," said the fox. "The little animals in the crates seem to get sold at different ports. Large animals like us, well, if they have a specific buyer for you, you're lucky, otherwise..." He motioned toward the swaying objects near the stairs.

Walter allowed his eyes to adjust more in the gloom. By squinting intently toward the stairs, he could make out several distinct shapes. Jumping back with a snarl, he rammed the back of his cage.

"Are those what I think they are?"

The fox nodded. "Skins. They're animal skins. They sell them in the South to make exotic throws and cloak linings."

Walter laid his head upon his paws, and then let out a growl.

MARTHA

Meanwhile, back in the dank stables onshore, Martha awoke from a deep sleep. The sun shone brightly in her eyes, causing her to blink. She let out a snort of disgust as she looked at the stall around her. With thoughts of Walter, she glanced in all directions, but there wasn't any sign of him. She struggled to her feet, calling his name, "Walter. Walter, where are you?"

As she emerged from the stable, she stepped into a dent in the wet mud. On the ground, she could make out the footprints of two different men. Worry began to eat at her as she continued to look for Walter. She quickly picked up a patch of black fur lying a few feet away.

"Oh no, Walter. What happened?"

She followed the two different sets of footprints outside the stables to where they left off and wagon tracks began. Walter had obviously been taken somewhere else. The wagon tracks led her to the docks, but when the wooden boardwalk began, she lost the trail. Frustrated, she scanned the scene before her. The dock bustled with activity. Men moved here and there loading and unloading ships. Sailors hung from riggings, patching up torn sails and preparing for further journeys. She'd never be able to find Walter in all this mess. With a sigh she looked down into her hand, which still clutched Walter's lost fur. An idea filled her mind, and she quickly ducked into an empty warehouse. Its old walls bore signs of water and termite damage, and she mumbled as she kicked debris out of her path.

"This might just work. I hope I can remember."

Martha filled a rusty old can half full of water. She then lit a fire, fueling it with the rubbish that lay strewn about. She hadn't tried a Seeking since her days in school. She pictured Walter in her head as she placed the can above the flames. Her strength gathered, she saw and spoke the word *seek*. The flames of the fire turned red and shot up around the can as she threw Walter's fur into the boiling water. Martha gazed into the steam rising up into the air. A fuzzy picture of Walter began to form. He was curled up in a ball lying inside a cage. Rage filled Martha, and another word filled with power issued from her lips. The picture shifted and then began to enlarge. Her vision focused sharply as the view flew from within the confines of Walter's cage to the outside of a sailing vessel. Painted ornately on the ship's side was the name Serina. From the angle of the sun off the deck, she could tell the ship was sailing southeast.

As she backed away from the fire, Martha's thoughts turned to rescue. These men were in for a big surprise. With a muttered word and a flick of her wrist, the fire went out with a swoosh. The door slammed shut behind her as she exited the warehouse on the way to "borrow" a boat.

"Just wait, Walter. I'm coming."

WALTER

W alter awoke with a start. He'd felt someone watching him and could swear he'd heard someone call his name. He instinctually knew it was Martha. A vicious snarl appeared on his lips as he thought of his captors. He'd have his revenge, but he'd have to get ready.

He signaled to a monkey a few cages away.

"You there, monkey."

The monkey eyed him warily. "What?"

"I need your help."

"Help with what? I'm stuck in my cage just the same as you."

"But what if you weren't stuck in your cage anymore? Would that be worth something to you?"

"What do I have to do?" the monkey asked.

"Do you think if you had the keys to the locks you could open the cages?"

"Of course I could!" the monkey replied indignantly. "What do I look like, a pig?"

Walter turned toward the barrels where the grain was kept for feeding the animals and spoke with power.

"Come out. I know you're over there."

A scurrying sound issued from behind a sack of oats, and a small mouse peeked its head out with concern.

"Are you speaking to me? Because if you are, you should know it's not normal for a wolf to be able to speak in mouse tongue. I think I drank too much cider last night."

Walter lowered his head toward the mouse.

"It's not the cider. I'm just a very special wolf."

"This could be a trick. I bet there's a cat somewhere around, and you're just trying to lure me out into the open."

"I wouldn't think of it," Walter replied. "I need to ask you a favor."

"What kind of favor? Does it involve cheese?"

"No, but I know someone who could get you some if you help me."

"I'm listening," squeaked the mouse.

"How many more of you are aboard the ship?"

"About thirty, give or take a family."

"Do you think you and some friends could sneak out to-night into the sailor's quarters and steal the key ring with the keys to our cages?"

"Maybe, but how would I know what keys to take?"

"When the guy comes to feed us tonight, remember what he looks like. It's his keys you'll need."

"I don't think it would be too much trouble. The sailors snore so loud, they wouldn't hear a cat screech."

Walter nodded his head in thanks and then called out to any other animals that could hear his voice. "Does anyone know if the sailors keep a pet aboard?" His words automatically changed into whatever language they spoke, a part of the natural magic of shape-shifters.

There was a general mumbling as animals talked among themselves. A voice spoke out over the din. Overhead, Walter noticed a beautiful parrot sitting in the beams. Its feathers were a vibrant green with reds and blue tips.

"There's a dog that's let loose on deck. I can hear it padding around above my head."

"Do you think you could get its attention the next time it passes over?" asked Walter.

With an affirmative squawk, the parrot flew over to a higher beam near the ceiling.

Wearily settling down to wait, Walter couldn't help but be impressed with his plan. He should be well on his way out of here by the time Martha caught up to him.

An hour passed in silence. It seemed the other animals knew something momentous was in the works. Suddenly the parrot squawked, "The dog is coming this way."

By sticking her beak up through the cracks of the ceiling, she pecked at the dog when it passed over. Unable to pass up the chance at a new game, the dog stopped and began trying to catch the bird's beak with his front paws. It bounced up and down happily, enthusiastically attacking the bird. Walter rose on his haunches, his growling rumbling up through the floorboards.

The sailors stomped their feet on the deck above, trying to silence the loud animal beneath. The dog, however, stopped playing and cocked an ear toward the floor. He let out a hesitant bark.

Under the boards, Walter answered back.

"Hey you, dog. We need your help."

The sailors stomped their feet again in annoyance while the dog circled the spot where he'd last seen the bird's beak.

"Who's there? Who's there?" he barked.

Walter knew he didn't have much time. If he spoke much more, the sailors above were bound to come down and whip him to keep him silent.

"If you want to know who I am, come down at the next feeding," he howled.

Angry shouts from the sailors rose in annoyance. Walter knew he'd have to wait until feeding time to see if the dog would accept the offer.

Several hours passed, and the sun began its slow descent upon the horizon. A loud clang announced the arrival of dinner. With a bang, the outer door opened and a large sailor carried down a bucket of slop. Walter noticed the mouse peek out from under the oak sack, taking note of the sailor's appearance. Just as the sailor's foot hit the bottom step, a brown ball of fur shot by him into the hold. With a shout the sailor yelled out, "Dumb dog," but he continued on his rounds to feed the animals.

Walter let out a hushed woof, calling to the dog. Several tense seconds passed before the dog found his cage.

"You're not a dog!"

"I've heard that before," said Walter. "Look, I need a favor."

"What kind of favor?"

Walter thought quickly. "It's a new kind of game I've invented. Will you play it with me?"

"Why didn't you just say so," barked the dog. "I love games. Do I get to chase my tail?"

"No. Something better. You get to pretend to attack birds."

"How would that be fun?"

"For every bird you catch, you'll get a dog biscuit."

Not realizing the con, the dog spun in a circle.

"A biscuit a bird. It's a deal. When do we start?"

The sailor got closer to Walter's cage. He had to make this quick. "Listen for the parrot. She'll squawk at you."

With a bang the sailor kicked Walter's cage.

"No dinner for you, you annoying wolf. Not till you learn to shut up!" The sailor passed by Walter's cage without dropping any food in his bowl. Walter growled. The sailor kicked the cage again and kept moving. From the corner of his eye, Walter could see the dog going back up the stairs. He had another wait ahead of him, and this time it wouldn't be so easy with his stomach reminding him of the passing time.

KYLER

Classes flew by as Kyler looked forward to Tuesday. He wandered around the school in a sublime bubble. He didn't even care that he'd been soundly beaten again in sword-fighting class. His carefree attitude ended when he got lost Sunday night.

Sundays were a quiet day for mental relaxation. He spent most of the time in his room practicing his letters. He aced them now. Many of the words he'd used growing up in the village; his aunt had just taught him a different way to write them. Things began clicking after his second week. He figured out Martha had taught him whole symbols for words, while in basic common a word was made up of different letters. He finished his homework early and decided to explore some more. The school was huge. There were rooms he didn't know existed because he hadn't thought to name them while passing through a doorway.

He'd had an idea a few days ago. He'd walk through a doorway and pick something out of the blue. Yesterday he'd thought of wine and ended up in a dank wine cellar. He could see wooden barrels full of aging liquids stacked on top of one another, and in the darkest part of the cellar there were metal wine racks filled with dusty old bottles. The air had been cold and wet and left a moldy taste in his mouth.

Of course sometimes he thought of things that didn't exist at the school, and by default he'd end up back in the dorm hallway. Once he'd been wondering about his bed sheets when he found himself in a room filed with large boiling vats of liquid. Large women stirred dirty laundry around in the steaming hot cauldrons. They used large wooden staffs to swish the clothing around and then fished them out of their soapy baths. Lines of rope strung across the top of the room where the laundry hung drying. The heat from the steam had forced him to head out quickly.

Today he thought he'd try to find something creepy like a morgue or tombs. As he walked toward the doorway, his thoughts shifted to his aunt. He could remember her teaching him the word for entrance. He had said it in common often enough when he wanted to go to the meeting hall. He crossed over the doorway, thinking, *What if I picture the word like Martha taught me to do?* No sooner had he thought this than he stepped into an unfamiliar, darkly lit hallway.

It smelled old and dry and the torches that lined the walls offered only little glimpses into the dark. He wondered where he was. Farther down the hall, he passed several doors deeply set into the stone walls. He tried to open a few, but they were locked tight. A little farther down, he came to an open door. What he saw left him frozen in astonishment. He had never seen anything like this room before. It had to be a library, but it was nothing like the student library. This one seemed to go on forever as row upon row of books extended into the

distance and vanished into darkness. *Why are there two libraries?*
Just then he heard voices. He moved back into the hall, out of
sight. When the voices faded, he cautiously peeked into the
room again. He could see the backs of two men walking down
a far aisle. They both wore robes of deep purple. He tried
to think what that color might signify, but he'd never seen
purple robes at school before.

Kyler got the feeling that perhaps this was not a place for
students. It felt different here, and his brain seemed to tingle. However, curiosity got the better of him, and he plunged
on down the hallway past several more locked doors until he
came to a fork in the passage. The right side looked well traveled, but the other path seemed dusty, and only a few lit torches showed the way. With a fast decision, he chose the dusty
path, figuring that if fewer people came this way, then he had
less chance of getting caught. The torches lit and went out
as he went farther down the hall. He wasn't able to see more
than ten feet in either direction. The path was uneven, and
his feet hurt as little pebbles bit through his shoes. Finally he
came into a large round chamber where several torches burst
into life.

It looked like an old throne room. A large wooden chair
decorated with intricate carvings rested upon a raised dais
at the head of the room. Crude chisel marks scratched into
its surface indicated where earlier visitors had tried to pry
out pieces of gold etching. Several pillars supported a dome-
like ceiling that had once been decorated with a nightscape;
stars and dark clouds still shone through some spots where
the frescoes hadn't chipped away. Marble statues of men stood
crumbling among the pillars; only their legs and torsos remained. Among the debris strewn about were chairs that had

rotted down to their nails. He headed over to one of the statues. Chiseled into its base, he read "Markus Kingborn 252." *Wow! That was nearly eleven hundred years ago.* He moved to the next statue, hoping to find more inscriptions, but the base had worn away. *What is this place?* He approached the throne. Carved into its intricate wooden frame was the word *Naterum*.

Kyler sat down on the dais with a thud. *This isn't real. Naterum was destroyed over a thousand years ago!* He remembered lessons from his aunt's history books. Naterum had been the capital city of the high king. A great battle had been fought, and though the high king was victorious, his city was destroyed. The battle had lasted almost a full decade. Most specifics about the war had been forgotten over the years, and only the name of the city and various legends remained.

I'm in the ruins of the ancient palace... He couldn't wait to tell Martha what he'd found. *But wait...who are the guys in purple robes?* Someone was using the ruins. *Maybe I should really get out of here.* He passed through the throne room's entryway, thinking of his dorm, but nothing happened. *Great...Guess transportation doesn't work in the ruins.* The eerie silence began to make him nervous, and he decided to move as quickly and quietly as possible. As he scurried down the hallway, he kicked a rock with his shoe and stumbled. He looked up from the ground, listening for any running footsteps, but all was silent. *Good. No one heard.* He was about to pick himself up when he noticed little green shoots poking up through a crack in the wall. By clearing away some debris, he was left looking at a plant he'd never seen before. He picked a few shoots to look at it more closely.

The plant was covered with a soft fur-like down. It made him feel calm as he rubbed his hands over the furry stalk. A yawn cracked his face, but he shook off the sudden urge to rest and looked a little closer at the plant. What looked like veins ran under the skin of the stalk. They seemed to throb with an eerie pulse. Considering he'd just picked it, it shouldn't have still been alive. *That is weird.* He put the shoots into his side pouch. It was too dark down here to do a sketch, and he wanted a specimen he could compare with other plants in the garden.

After creeping past the library, he finally made it back to where he'd entered. His fingers crossed for luck, he thought of his dorm room and passed through the doorway. He stepped into the living quarters. *Thank goodness.* He was done exploring for now. Inside his room he flopped down on his bed. In no time at all he was sleeping soundly.

KYLER

Tuesday finally rolled around. At 8:59 exactly, Kyler crossed through a doorway thinking of potions class. He ended up stepping into a room full of chaos. Students were everywhere. Some sat at desks. Others picked up cauldrons from a side table, and one group of boys held a frog up by its hind legs, listening to it croak in fear. The largest boy looked up from this animal torture and right at Kyler.

"Look who's here, guys," he said. "Looks like somebody got lost." The other boys stopped dangling the frog and looked up. Kyler stood firm, ready for whatever they were going to throw at him, but Master Avery chose that moment to enter from a side door.

"Take your seats, everybody. Take your seats." As students shuffled toward their assigned seats, Kyler just stood at the back of the room. The teacher finally noticed him.

"Ah yes, Mr. Kyler. Good to see you. Take a seat up here in the front row next to Mr. Henry." Avery gestured to a desk where an older boy sat. The boy had long straight brown hair pulled back into a ponytail. He had long fingers and a fair complexion, and a smile lit his face. Kyler thought he seemed to welcome the idea of having a lab buddy.

The teacher continued, "Today we are going to learn about healing draughts. I want each of you to pay attention. What you learn here today could save your life."

He went on to discuss the different plants needed and a few other rare ingredients. Kyler sat in rapt attention. He knew the name of most of the plants Master Avery discussed. After nearly thirty minutes of lecture, the teacher turned the time over to the students. "Now, let's see how well you all listened. If you don't have a cauldron, go get one. Then pick up the herbs you need. I'll come around and see how each of you are doing."

As students sprang from their desks, ready to start creating, Henry turned toward Kyler.

"I hope you're good at this stuff. Potions aren't my thing." He wiggled his fingers in the air. "I'm training to be a bard."

"That's great," said Kyler. "I'll do my best. Let's go get a cauldron."

The two young men headed to pick up a pot, but by the time they got to the side table with the cauldrons, the only ones left were old and rusty. Kyler shrugged. "Oh well, maybe rust will give the draught a bit of a kick?" The boys bumped fists.

Next came collecting the herbs, but Henry looked puzzled. "I can't tell one green thing from another."

"Let me take a look," said Kyler. "I recognized most of the things Master Avery was talking about." He selected a variety of herbs and guessed at a few he didn't know. The two boys returned to their desk. They began pounding and grinding the herbs. As they heated up their cauldron, a loud bang shook the room. With a glance behind himself, Kyler saw two girls standing before a smoking pot. Their hair stood straight up from the shock of the blast, and a sooty black residue coated their clothes.

"Remember, the pig sprout is blue and the chic weed is red," the teacher bellowed above the students' laughter. "Mixing the two will result in an explosion, as Ms. Anne and Ms. Sara just showed us!"

Kyler worked a little more carefully after that. He didn't want to end up missing an ear or something. Several more explosions echoed through the room before their time was up. Luckily none as big as the first, and only one resulted in an unfortunate eyebrow incident. Henry added the last herb to the pot, but nothing happened.

"Is it supposed to do something? How do we know if we got it right?" Kyler asked.

Master Avery walked up behind them. Carefully he leaned over and sniffed their potion. "Very good, boys. I think you're the first ones to get it right. You can start cleanup and head to lunch early." He winked at Kyler as he walked away.

"Wow! Master Avery really likes you," said Henry as he and Kyler tidied up. "I just got the best lab partner in class."

"Thanks."

The cafeteria was an oval room filled with long tables and chairs. Rich tapestries hung from the walls, depicting fairy tale adventures. Today's lunch special was chicken and noodles with fresh baked bread on the side. Kyler loved cafeteria food, and he didn't care what anyone else thought. He loved being able to eat something different every day. Plus, there was always dessert.

Henry chose an empty table near the back of the room, and the two boys set their trays down. Kyler wanted to learn more about his new friend.

"So, Henry, what's your story?"

Henry looked at him with a good-natured smile before beginning.

"Well, do you now where Rinna is?"

"Never heard of it."

"It's over on the coast. That's where I'm from. It's a little fishing village. It's been there forever. My dad's a fisherman and my mom had twelve of us."

"Twelve. Wow! How'd you end up here?"

"My grandpa was a bard, too. When I was little my dad used to take me out fishing on the boat, I was always so bored. One day Grandpa made me a little wooden flute. Dad was against it, he thought I'd scare the fish away, but he gave in to Gramps. I played that flute day and night, and the strange thing was, the fish liked to listen. I used to sit up on the hill overlooking the docks and play. All different kinds of fish would jump out of the water to listen. I used to play on Dad's boat until I realized all the fish that gathered to listen were being caught up in his nets. Dad tried to convince me my play-ing was actually a gift to fishermen, but it made me feel awful. Grandpa had a talk with Dad and convinced him I wasn't cut out to be a fisherman, and that I had a musical talent just like him. I've been at school ever since, though this is my last year. I'll be taking the journeyman test soon to become an official bard."

"Dude," said Kyler, "I've never even seen the ocean. It must be so cool, the sun, the sand, and the waves. One day I'd like to go see it. I'm just from a little farming village several days away. I'm staying here as a favor to my aunt until she gets back from a trip."

"That doesn't sound so bad. You're lucky you've got connections. My grandpa petitioned three times to get me accepted."

"Hey, what'd you get for dessert?" asked Kyler, his thoughts already turning to food.

"Looks like a berry cobbler. What'd you get?"

"I think it's a custard. You want to trade?"

"Sure, I love puddings and stuff."

"I think were going to be great friends," said Kyler as he shoved cobbler into his mouth.

WALTER

Moonlight shone through the rafters above, and all was quiet belowdecks. The animals slumbered in their beds—all except one. Walter lay still with one ear listening for the sounds of mice. Above deck the sailors on night duty paced back and forth, sending little rivers of dust floating through the moonbeams below. The floorboards creaked with each shift of weight.

As the night wore on, a shrew a couple cages away started moaning in her sleep. She began shrieking, and calling out for her family. Walter tried to wake her calmly, and whispered a few words of comfort. As he eased her into reality, he spoke softly, reassuring her. After a while he was able to get her back to sleep. If only he could get himself to sleep so easily.

Toward dawn he heard the scurrying of little feet approaching his cage.

"We did it! We got the keys," the two mice squeaked excitedly.

"Good job. Go give them to the monkey."

Hearing himself mentioned, the monkey awoke with a yawn. With deft fingers he took the keys from the mice and began working on his own lock. With a loud click, the door to his cage swung open. Proudly striding forward, he brought the keys over to Walter.

"What now?" he asked.

"Let me out first, and then let the other guys out. Make them keep quiet or the crew will know something's up."

The monkey went about his work in silence. Soon a large mass of animals was gathered at the base of the stairs.

Walter addressed them quietly. "This is our chance. Once the door is opened, everyone rush up the stairs and take the deck. Don't let anything stop you. The element of surprise is on our side." He turned toward the larger animals and continued, "Big guys, help the little guys. We'll need barrels and wood thrown into the water for animals that can't swim. The rest of you get into the water as fast as you can. We must be traveling on a river, so head for the shore." The animals took up places and waited for their morning feeding.

When at last heavy footsteps indicated the time had come. Walter signaled to the parrot to alert the dog. A loud barking sounded on deck. Several running footsteps heralded an attempt to silence the dog. With the morning watch sailors on deck distracted, the time was right for escape! As soon as the door swung open, the animals rushed the sailor carrying their breakfast. His feet flew up from beneath him and the contents of the bucket of slop landed with a plop on his head. He struggled to get up, but the animals charged over him, pushing him down again and again.

Once on deck the animals put the rest of their plan into action. The foxes pushed a few crates over the side before diving into the water themselves. A host of hens flew off the side of the ship, landing on the floating crates. The amount of noise being made brought sleepy sailors on deck. Many of the animals had stayed on board, intent on seeking revenge for their mistreatment. A family of muskrats attacked a sailor, scurrying up his pants legs and biting him every few inches. A few of the birds circled above, picking out their victims. With a rumble they dive-bombed the sailors, attacking with claws and beaks.

Walter did his best to help the smaller animals off the ship. He was showing a couple lizards off the deck when a pain shot up his leg. With a snarl, he turned to see a sailor swinging a rope at him. Walter leapt on him, his fangs digging into the man's arm and making him drop the rope. Scooting backward, the sailor looked for an escape.

"You're lucky I'm a humanitarian," Walter growled.

In utter shock the sailor looked at him and then with a whimper fell down through a bolt-hole in the deck.

Walter turned and saw another sailor brandishing a torch while trying to scare a few wolves back into the hold. With a snarl Walter leapt at the sailor, causing the torch to land on the deck. He made sure the other wolves got off of the ship and then looked around to check out the chaos. A loud bang sounded from below his paws, shaking the deck with a sickening heave. He looked at the door where the torch had landed and noticed a sign, "Yo, ho, ho and a bottle of rum." Alcohol! The whole ship was about to blow. With a powerful thrust of his hind legs, he sprang into the water. While paddling toward shore, he could hear the shouts of the men aboard ship. With a mighty roar the timbers were engulfed in flame and the vessel began to sink beneath the water. Because he was watching the disaster, Walter did not notice a small boat rowing up beside him. He jumped halfway out of the water when a voice spoke in his ear, "Leave it to you to send up a signal fire even I couldn't miss."

With a leap of joy, he bounded into the boat.

"Aren't you a sight for sore eyes," said Walter.

"Does that mean you missed me?" asked Martha.

"Only a little. I had things well under control." Another loud boom echoed from the direction of the trading ship.

"Yes, I can see you did. Would you like a ride then?"

"Definitely. I'm not big on soggy paws."

By paddling down the river, Martha headed away from the sinking ship. Animals on the shoreline sent up a caterwaul of appreciation as Walter went by.

"It seems you have quite a fan club."

"It was the least I could do to help. So, where are we headed?"

"We'll travel east as far as we can and then go on foot. I want to check out that drunken man's story about Orcs."

"There's another thing," Walter added. "While I was on the ship, one of the shrews kept having a nightmare. She screamed out about a big monster bird that was eating her family."

"Did you find out where she came from?"

"All I could get out of her was 'east.' She just kept saying 'east.'"

"Then it looks like we're on the right track." Martha uttered a word of power, and a stiff breeze kicked up and pushed the little boat's sails.

KYLER

A week later, Henry sat on Kyler's bed going over homework for potions class. Kyler sat back in his softly padded rocking chair and kicked his feet up. The room was totally different from a month ago. Ivy vines grew from his stone walls, twisting and covering every square inch they could find. His bed was now in the shape of a boat. A mast on the side reached up to the ceiling, and his favorite color, blue, was evident in everything from his bed linen to his bath towels. The only thing not completely decorated was his door. It kept switching back and force between vined plants and stormy gray wood. His homesickness obviously confused the powers of the room.

"Do you think we got the potion list right?" asked Henry.

Kyler stopped his rocking and thought for a moment. "I can't think of anything we've missed," he said. "If I could go out to the garden, I would have a better idea."

"You heard the announcement. No students are allowed outdoors without a teacher."

"That is so annoying. I wonder what's going on," said Kyler. "Has this ever happened before?"

"Not that I've ever heard of," said Henry. "I've been here four years, and nothing this interesting has ever happened. I did overhear Darcy talking about a problem in the kitchens."

"Who's Darcy?" Kyler interrupted. "Have I met her?"

"I don't know," said Henry. "She's on my grade level. She's got long red hair and a fierce attitude."

"Did you say red hair?" Kyler's thoughts shot back to the girl with the axe. *It couldn't be the same girl, could it?* "Does she chop wood?"

"Yeah, that's her thing," responded Henry. "Guess you've met her. Most people don't forget her. Anyway, she said in history class today that—"

"Wait," interrupted Kyler. "You said she's in class with you?"

"Yeah. Smarty. History class."

"You mean she's not one of the kitchen servants?"

Henry's face turned red as he grabbed his sides, trying to suck in air. It was no good. A mighty groan burst out from deep within his chest, followed by hysterical laughter.

"A...servant..." He tried to get the words out between breaths. "I'd like to see her face if you ever told her that!" He continued laughing so hard, he fell out of his chair.

Well you missed your chance, thought Kyler. He rolled his eyes. *No wonder she turned red as a tomato. Dude.*

Henry slowly calmed down enough to finish his story.

"Like I said, we were sitting in history class. She was telling everyone how upset the cook was yesterday. Evidently two cows were missing." He paused "Well, not quite missing. They found one out in the woods a little ways off. Something had eaten the bottom half of it."

"What do they think? Is there a wolf on the loose?" Kyler inquired.

"I doubt they know what to think. Just a few days ago, the boy that mucks out the stables said one of the horses was missing. He'd thought it had just run away, but who knows?"

"Now that you mention it, I remember when one of the midwives from the village came up to the garden to pick some herbs. She kept talking to herself, and I heard her mumble something about her husband and brother-in-law gone missing. You don't think it's possible..." Kyler let his sentence trail off, but the wheels continued turning in his mind.

"Who knows?" said Henry. "They've got us locked up in here for some reason. Maybe there are ghosts and ghouls afoot."

"More like werewolves and vampires," said Kyler.

The two were just getting back to their studies when they heard a knock at the door. They looked at each other, wondering who it might be. Kyler shrugged his shoulders. No one but Henry ever came to visit.

"Open," commanded Kyler.

As the door swung open, they were both surprised to see Master Ernie. He looked a little worse for wear, with a pale and haggard face. His normally smooth black cloak and pressed white shirt were badly wrinkled and looked as if they hadn't been changed in days.

"Good, you're both here." The bedraggled teacher wearily crossed the room. He paused, looking at Henry. "I've noticed you two have been spending a lot of time together. I was wondering if you both might be up for some research?" He smiled as he turned toward Kyler.

"What kind of research?" asked Kyler.

"Have you told Henry about your aunt?" Ernie asked. Kyler shook his head no.

"Well then, I guess this will all be somewhat shocking to him." Ernie turned toward Henry. "You see, Kyler's aunt believes that Mordrake the monster and his Griffin have awoken. She's gone after proof with an old friend."

Henry's face seemed to freeze mid-expression. "The only Griffin I've ever heard of was in a story my great-grandmother used to tell. She tried to scare us by saying the Griffin would steal us from our beds in the middle of the night."

"That's the problem," Ernie explained. "Everyone believes the Griffin is just some old wives' tale. Even the council of mages won't believe it without proof."

"Are you trying to tell me it's not?" Henry asked.

Kyler jumped in. "Martha went off to gather evidence to show to the council of mages. She thinks something bad is going to happen."

"Something bad is already happening," the teacher stated. "Animals and even some people have gone missing. I fear it's the Griffin."

"Are you kidding me?" asked Henry. "We were just joking about what was happening around the village."

"Afraid it's not a joke, boys. Something's out there...something big."

"Is it the Griffin you want us to find?" Kyler was now sitting up straight in his chair. A fun evening between friends had just turned into something a lot more serious.

"No, no, nothing like that," responded Ernie. "I hoped you two might help me out. I've barely slept over the last few days. I've been poring over all the books in my library looking for something, anything, about Mordrake and the Griffin. I've come to realize it's just too big a task. I need some help looking through the student library."

Kyler bobbed his head in obvious relief. Looking through books was something he could handle. With the mandate to stay indoors, they had nothing better to do anyway. "What should we be looking for?"

"Anything. All that's known about them comes from an old bedtime story about Mordrake being an evil tyrant. His pet Griffin was the same. It didn't care who or what it killed. It even snatched children from their beds." The teacher glanced over at Henry. "In the end there was a tremendous battle fought between the sides of good and evil. The entire kingdom was mobilized. Mordrake proved impossible to kill, so the mages came up with an ingenious plan. Whatever it was, it worked.

At least, that's how the story goes.

"What we need to find is the real history. The tale must have had its roots in the truth, but as time went on it's just become an old story. I need you two to check for anything in the library. Check the older volumes of history. We need to discover how to stop the Griffin before it's too late."

"I'm up for it," said Henry.

"I hoped you'd say that. I've got an additional task for you." Ernie looked at Henry with a serious expression. "I need you to check the bards archives. Some of the best history has been preserved through song. Unfortunately, a lot of those songs aren't sung anymore."

"I've not made journeyman status yet. I'm not supposed to be in the archives. What if someone finds me?"

"It's a chance we'll have to take. You're our best bet. I've already asked the master bard, but he refused, said he was too busy. We need to look everywhere."

"All right then, I'll do it," Henry pledged.

Kyler was just as determined. "I was trying to think of some way to help Martha, and you've just given it to me."

"Good luck, boys," Master Ernie said. "If you find anything, bring it directly to me." He left the room, closing the door behind him. Left alone, the two began planning.

"The bards archive isn't open till the morning," said Henry. "Maybe we should go start in the student library?"

KYLER

The library was a place Kyler loved. Its walls of books reminded him of his home. Now that he'd learned to read basic common, whole new worlds were open to him. He'd even been allowed into a few advanced classes. He glanced around at the shelves of books. *Where to start? This search could take months!* The library was quiet. Most kids were in bed now. Only a few diehard academics remained. Lights from wall sconces illuminated the room. Rich carved bookcases flanked the walls with etchings of fairyland creatures decorating the wood. Freestanding bookcases ran down the length of the room, while tables of all shapes and sizes were squeezed into whatever spaces were open.

"Master Ernie said to start with the old histories," said Kyler, as they walked toward the far wall of the library. He headed to a rarely used section. Most students wanted to read new books and weren't interested in going through huge old dusty volumes. Besides, the older books were said to have unique qualities all their own.

As the two boys continued down the central aisle, the lights became more spaced out and shadows more prevalent. The air seemed to grow thicker as they entered the ancient writings section. Specks of dust floated in the eerie light from the few candles. It didn't seem so quiet back here, either. Strange faint sounds could be heard coming from the books around them. Kyler glanced closer at the books on his left. One of them moved. He startled and bumped into Henry.

"Hey, watch it!"

"Sorry," Kyler apologized. "There's something really strange about these books."

"Would you please be quiet!" an angry voice shouted. "Some people come to a library to read!"

The boys looked around quickly for the source of the voice. Someone was down here with them, but where? The back of the library looked deserted.

"Maybe it was one of the books?" wondered Kyler.

"I said shut up!" yelled the voice.

Kyler turned toward one of the darkened corners of the room. He could just make out what appeared to be a table squeezed between two shelves. Slumped over the table was a dark shadow. It was definitely a person.

"Why don't you just show yourself instead of acting all high and mighty?" said Kyler.

The shadow straightened up, its posture stiff. Just as the person stepped into the light, Kyler realized who it was.

"Good to see you, Henry," said Darcy. "Why'd you bring him with you?"

"Real funny, Darcy. We have just as much right to be here as you," said Henry.

Darcy deflated. "You're right. Sorry about that. It's just that I've met this kid before. It was a bad first impression, but if he's a friend of yours, maybe he's worth a second chance." She looked over at Kyler. "So, what brings you to the old crusty section?"

"We're looking for some information," Kyler answered sheepishly. "I'm really sorry about calling you a servant before. Can we start over?"

Darcy looked straight into his eyes. After a moment she held out her hand to shake. "My name's Darcy."

Kyler smiled in relief. "My name's Kyler. Pleased to meet you." He attempted a mock bow, but he stumbled.

Darcy began laughing. She didn't seem so scary anymore. In fact, she had kind of a nice laugh. It was rich and breathy. Her auburn hair bounced in little ringlets from under her cloak.

"So, what kind of information? I might be able to help. I spend a lot of time back here."

"Um, well," Kyler struggled. *Should I tell her what we're looking for? She might be able to help out if she's familiar with this section.* "We're looking for any histories on Mordrake the monster and his Griffin." He waited for her response.

She looked at him quite seriously. "Well, that's going to be a hard one. I've only read about him once, and I don't remember where." She walked toward one of the shelves. "It was probably in a biography. Someone that fought against him probably mentioned it in passing." She started to pull books from the shelf, placing them on a table. Kyler noticed she picked up some of the books a little more carefully than others. "Let's start with these. I've read them in the last year."

Kyler sat down and pulled a book closer. It pulled back!

"Be careful with that one," said Darcy. "It's a little tempera-mental."

The book in front of him pinched his finger. "Ouch! It bit me!"

"Well, I said be careful. That's the biography of a mage. Any of these old books written by mages seem to have ab-sorbed some of their magic. Some of them are really fierce!"

Kyler looked down at the book in front of him. Its corner bent back in a snarl and its pages bristled. It didn't appear to want to be read. "Um?"

"Oh, just ask its permission. None of the books in the stu-dent library are that dangerous. They'll all let you read them," said Darcy.

"Do you mean there are books somewhere that won't let a person read them?"

"Yep, you won't find any here though."

A picture of purple-robed figures walking through an un-derground library entered Kyler's mind. Maybe he'd found more than he'd thought. Then, looking down at the book, he asked, "Hey, book, would you mind very much if I opened you up?"

The book relaxed its pages, its corner unbending. The night proceeded routinely from then on, though one time Henry nearly got his finger bitten off by a book about wolver-ines. Evidently it had been written by a shape-shifting mage who had gone feral. Some of the books actually purred as Kyler read them. After the group finished scanning the pile Darcy had picked out, they began browsing among the shelves.

Books fairly leapt out at Kyler in their eagerness to be read again. He had to fight with two books written on the history of mystical creatures. Neither was going to let the other be read first. Finally, he braced his feet against the floorboards and pulled for all he was worth. He landed on his rear with a smack. But in his hands was *Gregory the Great's Guide to Fantasy Beasts*.

As he read, the words started to blur before him. He realized it must be very late, and unfortunately they still hadn't found any mention of Mordrake or the Griffin. He could see Darcy's head drooping a little over her latest book. Angry at not being paid attention to, her book gave her a nasty paper cut down her index finger. She woke up with a screech. Henry's head peeked over from behind a tall pile of books. His eyes darted back and forth between them, and finding nothing amiss, his head disappeared again.

"I think we should call it a night," Kyler yawned.

Darcy sucked on her finger. "Being tired makes you careless. Let's come back tomorrow."

"You don't have to come back if you don't want to," Kyler said. "You've been a lot of help already."

Darcy looked at him with an icy glare. "If I've been that much help, you won't mind some more."

Henry emerged from behind his table carrying a stack of books.

"You don't have to put them away, Henry," Darcy explained. "The librarian does it. She has some kind of magic spell that puts things right back where they belong."

"Oh good, see ya tomorrow then. I mean today, whatever. You know what I mean." Henry shuffled along ahead of them.

Darcy leaned over. "I hope they let us go out for sword practice. They didn't mention it during the announcement."

"I wouldn't mind missing it. I hate sword practice. I'm always getting clocked in the head. But why would you care?"

"I mean, I like to watch."

"Oh," said Kyler. "I don't remember seeing you out there before."

"I'm there. I guess you're too busy getting whacked in the head to notice. Maybe you should find another style of fighting? Swords just aren't your thing."

"But they only teach swords."

"So, why should that stop you?"

Kyler continued on toward the doorway thinking about what Darcy had said. She'd told him how she'd read about sword fighting in the old section. Maybe he could find some other kind of fighting to read about. Maybe he didn't have to be the class wimp. It was frustrating. He was strong and tough from years of farming, but you wouldn't know it from the way he held a sword. Maybe he could learn something else.

KYLER

M uch to Kyler's dismay, the school allowed students outside the next day for sword practice. He looked around for Darcy, but soon realized students not in sword class would not be allowed outside. He cinched his protective chest strap tighter as the field slowly filled with other boys. The sun beat down on his head. Teachers with their black robes hanging like damp curtains stood watch around the practice circle. Their eagle eyes trained on the forest edge. Little beads of sweat ran down their foreheads, but they did not turn away.

The sword felt heavy in Kyler's hands, nothing like his old walking staff. The teacher blew his whistle and the boys lined up in rows, placing their swords in a pile. Class always began with forms. They would have to copy the teacher as he danced, moving his hands like blades, practicing ancient forms of combat. Kyler liked this part. He was very good at the forms, and his body flowed into new rhythms as he moved, twisting with skill. His feet danced on the ground, barely shifting any dust into the air. He could do the basic forms by heart, so he closed his eyes and went into a trance. His body knew what to do. When the time came for advanced forms, he opened his eyes to concentrate on the teacher. Later he would try to remember anything new and commit it to memory. Things went well. Many students dropped to the sidelines, the moves getting too advanced. Kyler hung on as long as he could, but he had to sit down when the teacher's moves got too difficult. The teacher continued going until only a few students remained. Then he blew his whistle. Sparring time!

Once Kyler felt the cold weight of the sword in his hands, it was all he could do not to run. All of his earlier fluidity vanished in seconds as his body completely rejected his baring a sword. The teacher separated them into pairs. Just his luck, he got sniveling John. The guy was a dork, but man, could he swing a sword. The teacher blew his whistle and John advanced. Kyler tried to ward him off, but it was no good. With one quick hit with the flat of John's sword, Kyler ended up sprawled in the dirt. At least he'd knocked off one of John's gauntlets. It had been an accident, but he was still going to take credit for it. John leaned over, offering Kyler his help getting up. After grabbing the offered hand, Kyler was pulled up with a snap.

"Thanks" he said. Kyler was so embarrassed to have once again ended up in the dirt that he couldn't look John in the face. All he could do was stare at John's hands.

John nodded. He never spoke during sword-fighting class. When John put his glove back on, Kyler noticed a bright red line running down John's index finger. The wound looked fresh, but Kyler knew he hadn't touched him. A thought pushed at the back of his mind, but he couldn't grab on to it. The whistle blew. It was time to switch partners.

That night, Kyler arrived at the library early. He had some extra research to do. If sword fighting wasn't his thing, he was going to find out what was. As he neared the ancient histories section, he could hear the excited rustling of the books. They knew he was approaching. As he reached his destination, a feeling of despair hit him. Where would he find a book on fighting? He wandered around the shelves, the books growing louder as he approached and their noise fading as he passed. A sudden thought came to him. *If these books want to be read, maybe they'll help.*

He cleared his throat. "Ah, hello, books." Was there a certain protocol when addressing books?

"I'm looking for a book on fighting." Tons of books pushed themselves out to the end of their shelves.

Great...this might work. "It needs to be a book about how to fight." Several of the books returned to their places.

"Oh, and it can't be sword fighting." Over three-fourths of the books slowly pushed themselves backward.

"It needs to be something I can do." His last question hung in the air. It was a long shot, but if these books had any kind of self-intelligence, there might be hope. Several books jumped back with a definite snap. Kyler wondered what those books were about to so firmly reject him. Only a few remained sticking out. He walked over to the far shelf where they waited. He looked at the various titles on their spines. There were some about knives, some about spears, some about things he'd never heard of, and then there was one about staffs. It quivered in its excitement to be picked. When he reached his hand out toward it, the book leapt into his grasp. He sat down at a table and began reading. The pages fell open quickly before him. He saw training diagrams, practice forms, and even a pictorial history of staffs. A shiver ran up his spine. He knew he had found what he was looking for.

Voices drifted back toward him. Henry and Darcy were on their way. He tucked the book into his side pouch, making a mental note to check it out before he left. Darcy walked in with a swagger. She grabbed a few books from a shelf and plunked herself down.

"Well, let's get started, boys."

Another long night of searching began. Around ten o'clock Kyler looked at the pile of books in front of him. Nothing. Their search might take more than months; it might take years.

Hey, why don't I ask the books? He stood up and looked around expectantly. Henry and Darcy stared up at him as he rose.

"Books," he began, "I'm looking for information about Mordrake the monster and the Griffin." He looked around expectantly, but nothing so much as budged out of place. "Anything, anything at all?"

Nothing.

"It won't work," Darcy said.

"Why not?" asked Kyler.

"A book probably has to be entirely about Mordrake or the Griffin to know its contents. Just a paragraph here or there won't be filtered out from the main subject. It was a good try though. I should have thought of that."

Kyler sat back down and began scanning the book where he'd left off. He was pretty sure the pain behind his eyeballs was the beginning of a killer headache. Potions class was first up tomorrow, and he wanted to be alert.

"I'm heading to bed. I've got class first thing in the morning." He turned to walk away but bumped into the pile of books stacked before Darcy. She caught a few before they slid off the table, but one managed to tumble to the floor. Kyler and Darcy both leaned over to pick up the book at the same time, and...their heads cracked together. While holding her hand to her forehead, Darcy groaned. Kyler knew there was no way to avoid that headache now. He finished picking up the book and handed it to her. As she reached out her hand to take it, he noticed something odd. Running down her index finger was a long red scab. He looked into Darcy's eyes.

"Good night, Kyler," she said. "I think I'll stay up just a little longer."

"Me, too," said Henry. "I think I've got at least another hour in me."

"Yeah. Okay," mumbled Kyler. How did he process this new information? Darcy was John? He needed to think about how to tell Darcy he knew her secret. His thoughts flew back to the axe that had gone sailing past his head. That is, if he decided to tell her at all.

WALTER

A s he sat in the front of the boat, Walter felt the wind ripping through his fur. He stuck his tongue out to taste the breeze. The river continued on its way, snaking slightly to the southeast. Trees lined the banks, oftentimes their branches reaching down to sweep across the top of the water. Walter's ears picked out all kinds of sounds coming from the brush. Birds sang, crickets chirped, and monkeys clicked their tongues. It was a symphony of sound.

Farther ahead he detected another slight southward bend in the river. The bends south happened much more frequently now. His sense of direction told him that soon they'd be heading completely south, not east. Even Martha's magic wouldn't be able to sail them across land. It was time to put ashore.

"I think we'd better stop at the next bend. We're getting too far off course," he said.

"You're right. I was just thinking the same thing, but I was hoping the river would turn east again."

"I don't think we'll have much luck staying in the boat. We need to start making our way across the land. We can head east much more directly."

"Let's put ashore up ahead, before the bend," said Martha.

Walter looked at the shore while Martha steered the boat. It seemed a little less cheerful than the previous shores they'd passed. The gloomy air clung heavily to the place, and a slight tickle in his nose warned him to be on guard.

The boat slid to a stop as a tangle of reeds grabbed hold of the vessel, allowing it to progress no farther. After jumping out with a splash, Walter surveyed the area. Tall marsh reeds jutted up in every direction, large green horsetails surrounded him, and the air smelled thick and rotten. His paws slapped into the ground, turning the water-drenched shore into slimy mud. All seemed silent and hushed, his ears not picking up the sounds of birds or chattering animals.

"Well, this wasn't quite what I was hoping for." He sniffed. "But there's nothing for it. We need to head east."

"Marshes aren't my favorite stomping grounds, either. Let's get started, the sooner we're out of here, the better," replied Martha.

"I'll take the lead. It'll be easier for me to find my way, and my eyes are keener than yours."

"Lead on, wise one. I'll follow."

As they continued on deeper into the marshes, the mud sucked at their feet, making each step harder than the last. Martha's dress became covered in muck and weighed down by water. Strange little insects climbed up the duo's bodies as they walked. Walter kept his eyes on the ground ahead, knowing one misstep could lead them into a sinkhole. He had a weird feeling that someone was watching their dismal progress, but every time he looked around nothing moved but the pesky bugs.

Soon the way grew more treacherous and their path through the bog less apparent. Walter stopped at a murky swamp filled with dark dirty water. He could tell crossing through was their only option.

"We're going to have to wade through the water," he moaned.

"There's no other way?"

"Not that I can see. It's not that far to the other side. We've just got to watch our step."

He paddled into the swamp. The smell of rotten eggs assaulted his nostrils, and he tried desperately not to drink any water. He turned back to signal for Martha to start. With a dainty step, she waded into the muck. When lifting her next foot, Martha flailed her arms as her other foot refused to unstick. With an ungraceful plop, she fell headfirst into the water. Walter swam back to her side, causing small ripples to lap at the bank. As she lifted herself out of the dirty water, Martha looked like a monster rising from the depths. Mud clung to her body and then dripped off in slimy torrents. Her ruined hair was smeared back, with tendrils of swamp grass sticking out at angles.

A sudden sound caught Walter's attention. "What was that?" Walter whipped his head to the side. He swore he'd just heard someone laughing, but it had stopped abruptly. Then, turning back to Martha, he let her wade beside him. "I think there's something out here with us."

"I heard it, too. It sounded like a child giggling," said Martha.

"Let's get through this and then find a place to dry off. I want to scout around."

"I think it better if we stick together. There's no telling what's out there."

Upon emerging from the swamp, Martha gathered her soggy garments and shuffled up the incline. With a leap Walter cleared the bank and landed beside her.

Martha and Walter struggled through the vines that littered this side of the swamp. Old-growth trees covered in slick moss greeted them at every turn. Martha used her staff to cut their way through the mess the best she could. As the long shadows of day's end approached, strange new sounds emerged all around. Unseen animals scurried underfoot, and even Walter's keen eyesight could only make out dim shadows in the brush. Walter's fur tingled in premonition.

After stepping into a large clearing, Walter stopped abruptly, causing Martha to stumble into his hind end. The lack of weeds and vines had confused him. The flat-pressed grass ahead of him suggested the presence of unknown creatures. Walter could only think that creatures living in the middle of this nightmarish swamp were not beings he wanted to meet.

Unexpectedly a sharp pain lanced through his right paw. Looking down he saw a tiny sliver of wood sticking out of his fur. Howling as another sliver shot into his shoulder, he tried to jump backward, but Martha appeared fixed in place and just stared directly ahead. Walter turned back and saw why she had frozen. A glowing green fire now burned brightly in the middle of the glade where only flattened grass had appeared before. It burned with an eerie light, casting no shadows upon the ground where it had spontaneously flared to life. Now was definitely a good time to leave, thought Walter. With a shove he pushed Martha back toward the murky swamp just as another sharp missile lodged into his left ear.

Walter's panicked shove must have knocked Martha out of her stupor, because she stumbled backward. He snarled when she found herself face-to-face—well, actually knee-to-face—with an angry pint-size creature. It stood only three feet tall and wore tattered clothes around its sticklike frame. Its long contorted fingers held a hollow reed to its puckered mouth while its long gnarly nose turned up out of the way like a twisted pickle. Its eyes glowed green like the fire in the center of the clearing. With a flick of its wrist, it gestured her back into the clearing, pointing the blowgun directly at her heart.

Walter checked out the Imp as Martha turned back. Its revolting appearance marked a change in their situation. They were not alone. Knowing they were surrounded, Walter turned grimly back toward the bizarre fire. The clearing now overflowed with strangely dressed Imps. Their gnarly forms hung from the trees surrounding the glade. Close to the fire, Imps swayed in a grotesque rhythm with green firelight glistening off their skins.

"Great," Walter growled.

"Quiet!" echoed a voice through the clearing. A large Imp appeared from within the midst of impish dancers. He wore fox pelts around his waist and ivy twined in his hair. His face was lined and withered, but his eyes glowed brighter than the fire.

"Why do you invade my domain?" His eyes pierced them straight through the gloom.

"We did not know," Walter replied. "We were just passing through heading east."

As Walter spoke the Imp king threw his arms up into the air and with a mighty roar declared, "East! East! Why do you travel east? What calls you in that direction? No good can come of heading east."

Taken aback by the king's ferocious response, Walter found himself unable to speak.

Martha stepped forward. "We head east in search of a great evil that threatens our land."

The Imp king leaned closer with interest. "What do you know of the evil that lies to the east?"

While clearing her throat, Martha searched for the right words. "We've heard stories of murders and vicious monsters appearing in villages to the far east. We seek to uncover the truth behind these stories."

The Imp king leaned back into a more relaxed position, but he eyed them cautiously as he continued, "My people have slowly disappeared over the last several weeks. At first I thought some new terror stalked the swamps, but two nights ago we caught one of my guards heading out of the swamps. When we questioned him, he said he had to go east. He couldn't tell us why, only that something called to him. We tried to keep him from leaving, but during the night he sneaked out of his dwelling and continued his quest.

"Since then I've questioned my subjects. Some feel a growing need to go east. One day they are here, and the next they are gone. I want to know what is taking my people!"

"Then your question is the same as ours," replied Walter. "We seek what is happening out east. If you let us go, we will search for the answer."

While nodding, the Imp king advanced toward Walter, waving a dagger at the wolf's throat. "I will agree to let you pass, but know this: if you lie, I will personally flay your skin.

You will be our guest this night. The swamps are not safe to travel in darkness. Strange new creatures darken its paths."

Humbly bowing, Walter responded, "We accept your gracious offer. We will wait till morning's light to continue our journey."

The Imps gathered around Martha and Walter and herded them across the clearing into the woods beyond. Darkness became absolute as they stepped out of the green fire's reach. The Imps continued on with unfaltering steps, their eyes sure of the dark path ahead. Several female Imps became entangled in Martha's skirts, curiously touching the fabric of her clothes. Others tugged at her hair, making shrill whistles of pleasure as they stroked her locks. Finally the lights of firepots appeared in the distance. They had reached the home of the Imps.

WALTER

Martha and Walter were led into a large hut covered with tree branches and twisted vines. The Imp king entered behind them, his chest puffed out in pride. "You will know the hospitality of my people!" he boldly decreed. And with a flourish of fox pelts, he sat himself down upon a pile of sticks that formed an odd-looking throne. With a clap of his hands, he summoned other Imps into the hut.

A short Imp with mud-encrusted hair gestured to a pile of limp leaves for Martha and Walter to occupy. Some Imps placed themselves down randomly upon other piles of leaves until those in the room formed a large circle. Other Imps then entered carrying sizzling trays of food. Walter's stomach growled as he smelled the aroma wafting from the platters. It had been a long time since he'd eaten. A female Imp with a necklace of mistylock blossoms placed a dish before him. He licked his lips and looked down to begin his feast, but the sight before him caused him to lose his well-earned appetite. The plate before him contained the head of a goat, its eyeballs still intact. The garnish for the main course appeared to be several fried worms and grubs. He looked sideways and spied the Imp king pluck out a goat eye with vigor and suck it sweetly after popping it into his mouth.

"Only the best for my guests. Will you not eat?" the king inquired.

With grim determination Martha picked up a grub in her left hand while nudging Walter with her right. With a look of reserve, she opened her mouth and placed the insect upon her tongue. The king smiled and continued his merry feasting. Next to Martha, Walter could hear the first squishy pop as she bit down firmly. There was nothing to do but eat. While nibbling at his dinner, Walter secretly smooshed as much as he could under the pile of leaves at his side.

The king raised a glass of reddish liquid and announced, "I have decided to aid these travelers in their quest. I will select six of my fiercest warriors to accompany them to the edge of the eastern swamp."

Martha nodded gratefully. "We thank Your Highness. A guide through these swamps will aid us greatly."

The king proceeded to point to six Imps who were standing erect at the entrance to the hut. They all held shiny silver spears at their sides, and each had a blowgun tied to its waist. While holding up the cup, the king gestured for them to advance. They walked proudly toward the king and then stopped at his side. Walter wondered what would happen next because the cup the king held was empty. He realized a second later that he should not have been so curious. With a rumble in his throat, the king spit into the cup. He passed the vessel to the first warrior next to him and then sat back as each warrior followed the king's example. All would have been okay if the strange ceremony had ended there, but with a narrowed eye,

Walter watched the last warrior advance upon him and hold out the cup for Martha and him to spit into. The warrior then swished the cup in a circle, blending the contents within. With a look of honor, he then took a greedy gulp.

Martha grabbed her stomach, but a warrior chose that moment to shove the cup under her face. Walter watched Martha's face turn green around the edges. With a thrust, the warrior tilted the cup into her mouth. A gag and a retch later, she swallowed a portion of the liquid within. Counting his blessings, Walter barely let his tongue touch the surface of the improvised drink, as the warrior next placed the cup under his snout. As each warrior and then the king took a sip in turn, Martha's complexion turned greener and greener.

The king raised the cup into the air. "Our common purpose is one. We have sealed it with our life's waters." With a bang he slammed the cup down and continued to eat his meal as if nothing had happened. The guards walked back to the entry and took up their positions.

Walter and Martha decided it was time to go to bed.

"Your Highness, we do not mean to be rude, but it has been a long day for us, and after such a wonderful meal, we feel truly overcome with exhaustion," said Walter.

"I understand," replied the king. "I will have Ruddo show you to your beds." He looked at one of the seated Imps and then let out a loud belch. "It is too bad you will miss dessert. Perhaps you will change your mind when you see the pig intestine gelatin that my wife has made."

"We are thankful for your generosity, but I will fall asleep sitting up at any moment," said Martha.

Ruddo rose and impatiently grunted for them to follow. Obviously he wanted to finish his meal. He led them out of the hut and into the dark night. After walking down a path to the right, he ushered them toward a lean-to against two tall trees. Another pile of leaves greeted them upon the rough ground. They sunk down with great weariness, and both Walter and Martha were asleep in moments.

A sharp poke in the side awoke Walter. The morning sun peaked through the trees above as he opened his eyes. One of the warrior Imps prodded him with his spear. "The sun is up. We leave." The Imp turned and walked away. With a gentle lick to Martha's face, Walter stood upon all fours, shaking his coat briskly in the morning dew.

"Is it breakfast time?" Martha's weary voice asked.

"Do you really want to eat breakfast here?" laughed Walter.

With a smile Martha rose and dusted herself off. "If we hadn't been surrounded last night, I would have made our meal a little more pleasant." She pulled a piece of moldy bread out of one of her patchwork pockets and held it up into the sunlight. "Voilà." With a fierce look of concentration, Martha muttered some words under her breath, and instants later the old bread was no more. In its place was a large blueberry muffin. She closed her eyes as she bit into it.

"I'll find my own breakfast," said Walter as he headed off into the woods to hunt.

After a quick scrub with some not too clear water, they were ready to go. Walter loped at Martha's side as they followed the double line of six Imps in front of them. The going through the swamp this time was much easier than it had been the night before. The Imps followed paths that were difficult to view with human or wolf eyes. They traveled most of the morning. The warriors kept up a brisk pace, which Walter had no problem matching; however, Martha began to lag behind after an hour. When they noticed that they were losing sight of one of their guests, the Imps decided to stop for a break.

Walter waited for Martha to catch up before sinking to the ground, but he startled the next second when a spear whizzed by her head. With a start of fear, Martha jumped to her feet, but Walter noticed the Imps weren't attacking but were slapping one of their own on the back. Walter glanced behind Martha and saw a large black hairy spider with yellow flecks on its legs impaled on the tree where she'd been leaning. Walter cautiously approached the spider, sniffing at the yellow ichor that seeped down the tree trunk from its body.

"Poisonous," he replied.

"Thank you!" gasped Martha. She realized how close she'd been to dying. The guardian Imp merrily walked to the tree and removed his spear from its two-inch target.

They continued their trek into the late afternoon, resting only as needed. The warriors protected them from several unknown hazards as they went. Toward sundown they came to the end of the swampland. Before them the land hardened into small hills and then continued on as open terrain.

"This is as far as we go," spoke one of the Imps. He pointed a gnarly finger over the hills in front of them. "A human trail passes by not far. It will take you east."

"Thank you," Walter said. He wasn't even sure the Imps had heard him, because when he looked behind himself he could already see their backs fading into the swamp.

KYLER

At school, two weeks went by and more people went missing. The city was in a real panic. It looked to the school for protection. After all, there were mages here. Unfortunately, none of the spells of protection that they'd tried had worked. Sword practice outside had been canceled and relocated to the arena. None of the students could remember there having been an arena before, but who knew in this place? The arena's interior was a large oval with a running track circling its edges. Two large pits took up equal space in the center of the room. It was in these spaces that forms and sparring were practiced. It was also the perfect place for Kyler to practice with his staff.

He spent each night working out, perfecting his skills. One evening he walked in on Darcy practicing with her sword. He'd been tempted to back out of the room, but she'd just looked at the staff in his hands and nodded. Sometimes he watched her practice. She was amazing. Her forms were smooth and her sword arm strong. The silence was finally broken one day when Darcy came over to Kyler with her sword raised.

"En garde," she mouthed.

After a second, a grin spread over his face. They circled each other, and then Darcy feigned to his left. Kyler knew she was bluffing. He swung to the right. The battle began.

Sweat poured off Kyler's forehead as he matched Darcy move for move. The forms flowed from his subconscious. As he held the staff in his hands, he felt the pounding of blood in his ears. Everything seemed to be clicking. His forms and his staff worked together to block Darcy's attempts at an easy victory. He pivoted on his left foot, avoiding a passing swing. After raising the staff up before him, he jabbed at her mid-section. She twisted to her left, avoiding the jab. He swept the staff back and forth, trying to knock her off her feet, but she jumped to avoid the blow, landing with her sword at the ready.

As time went by, Kyler slowed. He was in great shape, but Darcy was in better shape. In a heated moment, she thrust, blocked his staff, and sent it flying out of his hands. She stopped with the edge of the sword near his throat.

"I knew you had it in you," she said between gulps of air.

While panting he replied, "I knew it had to be in there somewhere," and then smiled.

They both started laughing. With their arms around each other, they walked out of the arena. Kyler took a moment to add, "I knew you were pretending to be John."

Darcy bumped into his hip. "I knew you knew."

Today Kyler walked to sword practice in the arena, carrying not a sword but his staff. He was tired of practicing in secret. Darcy had her own reasons, but he did not. Continued practice with the sword was a waste of time. He needed more experience with his staff.

As he entered the arena, he could see the other boys milling around. Their protective gear strapped firmly in place, they were ready for lessons. Kyler silently approached. Nobody glanced his way, and why should they have? They had nothing to fear from him. Master Dirk blew his whistle and the students went to their assigned rows. Kyler placed his staff beside the pile of swords and took his place in line. While moving, he pictured himself doing the steps with a staff in hand, not a sword, and lasted until the teacher blew the final whistle. With a look around, he saw three other students still in the circle. One was Darcy disguised as John. The teacher blew the whistle again, causing a flood of students to run and get their swords. Some jumped quizzically over his staff, while others simply passed by.

Kyler walked slowly toward the pile of weapons. He noticed Darcy/John waiting for him. He took a deep breath. It was now or never. He bent over and picked up his staff, grasping it firmly in his hands. Its smooth exterior felt familiar and warm. He lined up with the other boys waiting to get their partners. When the teacher reached him, he held his breath, but there was no disapproval. Master Dirk eyed the staff and then, with an approving nod, sent him to spar with Tom.

Tom didn't last long. Kyler knocked him flat into the dirt with his first move. Other boys ended up in the same position as they faced Kyler. He wouldn't be underestimated again. But that was fine by him. He wanted them to bring it on.

That evening at the library, he couldn't help gloating about his success. It was the only success he'd had in weeks. The students' search for information about the Griffin seemed fruitless. It had taken some time, but they'd finally found the reference to Mordrake that Darcy had remembered. Unfortunately, that's all it was, a reference. Henry began spending more time in the bards archive. Kyler didn't know how he'd done it, but Henry had obtained a pass into the bards' inner sanctum, the place where they kept their priceless records.

One afternoon Kyler returned to his room after lunch to find a note floating above his desk. Surprised, he saw that Henry had sent the note. It said to meet him in the library at eight o'clock. He'd found something. Kyler whooped with joy and fell back onto his bed. He looked at the ceiling and noticed a rainbow appear in the sky. Ever since his ceiling had decided to mimic the outside heavens, it always tried to match his mood. The other day when he'd stubbed his toe on the comfy chair, the sky had turned dark and filled with clouds. He'd actually ducked under his covers, as if to avoid being drenched by a sudden downpour.

Henry was already waiting in their normal meeting place at eight o'clock. A huge smile filled his face. This was going to be good. Kyler just knew it. Darcy arrived not a moment later. Upon taking their seats, they waited for Henry to begin, but his big silly grin just grew larger.

"What is it?" Kyler could contain himself no longer. "What did you find?"

Henry pulled a rolled-up parchment out from below his cloak. It looked yellow and brittle, the writing faded and worn.

"I had a breakthrough," he announced. After rolling the parchment out on the table before him, Henry began to sing the words to an old song. His voice was pure and flawless to Kyler's ear. Henry's finger followed along the parchment as he sang. About halfway down he paused. He looked up to make sure the others were both paying attention before continuing,

And the battle against evil was won,
Mordrake and Griffin were undone.
Cast into slumber in a bottomless pit.
Never to wake while the guardians sit.
And the world recovered from strife.
Remembering once again the good life.

He stopped singing.

"The rest of the song goes on to describe the attributes of a well-lived life."

Henry smiled at them again. He'd found their first clue.

But Kyler wasn't so impressed. "It just tells us what we already know."

"Look closer." Henry pointed to the verse about Mordrake and the Griffin. After their names was an asterisk.

"What does it mean?" Kyler questioned.

Henry moved his finger down to the bottom of the parchment and stopped at another asterisk. "The writing is so faded I can't read it, but I know it has to be about Mordrake."

Darcy elbowed her way in to look at the parchment. "Let me look. My mom tells me I have eyes like an eagle." She studied the writing. After a while she threw her hands up in exasperation. "I can see symbols. I just don't know what they mean. I think—"

"Let me try," Kyler interrupted. He looked down at the writing. The words glared up at him. It was easy to read. "*Milford's Magical History 6*," he said.

Darcy looked at him in shock, "But, I think it's written in the ancient language."

"What ancient language? I asked if there was another language when I got here, and everyone told me no, only basic common," said Kyler.

Henry eyed Kyler warily. "That's because none of the students on your skill level know about it. It's called the ancient language, but it's also known as the mages tongue. It's what all true magic spells are written in. We only learned it existed this year, and they only teach it to students who pass the senior journeyman test. It takes years to learn. There's a symbol for every word. Even then only a few are able to speak it with power." He looked at Kyler more seriously, pointing at the scroll. "Are you telling me you could read that?"

Things were slowly dawning on Kyler. He thought of his aunt, her teaching him to read and write, and her lectures on books and reading. He'd been taught to read and write the mages tongue. No wonder he'd been unable to read basic.

"My aunt taught me."

Henry's mouth dropped open in awe. "You mean you're fluent in it?"

"I think so," Kyler responded. "Am I screwed?"

"No way!" Darcy answered. "They're always looking for people with mage potential. And you seem to have it in spades."

Ideas started rolling through Kyler's brain. His thoughts returned to the placement test in the headmaster's office, but Henry interrupted his remembrances.

"So where do we find *Milford's Magical History 6*?"

"If it's written in the ancient language, we haven't got a shot. I don't know a single senior in the whole school who has seen a book in the mages tongue," said Darcy.

"I might have some idea where we could look," Kyler added. "There's another library."

"You're kidding?" Darcy clapped her hands.

Just then the librarian came into view.

Did she hear? Now I'm in for it. Kyler waited for the shoe to drop, but instead the librarian turned to Darcy.

"You're wanted in the headmaster's office."

"Why?" asked Darcy.

"I don't know. A Searching note appeared over my desk a few moments ago, and I remembered seeing you head back here."

The librarian put her arm around Darcy and steered her away. "It must be pretty important. Come along now."

Darcy turned back to the boys. "I'll be right back. Don't finish your explanation till I return. I want to hear everything."

The boys waited for a whole hour, but Darcy never came back.

DARCY

Darcy followed the librarian toward the doorway. Her mind shifted over everything she'd done the past few days. She remembered knocking that jerk Howard down in the dorm hallway when he'd teased her about being a she-male. She didn't feel sorry at all. He'd got what he deserved. Besides, she'd never gotten into trouble for knocking kids around before.

She remembered her first week at school and the boy who'd called her "princess."

Leroy later told her the kid had probably just meant it as a statement of fact, but Darcy didn't care. She was no lily-livered princess. All the princesses she knew loved to embroider, talk about boys, and take dance classes. Her cousins were always trying to teach her how to waltz. She hated it! All those frilly dresses and hair bows. It had been a wonderful day when her father had decided to send her to school with Leroy. He thought she'd be forced into line, but all she'd thought about was freedom, and no more dance classes. She'd been right about more freedom, but not about the dance classes. They still forced her to learn all the required dances and steps necessary for a royal ball.

She couldn't figure out what the headmaster wanted with her. *Maybe my dad wants me back home? That would so totally bite!* She'd finally made friends here, and Leroy wasn't bothering her anymore. Things had started falling into place, and she was enjoying herself. The librarian stopped in front of the doorway.

"Just head straight to the headmaster's office. They'll be waiting for you."

Darcy took a deep breath and crossed over the threshold. *It couldn't be that bad, could it?*

The headmaster's office felt warm and cozy. The backs of three men faced her. She recognized Leroy at once with his tattered old brown fuzzy slippers. The other two men reminded her of her father. They stood tall and erect with perfectly tailored uniforms. The air of tension around their shoulders projected alertness. They both wore the royal-green sash of her father's house draped across their chests and carried sharp swords that glinted in the firelight. The headmaster sat behind his desk facing her. His old face looked haggard, and his eyes lacked their usual aura of power. When he caught sight of her, he gestured for her to sit.

Darcy wasn't sure she wanted to sit. Whatever the problem was, her brother stood, so why couldn't she? She was about to voice her defiance when Leroy noticed her presence and turned to look at her. His face was ghostly white, and tears ran in a stream down his cheeks. Things looked bad. Maybe she'd take a seat after all.

"Darcy, it's terrible news," Leroy began, but he couldn't finish.

One of her father's personal guards turned toward her. His voice sounded so dry and unemotional, like sandpaper, that she missed his first few words, but then the world came rushing in. "You're brother William is dead. It was a hunting accident."

How can that be? William is always around. He used to bind her scraped knees when she fell out of trees while trying to spy on the boys. He'd been the one to suggest she go off to school with Leroy. He understood her need to be who she wanted to be, and now he was gone. It couldn't be true. There had to be some mistake.

"But how? I don't understand. William started hunting when he was four years old. How could there have been an accident?"

"All the details aren't clear yet," said the other guard. "It seems he was hunting pheasant with other members of the estate when an arrow struck him in the chest. As far as we can figure, an arrow meant for a bird went astray. It was a horrible time for an accident. The healer had left the day before to attend a risky birth in the next village. The local midwife did all she could, but the bleeding was too severe. By the time the healer arrived, it was too late. I'm sorry, miss."

Darcy felt things grow dark around the edges of her vision. This was too much information for her to process. She'd read hundreds of stories about heroes and death, but this was the first time it had personally touched her life.

"Does Father wish us to come home?"

"There will be a family service in four days," began one of the guards. "After that, you may return to school." He turned toward Leroy. "You are now the heir. You'll need to remain at the estate. As you both know, unless your uncle has a male child, the throne will pass to your father."

Darcy nodded. She thought about her uncle, the king. He'd been blessed with a whole bunch of daughters, her annoying cousins, but so far, no boys. Dad was his younger brother, and unless a male heir was born, the rulership would pass to his line. No one actually expected this to happen. The way her uncle had children, a boy would be born sooner or later, but until then, Dad's line needed protecting. Leroy would have to go home and start learning about politics and diplomacy. Her brother looked toward the guards.

"When do we leave?" he questioned.

"In the morning. Pack your bags and get some sleep. We'll head out at first light."

A guard escorted them both to their rooms. Darcy hated the idea of leaving, but for William she'd brave the fiercest tempest. *Stupid accident! Why him?* Tears rushed down her face.

The next morning she set out with her brother before her schoolmates were even awake. She'd wanted to say good-bye to Kyler and Henry, but there had been no time. The guards forced her to ride in the royal carriage while Leroy got to ride his horse. Her emotions were so strung out that she didn't argue. Well, for the first few hours. After lunch, she insisted on a horse of her own. The guards ignored her, but Leroy took her side.

"Give Darcy a horse. She'll be a much better companion if she gets her way."

"Thanks, Leroy." Then Darcy laughed. She couldn't remember the last time she'd thanked her brother for anything. However, the guards held firm, and Darcy spent the next several days in the carriage. Her only breaks came at the inns where the stopped for the night.

As they rode up onto her uncle's lands, Darcy couldn't stop her feelings from overwhelming her facade. However, when the castle loomed before them, a bitter feeling of injustice replaced her grief.

"There is no way it was an accident. William is—was—the best hunter in the land."

Once inside she was swarmed by her cousins. They sobbed and moaned and told Darcy how sorry they felt. She spent the next several hours going through protocol in the ladies solar. Her mother was devastated, unable to do more than hold Darcy in her arms and whimper. In return, Darcy hugged back just as tightly. Several times she tried to ask her mother about the accident, but her mom just cried harder. Darcy decided she would need to talk to her father.

The one time she spotted him, he was in the throne room with Leroy, talking to the king's personal advisor, Chancellor Usborn. He looked ashen, a pale version of his normal robust self. His arm was draped over Leroy's shoulder, and from her brother's stance, she could tell her father was placing his weight on him. Darcy wanted to run to his side and hold him tight, but it wasn't proper right then. She waited, but the intense conversation would brook no interruption. Reality was like a swift kick in the gut, as she realized that from now on Leroy would be just as distant as he was now.

The funeral took place the next morning. Every noble within a three-day ride was there. She'd done her part and stood silently by her mother's side, accepting condolences and well wishes. The ceremony was long. The king spoke first. Darcy knew he had loved William like a son, and the tears he shed were true. When her own dad spoke, she felt her heart clench. His despair was deep and unrequited. Her mother had sobbed, "My son," before she'd collapsed into a maid's arms. Chancellor Usborn had spoken of her brother's loyalty to the kingdom and his passion for life. The last person to speak was Leroy. Darcy watched her brother struggle to stay composed while the mantle of leadership descended upon him.

William was buried in the royal vaults beneath the castle. Her uncle had led the procession through the courtyard and to the lower levels. Only the royal family was allowed at the final closing of her brother's tomb. Darcy would never forget the sound the solid stone made when its final corner was set in place. It was after this that her entire family retired to their suite. She knew it was not the time to raise questions, but she could only wait so long.

KYLER

The boys didn't see Darcy until over a week later. Rumors had gone around the school about a death in the royal family, but no one knew any specifics, and Kyler hadn't associated Darcy with the news. Henry and Kyler were studying in Henry's room when she walked in and sat down on the bed. Both boys looked up, astonished.

"Where have you been?" asked Kyler. "You've been gone forever."

Henry gave Darcy a hug, and Kyler began to think he'd known more than he'd said.

"Life happened." Darcy moved over, fluffing the pillow next to her. "I don't often tell people about my family. It makes them start acting funny." She looked at Kyler. "It was nice, you not knowing and treating me normal."

"Not knowing what?" asked Kyler.

"Um," mumbled Darcy. "You see, my uncle is the high king."

"Huh?" said Kyler. "No way. Who else knows?" Henry raised his hand halfway into the air. Kyler gave him a shove.

"My brother William was murdered. I went home for his funeral."

"That's terrible. I'm really sorry, Darcy," said Kyler.

"Wait," said Henry. "I heard he died in an accident, but you just said he was killed."

"Yes." Darcy nodded, and then she punched the fluffy pillow. "What's really sad about it is that no one will listen to me when I tell them it wasn't an accident."

"What do you mean?" asked Kyler.

Darcy looked fierce. "Well, William was a great hunter. I saw where the accident took place. It was in a wide-open area. I don't see how someone could have missed a pheasant and hit him. There's other stuff bothering me, too. I just need some time to sort it out in my head. I can't go back to my father without real evidence this time. He just thought I was depressed before."

Henry looked troubled. "If there's anything we can do to help, let us know."

"Thanks, guys. But right now I just want to get my mind off things. Where are we on our hunt?"

"Ahh," Kyler began. "Before you left I was telling you where I think more information could be found. There's another library here."

Darcy brightened. "I've thought about that the whole time I was gone. What's the deal?" Her enthusiasm was contagious.

"Well, a while back I explored the school," said Kyler with grin. "I ended up in the ruins of the old high king's castle at Naterum. I think the school has a portal directly to it!"

"Really? Are you sure?" asked Darcy.

Kyler nodded. "I saw the throne room and everything. I think the mages have rebuilt a good portion of the building. That's where I saw the library. It's enormous."

"Did you two go while I was gone?"

"We tried to sneak down there on a couple of occasions, but there were too many mages roaming the halls. We were going to give it another go late tonight. Now that you're back, it'll be perfect," said Kyler.

"Sounds like fun to me." She turned to Henry. "Did you find out any more information in the bards archive?"

"Nothing else. But Kyler's worked on some stuff. Show her, man."

Kyler smiled and went to Henry's closet. He brought out an old box filled with candle stubs. Smiling, he lifted one out and held it before his eyes.

"For the longest time, I couldn't figure out how I was supposed to light a candle by just looking at it. After you guys told me about the mages tongue, I gave it another try." While staring intently at the candle, Kyler spoke the words "Candle, light" under his breath. Immediately the candle flared to life. He looked up, grinning. "I had things all wrong. During the placement test, I thought about fire, not light. You have to be specific in the words you choose. Watch this."

Kyler handed the lit candle to Henry. He looked directly at their potions notebook siting on the table. Holding out his hand, he said in the mages tongue, "Potions notebook." The notebook lifted off the table with a jerk and flew directly into his hand.

"Cool," marveled Darcy. "How did you figure it out?"

"Well, when you guys told me the symbols I knew were really a form of magic language, I started thinking. Aunt Martha had talked to me about focusing on an object, imagining its symbol in my mind, and then speaking its name. So I tried with the candle. I think the reason so many mages have trouble with it is that you have to be very specific. If you're fighting a Bavarian monkey, you can't just think "monkey," you also have to know the word for Bavarian. Just like with the notebook. I couldn't say "Book, come" because that isn't being specific about any one book. There are tons all around. I had to know the words for potion and notebook."

"This is really great," said Darcy. "We should tell someone."

"I was going to tell Master Ernie, but I decided to wait until we have more information about Mordrake from the mages library. That way he'll be real stoked.

"When I first started practicing with the candle, it was really hard to keep my thoughts fixed on both thinking about the symbols and saying the words at the same time. I tried to teach Henry, but nothing seemed to happen."

"Well, let a girl show you how to do it!"

Kyler explained the symbol to Darcy. He had her focus on an unlit candle, think of the symbols, and say the words. As hard as she tried, nothing happened.

"Maybe it just takes some time to learn," said Kyler, but he couldn't help but feel a bit of satisfaction.

"That's okay. I'll keep working on it though. That would be a cool trick to pull on Leroy," said Darcy.

KYLER

The three friends continued discussing their plans to raid the mages library. Darcy was excited just to see it. After lights-out the three accomplices snuck out of their rooms and met at the doorway to the dorms. They were each dressed in dark clothes, and Kyler took the lead. Darcy had her bright red hair squashed down under a knit cap. Henry had gone the extra mile and applied dark coal under his eyes. He looked like a zombie. While holding hands they stepped through the doorway as Kyler thought of the word for entrance in mages tongue. They stepped into an ancient dark hallway. It was eerily silent this late at night. The shadows on the walls flickered like watching ghosts.

"Come on," whispered Kyler. "It's this way."

They passed several doors before they came to the library. The wide-open portal looked inviting, but Kyler held back. He pointed to an inscription above the doorway while stopping the others in their tracks.

"I only peeked last time. I didn't go in. The carving there says that those who seek the library may enter at the 'word.'"

"What word?" Darcy asked. "Is there a word written there?"

"Not that I can see," said Kyler. "It's written in mages tongue, so it must be something only mages would know."

Kyler thought hard about what the riddle meant. He was sure that if he walked through the door without uttering the magic word he'd be blasted. Who knows what the mages used as a security system? Maybe bells would start ringing throughout the school, perhaps he'd turn to stone, or maybe a powerful lightning bolt would fry him to the bone. Nothing Kyler thought of sounded like a positive experience.

He stood up and began feeling around the door frame, looking for a clue, for anything. There was nothing else carved into the wood. Standing upon Henry's shoulders, he traced the lines of the riddle with his finger.

"We've got to hurry up," said Darcy. "We don't know who else is down here."

What word was he supposed to say? This whole mission depended on him. He thought and thought as Henry lowered him down. Then it came to him. Maybe it was just like in the school, where you had to think of where you were going as you passed through a doorway. What if the word he needed was *library*, but he just needed to think about it in the mages tongue?

"I have an idea, guys," he spoke. "Do you trust me? We've only got one shot at this."

"We came this far with you," said Darcy.

"We'll go the rest of the way," continued Henry.

Holding hands the three stepped over the entryway with Kyler speaking the word library in the ancient tongue. A brief tingle surged up their spines as they stepped into the room. Kyler waited for more, but nothing happened. *Score!*

"Let's go, guys," Kyler said.

"But where do we look?" Henry asked. "This place is huge. Do you think it's alphabetical?"

"I doubt it." Darcy laughed. "Let's just see what's in the first bookcase. That way we can get out of the open."

They headed to a large row of books. All of the books were squirming and wiggling. Several were actually chained down to prevent them from moving. One of the books opened a pair of eyes and stared at them as they approached. It followed their movements with dark pupils.

"This place is creepy," said Kyler. "I think we'd better be careful how close we get to the bookshelves."

Just then one of the books leapt out at Henry and bit his arm. Scarlet blood ran down his elbow in rivulets.

"Dude!" Henry screeched.

The book returned to its place, happily chewing away. While trying to help Henry and keep him quiet, Kyler didn't notice the footsteps that approached him from behind.

"Can I help you?"

Kyler jumped into the air. They'd been caught. His heart pounding in his chest, he looked into the face of a very old man. He was very tall and wore a purple cloak that hung to the floor. Wrinkles were at home on his waxy face, and his blue eyes looked right into Kyler's.

"We're sorry. We got lost," Kyler fibbed.

"Nonsense. You couldn't have entered the library if you didn't have the skill level to be able to use it. So, how can I help you?"

Darcy had finished bandaging Henry's arm with a piece of her shirt. She looked at the old man. "We're looking for a book called *Milford's Magical History 6*."

The man nodded his head. "No one's looked at that book in years. It's going to be really excited to get off the shelf."

"Ah, guys?" interrupted Henry. "A little help?"

"Oh, allow me." The old man murmured some words over Henry's arm and—poof—the wound healed. "Now then, follow me," he gestured. "Everything is sorted by the century it was written and by the author."

They followed the librarian deep into the library. It was an amazing place. They passed a table where two books were playing chess by moving the pieces with bookmarks that hung out of their pages. There was an area where moonlight shined through a high window into a pool of silver. Several books lay about, basking in its glow. A few mages in purple robes sat at tables with piles of books beside them. They were so engrossed, they didn't bother to look up as the small group passed. One of the mages was writing with his left hand while fighting off a book with his right. The whole place seemed magical. It was like entering a whole other world full of wonderful and amazing ideas. Kyler felt a pulse of energy running through his veins. He belonged here. He could hear books calling out to him, wanting to be read.

They passed a section of cages that were bolted to the floor. Inside, books growled and threw themselves against the walls of the cage. Others attacked one another with snarls and lashed out with pages sharpened into teeth. The old man stopped.

"Be careful here. Don't get close to the cages. These books have been tainted by dark magic. We have to keep them locked up for everyone's safety. They'd like nothing better than to get their hands, um, I mean pages, on a person. If you ever need a book from here, we have a team of mages that help hold them down while you grab the one you want. We sprinkle them with a little sleep dust first, of course."

The man continued to lead them through what seemed like a maze of passageways. He finally stopped in a section full of old dusty books. Several of them were snoring. "They don't get much action back here. Stuff written a millennium ago isn't as popular as you'd think." He wandered over to one of the shelves of books. "These are Milford's writings. You should find what you're looking for here. If you need me, just call my name: Alfred. I'll hear you anywhere in the library."

Before leaving he turned to look at Kyler more closely. "Have I met you before? You remind me of someone."

"No, I'm sure we've never met."

The old man snapped his fingers. "Aha! I've got it. You look just like your father. He used to sneak down here, too."

"My father!" exclaimed Kyler "You knew my father?" Ever since Kyler'd come to the school, he'd been looking for information about his dad. It had taken him a while to start, having to learn basic common and all, but he'd searched through old school newspapers in the library upstairs. Unfortunately he didn't know exactly when his father had been there, so he just started twelve years before and started working back. So far he'd had no luck.

"Yep. I'm sure you're George's boy. You look just like him. You have the same aura, too."

"What's an aura?" asked Darcy.

"Tell me about him," pleaded Kyler at the exact same moment.

The librarian chuckled. "He was a really smart boy. Always getting into trouble. But he had such a gift. To see him work a spell was like watching a dream. He had an older sister here, too. Used to play the worst practical jokes on her. I remember when he replaced her shampoo with glue. Her hair stuck out straight for days. The other teachers hated having him in their classes. He always contradicted them and asked questions that were too complex for the other students to understand. So, he spent a lot of time down here. The ancient tongue seemed to come naturally to him. After a time, he stopped going to classes and spent all his time down here going through advanced spell books. The headmaster didn't dare expel him. They hadn't seen anyone so gifted in ages.

"That all changed when he met Sally, of course. He fell head over heels. His studying slowed down as he courted your mom, and then he left the school to settle down. Others were shocked, but I wasn't. He knew more than most of the teachers anyhow. What was the point in staying?"

"How long ago was that?"

"I'd say about twenty years ago. I'll let you kids get on with your research." Alfred caught Kyler's eye. "We can talk another time."

Reluctantly Kyler turned to the rows of books written by Milford and began searching. Henry and Darcy did the same. Both of them carried pieces of paper with the title spelled out in mages tongue.

Time passed in silence until Darcy called out, "I found it."

The book she pulled off the shelf sighed as she brought it down. When she rubbed the front of the book to get the dust off its cover, it folded its pages into a smile. "It seems happy to see us. Let's sit down and dig in." She laid the book down on a nearby table, and Henry and Kyler dragged chairs across the floor so they could see as well.

Darcy pointed to the book. "I guess it's up to Kyler now."

With a nod Kyler began to read. The book didn't have any type of index, so it was impossible to tell where to look, so he started at page one. He scanned for any mention of Mordrake or the Griffin. Halfway through, he began reading about a war that had taken place for the city of Naterum.

A grunt broke his concentration. "What's it say?" asked Darcy. "We can't read it ourselves you know."

"Oh, sorry. Hold on. I'll paraphrase."

"Around a thousand years ago, a mage warlord rose among the outland tribes. It was Mordrake. He was ambitious and wanted to be king, so he started using dark magic to gather an army. His words were like honey, and people came from miles around to join him. It says he was known for his violent temper, and that during fits of rage he would kill anyone unfortunate enough to be close to him. His constant companion was a monstrous creature that had been pieced together using dark magic. It had the body of a lion and the head of a bird. It came to be called the Griffin and is thought to be the only one ever created. It had the same bloodlust as its creator and hungered for flesh of any kind. The only thing that could control it was the call of its master."

Kyler paused in thought. "Oh, that explains what happened to Walter."

"What?" asked Henry.

"The Griffin left him half-eaten and flew off."

"Yuck," said Darcy. "Keep going."

"Together Mordrake and the Griffin fought their way toward the high king's city. Their army razed everything in its path. Desperate to stop him, the high king called together a council of mages. They entered into an agreement to stop Mordrake at all costs. Most of the council died in the attempt to kill him. In the end, the remaining members of the council concluded that if there was a way to kill him, they didn't know what it was. So they devised a plan to put Mordrake into a deep sleep and place him in a hidden location to sleep for eternity. The Griffin was another story. It was known to have two flaws. One, its soul was connected to Mordrake; and two, it could only die by fire. Being a creature of magic, the Griffin proved immune to the attempts of man to burn it. Even though mages threw fireballs at it and the villagers poured tar over it, the creature's protective skin repelled the fire and the mages could not figure out how to burn it. It was hoped that the Griffin, being tied to Mordrake, would sleep as well."

"Wow, that's some story," said Kyler. "I guess it worked though. Mordrake disappeared from history."

"It worked until now, you mean," said Henry. "Now they're awake."

"Hey, guys, look at this next paragraph. It says the location of the hiding place of Mordrake and the Griffin is watched over by ever-vigilant guardians and that details of how they put Mordrake to sleep and how to get to his hidden chamber are in a sealed volume of the minutes of the council of mages."

"I bet those records were destroyed when the city fell," said Darcy. "Maybe that's why the council of mages doesn't know any of this stuff now. Let's take this book up to show Master Ernie. Maybe it will get the current council of mages to believe your aunt Martha."

WALTER

Martha and Walter walked over the low hills looking for any signs of a human trail. They heard people on the path before they saw it. After cresting a rather barren hill, they came upon a merchant caravan. Brightly colored wagons circled around a central bonfire, and loud music played to an enthusiastic crowd. Well-armored guards stood post around the camp.

"We better go slowly. We don't want to excite the guards," warned Walter.

Cautiously they approached the camp. As they came nearer, one of the guards detained them.

"Who are you, and what are you doing here?" he demanded.

"I'm a healer, and this is my pet wolf," said Martha. "We were hoping to join with this caravan and head east."

"I'll take you to Boyd. He's the head merchant."

They followed the guard into the circle of wagons, coming to a stop in front of a squat balding man. He wore the rich robes of a merchant and had the belly of a man accustomed to the comforts of life. He turned toward them as they approached.

"What do we have here?" he inquired of the guard.

"I caught these two approaching the camp from the west. She says she's a healer looking for passage east."

Boyd looked questionably at Martha. "Why would you want to go east? There are rumors of war and trouble."

Thinking fast, Martha answered, "I'm a healer. I go where I am needed. I also have some rudimentary magic skills." Walter let out a cough, though Martha knew it was really a chuckle.

"What would you offer my caravan if we accept you into our group?" Boyd asked.

"I would offer my skills. Plus, my pet Walter is a fierce fighter. He will help guard the camp."

Boyd nodded in agreement, and gestured a welcome. "A healer will be most helpful. Make yourself at home." He pointed to a wagon painted with bright pink flowers. "You can ride and sleep with Dorothy. She's traveling with her little boy and has extra room in her wagon."

While walking around the strange assortments of wagons, they looked at the different wares for sale. There were wagons full of jewelry, dry goods, leather jerkins, and boots. Walter was interested in a wagon full of jerky. The smell seemed like heaven to him. He could make out beef, pig, and venison jerky. His stomach rumbled with hunger, but the wagon was closed to guests, so he looked at the display of knives in the next wagon over. He could tell most were shoddy imitations, but a few had the look of well-crafted blades. He loped off and caught up to Martha at Dorothy's pink wagon. She was already deep into conversation with the owner. He looked inside and saw colorful weavings hanging from hooks. Blankets stacked in neat piles lined the sides, providing extra comfort for extra-bumpy rides. A little boy sat on top of the biggest pile, staring at Walter with wide eyes. Walter gave him a wink and then turned back to Martha.

"Why are you heading east then?" Martha asked Dorothy.

"Wares are always necessary, so we decided to head out despite the rumors. Boyd hired extra guards for the trip, so I'm sure we'll be safe enough."

"We'll help out all we can on the journey," said Martha.

"You're more than welcome. It'll be nice to have someone to talk to. Do you want me to show you around camp? There won't be much time to meet anyone when we move out tomorrow."

"Sounds good to me." Martha joined Dorothy as she headed off to the next wagon. Walter took a look around and decided it was a good time for a nap. He circled in place, then curled up into a ball.

The first two days of travel passed in doldrums of boredom. The caravan traveled slowly, wary of danger. Martha and Dorothy became fast friends. Walter decided to leave them alone and scout the route ahead.

As dusk approached on day three, Walter slowed down to wait for the merchants to catch up with him. He liked running ahead. It gave him the freedom to race the wind. As he sank to his haunches, a strange smell floated past his nose. The odor of decaying meat and rotting vegetables assailed him. His eyes narrowed in on a small brushy area to his left. In a crouch, he silently began stalking the smell. Behind a scrub brush, he found a deserted campsite. The smell of refuse and bodily waste filled the air. He felt the fire pit with his paws and noticed that warmth still lingered in the gray coals. Whoever had been here wasn't long gone. His thoughts turned toward the caravan and Martha. He had to get back and warn them of the suspected danger.

He raced back along the path he had come. His tongue lolled out of his mouth as he fought for air to breathe. Suddenly screams broke through the air around him. He rushed past the last rise to find the caravan fully engulfed by ferocious Orcs. The monstrous giants towered over the humans. Their faces appeared disfigured and scarred, so ugly not even a mother could love them. Their skin, which was pale green and as thick as alligator hide, was covered with mismatched armor collected from previous victims. He was too late!

He charged into the fray, searching desperately for Martha. The poor people around him stood little chance against these monstrous seven-foot-tall beasts. The Orcs swung their cudgels and swords at all they encountered. Their strong blows sent people flying through the air to land in motionless lumps. Walter fought his way past a bellowing one-eyed Orc heading toward Dorothy's wagon. Up ahead he could see a small group of humans gathered together, trying their best to resist. In their midst stood Martha, her plump frame standing tall and rigid, her arms reaching out toward the deadly Orcs. He saw her mutter a few words, and sparks shot out from her hands, striking an Orc square in the chest. It looked down in surprise to see a hole passing through its armor. With a gasp of disbelief, it then fell to the ground dead.

After reaching Martha's side, Walter joined the battle. He darted in and out of the Orcs, tearing chunks of skin here and ripping appendages off there. A feeling of blood-lust washed over him as he saw the havoc being made of the merchant caravan. He returned to Martha and watched her destroy another Orc with her magic, but this time her proud stance faltered and she sagged heavily against Dorothy. There were too many for one mage to handle, and her energy was draining fast. Walter saw Dorothy's little boy cowering under their wagon, tears running down his face. He grabbed a blanket in his jaws and dropped it over the boy, blocking him from view. The scene before Walter was horrific. Bloody corpses lay strewn around the road while Orcs rampaged over now vacant wagons, setting them on fire and breaking wheels with their bare hands. Walter knew they were in a fight they could not win. He had to save Martha and escape.

He hurried over to her side and began tugging at her skirts, but she brushed him away and shot another bolt of fire from her hands. This time she fell where she stood. Walter bit the scruff of her dress and began pulling with all his strength. Martha struggled from Walter's grasp. She turned toward Dorothy and the boy. While stumbling toward her friend, she missed the Orc approaching on her right. Walter gave a terrible snarl and jumped, but he was too late. The Orc clubbed Martha across the head, dropping her into a slumped pile upon the ground. The Orc raised his club to finish her off, but another Orc snarled at him from across the field.

"She's the mage! Take her! Mordrake needs all mages for the solstice."

Walter saw his chance and jumped at the Orc. His teeth sank deep into the Orc's muscular wrist. The Orc shook, trying to dislodge Walter's fangs, but Walter dug in even deeper. With a final thrust, the Orc slammed Walter against a large rock. He slid to the ground, whimpering, the bitter taste of blood in his mouth. There was something wrong with his vision: everything seemed to swerve, and every image he saw seemed to double. He vomited just before losing consciousness.

KYLER

Master Ernie whooped with joy when they showed him their discovery. He pored over Milford's book like an eager child.

"Tell me again how you got this book?"

"I found a reference to the book in some old lyrics in the bards archive," began Henry.

Kyler interrupted. "Then I remembered that I'd seen another library at the school. We thought we should find out if there was any more information before we let you know about it."

Master Ernie stared at Kyler. "How did you enter the library?"

"I figured out the riddle above the door."

"You're telling me you could read the writing carved above the door?"

Kyler squirmed.

"I kinda figured out that I already knew it. Aunt Martha taught it to me."

"Your aunt Martha taught the language of magic to a child who had no idea what he was learning? That goes against the very code of magic. That—that..." Master Ernie puffed up huge, but then slowly deflated. "We're very careful about who learns the true ways of magic. It takes most students years to even be considered."

"Sorry, I didn't know. I just thought it was normal."

"Kyler," Master Ernie questioned, "have you performed any magic?"

"Um, would you be mad if I said yes?"

"No," Ernie replied.

Kyler smiled. "Do you want me to show you?"

Ernie leaned back in his chair. "If you're anything like your father, this should be good."

Kyler glanced around the room, looking for something he could use. Hundreds of candles rested in sconces along the wall. After taking a calming breath, he held a picture of all the candles in his mind and imagined them all going out. He spoke the words for "candles, go out" while seeing the symbols in his mind. The room was immediately cast into darkness. He thought of the candles again, this time burning bright. He spoke and thought, "candles, light," and the room grew bright again.

"That's amazing," exclaimed Master Ernie. "Do you feel any side affects at all?"

"What type of affects?"

"Headache, nausea, dizziness?"

"Not that I'm aware of. I used to feel tired, but now that rarely happens."

"Incredible. Any other student attempting to do what you just did would have to sit down now. Only mages that have

DORINE WHITE

practiced for years can expel large amounts of energy without feeling depleted in some way. We're going to have a talk later. Got it?"

"Yes, Master Ernie. Got it," Kyler replied.

"The school can't have you wandering around with that much power and no knowledge of how to use it. In the meantime, I'm going to present this book to the council of mages. They need to take action right away. I'll also see if there are records remaining of past council of mages meetings. A thousand years is pushing it, but you never know."

As they talked on the way back to their rooms, Kyler smirked. He felt ten feet tall. They'd actually done it. They'd found what everyone else had looked for but couldn't find. Caught up in the emotional high, Kyler forgot to pay attention to where his feet took him. It wasn't until a sobbing kitchen servant plowed into him that he returned to the real world. Darcy reached out and grabbed the girl's arm to steady her.

"What's wrong?" asked Darcy.

The girl's lips trembled as she talked. "It's Ralph, he was on kitchen duty with me this evening. He, he..." she stammered, "...he went out to get more wood for the oven pit. The previous boy forgot to do it, and we had to keep the fire going. I told Ralph not to go out there alone. I told him to let me get the groundskeeper. But he didn't listen. He just went out anyway." Sobs raked the girl's frail body.

"That's when I saw it. This huge birdlike thing swooped out of the air and grabbed him by the foot. Ralph screamed and screamed, I didn't know what to do. The groundskeeper is supposed to be in his room, but I can't find him. I have to tell someone. They've got to help Ralph!" The girl broke into hysterics.

Kyler was already in motion. He propelled the girl down the hall and told her to find Master Ernie and tell him what had happened. Then he headed toward his room.

"Well, what are you waiting for? Get your stuff!" he yelled.

"Are you insane? You're not going after it?" called Henry.

"You better believe it. I know Ralph, and I'm not about to let him get eaten by some cocky bird! The least we can do is try to rescue him. Maybe the Griffin will be out hunting again."

"What? You think the Griffin is just going to leave him alone?" asked Darcy.

"No, but it might just beat him senseless and save him for later. There might be a slim chance, especially if we get him right to a healer," said Kyler.

"What am I supposed to do," asked Henry, "sing it to sleep?"

"You can carry a sword, can't you?" replied Darcy. "I've seen you fight. You're not too bad."

"Yeah, but that's only fighting in full body protection with dull blades. I've never fought for real."

"Well now's your chance. Go get your stuff!" Kyler yelled as he raced into his room. He didn't have to tell Darcy twice.

The night was dark and bitterly cold. Kyler took a second to breathe the crisp air into his lungs. The light from the kitchen windows cast an eerie gleam upon the woodpile. Not three feet away lay Ralph's shoe. It looked sad, sitting there all alone covered in mud. It was even sadder to see the trail in the dirt leading into the forest. The only ray of hope was that the Griffin had decided that flying through the dense forest would be tricky and had decided to drag poor Ralph.

"At least it'll be easy to follow," said Kyler.

He led the way into the eerily quiet woods, carefully following the path of broken branches and pressed grass. The wind chose then to pick up and gusted frigid air into his face. Dark storm clouds rolled across the sky and partially blocked the pale moonlight. While moving as silently as possible, Kyler led his friends, swords and staff alike held at the ready, and determinedly moved deeper into the woods.

They traveled for over an hour, heading farther away from the school. The dark woods pressed down on them, slowly smothering their spirits. Kyler was glad when they suddenly came to an opening in the trees. Stopping abruptly to stay hidden, Kyler scanned the clearing. Toward the middle he spied a large bird's nest made of sticks woven together and patched with mud. On the ground lay the rotting bones of animals and humans alike. His nose rebelled at the putrid scent lingering on the wind. Kyler gagged, desperately trying not to vomit. It wasn't easy.

He gave the other two a sign to wait and then advanced on his belly through the shrubbery. The ground was rough, and the rocks and twigs bit into his flesh. Pushing the skeleton of a small squirrel out of the way, he inched as far forward as he dared. Looking around he tried to spy the Griffin, but there was no sign of it. With a signal to Darcy to approach, he took cover behind the dead body of a cow.

"I don't see the Griffin around," he whispered over his shoulder.

"Any sign of Ralph?" Darcy asked.

Kyler carefully rose into a crouched position. He glanced toward the nest, looking for signs of any recent additions. Over on the right side, he could barely make out what looked like a shoe poking out of the nest. He hunched back down quickly.

"I think he's in the nest. We'll have to move closer to find out for sure. Henry, you stay there. Darcy and I will approach the nest. If you see anything move, yell."

He signaled for Darcy to follow him again, and the two crept their way toward the nest. Kyler's heart seemed to beat more loudly with every step he took. The snapping of twigs echoed through the woods. Kyler looked cautiously around. *This is insane!*

Approaching the nest on tiptoe, he pulled himself up to peek inside. Ralph's body lay bent at a weird angle with his foot hanging out of the nest. Kyler could see raw claw marks raking Ralph's flesh and what appeared to be bite marks on his side. It was a horrible sight, but just when Kyler had concluded he was a lost cause, Ralph took a shallow breath.

"He's still alive. We've got to get him out of here," said Kyler.

"If we get him to the healer in time, there's still hope," said Darcy.

Kyler pushed himself over the rim of the nest. He struggled to place himself under Ralph's shoulders and hoist him upward. It was slow going. Ralph's limp body felt like a sandbag. While lifting Ralph's torso up toward Darcy, Kyler saw Ralph's eyelids flicker in pain.

"Grab him under the armpits. I'll push him from in here," said Kyler.

The two heaved and hoed until Ralph's body slid out of the nest and landed on top of Darcy's tired form.

DARCY

The night grew darker as a storm cloud passed over the moon. Darcy and Kyler backed up toward Henry, carrying Ralph's body. They were almost halfway across the clearing when Henry screamed.

"Look out! It's above you!"

Dropping Ralph to the ground, Darcy and Kyler took up defensive positions back-to-back, her with her sword and him with his staff. They fearfully looked toward the sky. Darcy could make out the outline of a great beast hovering above the ground, watching their rescue attempt. The Griffin let out a mighty shriek and charged. Its powerful body streaked downward, it sharp claws extended to rend flesh.

"Henry," yelled Kyler. "Cover Ralph."

As the monster approached, Darcy lashed out with her sword, aiming for its underbelly. Kyler ended up deflecting a claw that had been intent on ripping his eyes out. Together they managed to keep the Griffin from landing. Swinging with all her strength, Darcy sliced into the monster, leaving a trail of blood dripping from its hind leg. Henry ran into

the fray, taking up a protective position over Ralph's unconscious body while Darcy kept up her attack. She swung and
thrust her sword, forcing the beast back, until it found ground
enough to face her.

With a berserk holler, Kyler swung his staff at the beast,
knocking it a stinging blow to the head. Unbalanced from
Darcy's attacks, the Griffin flew backward and landed with
a loud crash on its nest. Darcy and Kyler took up defensive
stances across from the wrecked nest as the Griffin slowly regained its footing, ruffling its feathers in irritation. The beast
eyed both its young attackers, anger flashing in its green eyes.

Darcy watched the Griffin approach, and gave Kyler a cautious look.

"Back me up," she said through gritted teeth.

She stood at the ready, her sword tight in her grasp. The
Griffin's glare narrowed in on her. She could smell its fetid
breath as it drew nearer. She ran forward, swinging her sword
valiantly before her. She blocked one of its clawed feet, but
the other knocked her to the ground. The Griffin pounced
on her, ripping into her protective gear and gnashing at her
thigh. It batted her around like a rag doll as she tried in vain
to block its attack. Kyler ran to her aid, bashing the Griffin
on the back, but it contemptuously kicked its hind leg and
struck him a heavy blow across his forehead. He stumbled
backward, digging his staff into the ground. The Griffin gave
him a glance before turning back to its attack. Darcy lay on
the ground, unable to move. She watched as the beast approached. Its face loomed larger, and she could actually see
the individual scales that lined its taloned feet.

Henry shouted at the beast, trying to distract it. "You! You
big piece of stinking hybrid trash. Over here!"

Darcy watched him wave his sword in great circling arcs while calling out for the Griffin to come and fight. The Griffin slowly turned and began stalking toward Henry, its body low to the ground. Darcy tried to inch away, but she couldn't move. Every breath she took seemed to burn like fire, and she knew something was badly broken. All she could do was watch as Henry trembled before the Griffin.

Henry's sword was unsteady, and she let out a squeak when he dropped it. Quickly he pulled a small flute from his pocket and placed it to his lips.

"Maybe if it worked with the fish, it'll work with the Griffin!" he yelled, bringing the flute to his lips and playing.

He played his flute slowly, missing several notes and producing a wobbly sound, but then he doubled his efforts and played for all he was worth. At first nothing happened, and Darcy thought Henry was Griffin meat. The beast began to raise its sharp claws into the air, ready to strike a killing blow, but when they were halfway up it stopped, pausing to listen to the haunting melody.

Darcy watched as the air around Henry shimmered. Noticing the Griffin's pause, she had a moment of hope, but it was suddenly dashed as the monster shook its head with a fierce snarl and charged forward. Henry played harder, his eyes focused upon the glimmering shell surrounding him.

Waiting for the blow, she saw Henry give in and close his eyes, but he refused to stop playing. Darcy's vision began to blur and she knew that she wasn't getting enough oxygen into her lungs. Any second now and she would black out, but she fought to keep her eyes on Henry. The Griffin stopped in midair, clawing uselessly at the space right in front of him. Henry cracked open one eye, and seeing the shield blocking the Griffin, played like there was no tomorrow. A small sigh of relief was all that Darcy could utter before the world grew black.

KYLER

While Henry played his flute, Kyler rushed toward Darcy, losing no time in dragging her as far into the bushes as possible. The Griffin, sensing movement, began to back away from Henry. Kyler ran in the opposite direction, hoping to draw the animal's attention from Darcy, but the beast went after the easier prey.

When Kyler saw the Griffin focus on Darcy's limp form, he leapt into the way, staff at the ready. As the beast lunged, Kyler thrust his staff forward. He felt a connection with the animal's gelatinous eyeball. With a howl of pain, the beast threw itself back, its anger growing.

It came at Kyler again, blood weeping from its poked eyeball. Kyler weaved his staff before him, allowing the monster no room to maneuver. He knew his weapon had no chance, but he was not going to give up. As Kyler advanced, the Griffin stumbled backward.

Suspicious, Kyler stopped, but the beast wasn't faking an attack. Instead, it staggered sideways now, its steps uneven. "I think blinding it messed with its depth perception!" yelled

Kyler. He knew now was the time to advance. With quick thrusts and jabs, he aimed for where the Griffin was the weakest, the underbelly and the face. The beast had trouble deflecting the blows, and Kyler scored several vicious punctures.

Then the Griffin roared and swung his right foot at Kyler's staff. The sharp talons dug into the wood, and Kyler was forced to let go as his weapon was yanked from his hands. He began to back away as the Griffin shook his claws to get free of the staff.

Suddenly a crash sounded in the bushes near the creature's nest. Just emerging from the woods at a run was Master Ernie, his cloak billowing behind him, his face filled with determination. He ran at the monster with his magical staff pointed before him. With a loud cry, he uttered words that were lost upon the winds of the rising storm. A bolt of energy shot from his staff, impaling the beast. It staggered back into the bushes, and Kyler's staff flew into the gusty wind. Without losing momentum, the master mage shouted again, this time causing the wind to lift the stunned beast into the air and spin him around like a small toy. The gust threw the creature to the ground with a mighty thud.

Master Ernie yelled over the storm, "Quickly, children, get out of here!"

But Kyler knew there was nowhere to run. He would not leave Darcy and Ralph to be the Griffin's dinner. As he thought this, he saw Darcy stumble to her feet, looking uncertain. She limped toward him, clutching her side, desperate for rescue. The Griffin saw her, too. With a giant heave, it thrust itself through the bushes and collided with Darcy's figure. With a bone-jarring crash, it knocked her to the ground. Kyler winced, and hoped that Darcy was still alive.

Master Ernie raised his staff again, this time sending waves of hot fire toward the beast. The Griffin lowered its head and fought its way through the fiery currents, its magically constructed body reflecting the fire back to its summoner. An aura of heat shimmered around the teacher, and sweat ran down his forehead. He fought desperately to keep himself from burning and the Griffin from advancing, but his power began to wane. With a leap Master Ernie jumped to his side, summoning barely enough power to place a weak shield around his body as he hit the rocky ground.

But Kyler was ready, having found his staff dented, but unbroken. When he saw the Griffin turn toward Darcy again, he struck. He stabbed the beast in its side, digging his staff into hard flesh, but it was no use, the Griffin's magic hide protected it from any severe injury. It stood on its hind legs and lifted its frame into the air. It stood nearly eight feet tall, its sharp claws ready to impale Darcy on impact.

Kyler frantically racked his brain for any way to help, battling as the storm gathered strength around him and the wind tried to force him over. Large raindrops splattered on his face. He could not let this happen. He had to save Darcy.

The Griffin began its strike. Its beak opened in disgusting pleasure as it readied to end the life of its prey.

Kyler screamed and pointed his staff at the Griffin. From some primeval source deep within, words ripped out of his mouth and he envisioned the symbols for a lightning strike.

A bolt of white electric heat cut through the sky. It slammed into the Griffin's chest, leaving a sizzling trail as it exited through the other side. The beast screamed in pain. Its body burned from within as powerful electric currents ravaged its frame. Then the monster burst into flame. The three conscious onlookers shielded their eyes from the sudden heat. Darcy managed to roll out of the beast's way as it collapsed onto the ground, writhing in agony.

Kyler watched in shock. His head felt fuzzy, and black spots danced in front of his eyes. His strength left his body, and he leaned heavily on his staff while watching the scene unfold before him.

The Griffin's magical skin could not protect it from the fire already within its folds, and the beast burned from the inside out, its organs roasting as it rolled on the ground and howled. Soon the fire subsided, leaving only smoldering ash that occasionally spit tiny blue sparks. Only scorch marks remained on the ground when Kyler moved to help Darcy to her feet.

The lightning bolt had roused Ernie, and he rolled into a sitting position looking at the smoldering marks around him. Kyler struggled with Darcy as Henry pulled an unconscious Ralph away from the burning grass where the Griffin had died.

"Kyler, you did it!" shouted Ernie.

"It wasn't just me. It took all of us together."

Along with Master Ernie, they struggled their way back through the forest, pulling Ralph on a makeshift travois. Kyler was forced to take much of Darcy's weight onto his own shoulders, but he didn't utter a word. In fact, none of them spoke. The experience had drained them all. As the bedraggled group approached the back entrance to the kitchen, the servant girl from earlier flew toward them.

"Oh, thank goodness. I was sure you were all dead!"

Darcy rested against the woodpile as Henry lowered the travois and placed Ralph's still unconscious frame onto the ground. Master Ernie leaned heavily on Kyler's shoulder, struggling to stand upright. The black-cloaked figure of the school's master healer came running out the kitchen door, taking in the situation with practiced eyes.

"Let me take Ralph. I'll send help back for Darcy." He knelt and lifted Ralph gently into his arms. "I thought I'd never see you kids again. The council of mages declared it unsafe to follow you and forbade anyone to leave the school. Luckily Ernie had already gone after you. The council's been behind closed doors for over an hour discussing what to do."

"We fought the Griffin," Kyler coughed out. "We'd only hoped to rescue Ralph, but the monster surprised us."

"You're lucky to be alive," said the healer as he started off with Ralph. "Where is the Griffin now?"

"I killed it."

"You what?" The healer paused in mid step.

"I killed it. It was about to kill Darcy and I couldn't let it. I just…I just had to. I called down lightning from the storm to strike the beast. It burned to nothing right in front of us."

"That must have been a very powerful lightning bolt you cast if it penetrated the Griffin's skin." The healer eyed Ernie. "That's some boy you've got there. Now let's get you guys inside and out of the storm."

The healer carried Ralph's unconscious body into the school as another healer came outside and attended to Darcy. Kyler's brain could barely comprehend all he'd been through that night. He sighed as he slowly made his way into school, yearning for a bed to rest upon.

KYLER

Kyler visited Darcy in the hospital room every day that week. Though still not able to leave her bed, with the healing magic she'd received, she was recovering steadily from her injuries. Ralph lay in the next bed over. He'd been placed in a magical coma to give his body time to heal. His prognosis was good, though the healers weren't sure what mental state he'd be in.

Darcy smiled up at Kyler.

"Henry came to visit me earlier. He said things are back to normal."

"Mostly," said Kyler, "but the council of mages has been meeting late every night. Master Ernie is trying to convince them to take the threat of Mordrake seriously, but many of them are too comfortable in their way of life. They don't think the appearance of a strange animal means that the stories of Mordrake are true."

"Morons!" scowled Darcy. "Has there been any word about your aunt?"

"No, nothing." Kyler's face fell. "It's been so long. I can only hope she's okay. Plus, we need her to bring back proof to prod the council into action."

Running footsteps echoed through the room, and Kyler and Darcy looked up to see Henry headed toward them at a dead run.

"Kyler! Kyler! Follow me. Something's happening."

"What's going on?" Kyler questioned.

"I don't know. Master Ernie just told me to find you quick, something about your aunt."

"Maybe she's back!" Kyler took off after Henry, forgetting to say good-bye to Darcy. The boys raced down the hallway, heading toward a doorway.

"Where is Master Ernie?" Kyler questioned.

"He said to meet him back at your room."

The two boys flew through the doorway, both thinking of the same destination. They arrived in front of Kyler's door panting for breath. Waiting for them inside was Master Ernie, and wrapped up into a comfortable ball on his bed comforter was a large black furred ball. Master Ernie looked up as the boys came to a screeching stop.

"I've got some bad news, boys."

Kyler walked slowly toward the bed, recognizing the depleted form of Walter. "Is it Aunt Martha? Where is she?" He looked down at Walter, but the wolf was in a deep sleep.

"Walter returned late last night. The council wanted to see him immediately. This is the first time he's been able to sleep in days." Ernie stroked Walter's fur.

"Did Aunt Martha come with him?"

"No, Kyler, I'm afraid that's the bad news. Mordrake's minions captured her. Walter managed to escape and headed straight here for help."

Kyler ran to his closet, pulling out his staff and traveling case.

"What are you doing?" Henry wanted to know.

"I'm going to find her. I won't let Mordrake hurt her."

"Calm down, Kyler," Ernie cautioned. "I agree we need to go find her, but first we need to prepare."

"Prepare what?" asked Kyler.

"We need time for Darcy and Walter to fully recover. They'll both be an asset to our quest. Plus, Henry has his journeyman test in one week. If he passes he'll have all the rights and privileges of his status, plus a new instrument. Now that we know he has magic talent, there's no telling what instrument will pick him."

"He's right, Kyler," explained Henry. "I can't leave until I pass the test. Then I'll have full bard rights. I'll have free access to the archive and all way stations in the kingdom. Plus, I get to go into the bards conservatory and pick an instrument."

"I thought Master Ernie said the instrument picks you?"

Henry shrugged. "I'm a little unclear on the whole thing. They keep it hush-hush."

"As well they should," said Ernie. "Besides, if they've taken Martha to Mordrake, we'll need all the information we can find. The old text you found mentioned the possible existence of sealed notes about Mordrake and his prison in old mages council transcripts. The only place I can think of where they might still exist would be in the royal archives."

"But it'll take weeks to get there! What about my aunt? He'll kill her by then!"

"Walter doesn't think so. He says Mordrake needs her for some magical ceremony he's planning. It doesn't happen until the summer solstice, three months from now. I'm going to try to get the council to lend us their support, but they're still behind closed doors discussing Walter's information."

Kyler looked at his companions and saw strength, intelligence, determination, and power. "I'll wait two weeks, no more. Then I leave to find my aunt."

Henry looked around. "Then *we* leave to find your aunt!"

Kyler went to Walter's side and patted his fur. Looking out through the window into the world beyond, he wondered where his aunt was and what was happening to her.

MARTHA

Meanwhile, on a bumpy old road, Aunt Martha bounced up and down in a rickety wagon. Her captors had bound her hand and foot, and to prevent her from speaking any spells, a piece of cloth cut deeply into her mouth. An Orc looked down at her, its drool hanging from the corners of its mouth like slime.

"Master will be happy with me." An evil grin spread across its face. "Maybe I get to keep human as pet?"

The rotten cabbage–like odor of the Orc's breath buffeted Martha, and she squirmed away from the foul creature, but after only inches, her back hit hard wood. The Orc howled in laughter, pointing at her bound form.

"You funny. Remind me of pig I eat for dinner last night."

Martha knew she was in trouble, and for the first time in her life she had no idea what to do. Walter was not with her, and she could only hope he had escaped the attack. She felt wetness on her cheeks as tears fell.

She rolled over onto her back and looked up into the blue sky. The crude wooden slats sent splinters into her exposed skin, poking like mini toothpicks. With the Orc again focusing ahead, Martha struggled to twist her hands out of the ropes. Soon she felt rope burns cut into her skin, and her flesh became slick with blood. The Orc began sniffing the air, noticing the metallic twang, and Martha stopped her painful attempts.

Alone in the wagon, unable to see much, Martha had to use her other senses to figure out what was happening around her. She could hear the grunts of many Orcs around and in front of the wagon, and guessed they were marching toward their goal. As the day moved on, the sun began to grow too hot. She had nowhere to go and nothing to cover herself with. As the sun baked her skin, she consigned herself to the discomfort.

Without warning, the surrounding Orcs raised their voices, and Martha heard the thumps of their footsteps as they began to run. The Orc driving her wagon whipped the horses, and soon she was bouncing across the land like a sack of potatoes.

Somewhere up ahead she heard screams of agony and smelled burning wood.

"Urg!" she yelled. Perhaps she might be rescued?

"Shut up!" yelled the driver, and he smacked her with the back of his hand. She took the blow, but didn't back down.

"Hmmph!"

"Lady mage, be quiet or I make you be quiet!"

The sounds of battle echoed around Martha, and she cringed each time she heard an Orc roar in victory. She could tell the wagon was not close to the fighting because bodies weren't bashing against its sides, but the horrible noises were near. She endured the screams for half an hour before silence fell. Whomever the Orcs had attacked had fought back well, but they had lost.

Feet stomped toward her, and then the wagon shifted as a body was dumped over the side. The prisoner was bound like she was, but unconscious. A line of blood trailed down his forehead, and one of his eyes appeared sealed shut. She studied the swollen face, a feeling of familiarity growing within her.

Donald!

The man's pupils moved violently behind his closed eyelids, but he did not regain consciousness.

Martha did indeed know the man. He'd been one of her students at the school. The poor boy had little talent for magic, but had graduated with enough skill to practice what he could. The last she'd heard, he was on the town council of a small hamlet. If he had been captured, then things were not going well.

KYLER

Kyler walked into the arena, gripping his staff like a starving man holding a sandwich. That morning a note had appeared over his bureau with a request from the weapons instructor to meet at eleven a.m. in the arena. Big bold print read, "BE PREPARED."

As he stepped inside the oval area, he spied his fully geared instructor, waiting in one of the fighting pits. Kyler's steps slowed as he approached. He had spent the last week healing from the beating he had taken from the Griffin, and though he was feeling better, he didn't know if he was prepared to spar.

"Get in here!" yelled Master Dirk.

"Yes, sir!"

Master Dirk nodded when he saw that Kyler had brought his staff and was ready to fight.

"Your normal school schedule is postponed," said Master Dirk. "As of right now, you are to focus on two classes only, weapons and advanced magic."

"What?"

"There is a bit of disagreement within the council, but some among us feel your time needs to be spent in better ways. I feel you need more weapons training than book work. So, you'll meet me here every morning at eleven, and be prepared to work out."

As Master Dirk's words sunk in, Kyler began to nod his head. He had every intention of leaving soon to find his aunt, and more weapons training would come in handy.

"Let's start with forms. Take up position next to me," said Master Dirk.

Two hours later, Kyler dripped sweat from every pore, and left to go shower. He stumbled away, his legs shaking. Never before had he undertaken such intense training in battle forms. He had thought he was prepared, but when it was just Master Dirk one-on-one, he picked apart everything. They hadn't even sparred. Kyler had no idea if he would survive a week of this much attention.

Just as he finished lunch and returned to his room, another note popped in above the desk. This time he was to report to Master Ernie in the advanced magic room. He'd never been to the advanced class area, let alone a magic class. The only people he knew of that trained in the advanced wing were the senior journeymen.

He crossed the door threshold with worried thoughts cluttering his mind. Only days had passed since he discovered that he spoke the mages tongue. He had no idea what would be in store for him. Master Ernie stood alone in a large oval room, a smile nipping at his face.

"Ah, Kyler," said Master Ernie. "I've been looking forward to this all day."

"Um, okay." Kyler took his time walking toward the center of the room. He noticed scorch marks burned into the stone walls around him. The air felt heavy and thick, almost like a blanket. Kyler waved his hand before himself, feeling a slight tension push back.

"That's the shielding," said Master Ernie. "The things we do in here can sometimes go haywire. We don't want to blow up the school."

"Sounds like a good idea," said Kyler, stopping before the teacher. "What exactly do we do in here?"

Master Ernie threw his arms wide, gesturing to the empty space. "In here is where you learn how to control your magic, and in your case, learn to fight with it."

"Wow. I'm liking this already."

"Don't get ahead of yourself," said Master Ernie, and then he wrapped his arm over Kyler's shoulders. "I know you speak the mages tongue, but I have no idea how powerful or how focused you are. First we need to run some tests."

Kyler was ready to break into a dance. After months of basic classes and other students questioning his intelligence, he was about to own this. He had no doubt whatsoever that he could handle whatever Master Ernie threw at him. What he didn't expect was two hours of reading. Just like Kyler's aunt, Master Ernie was a big fan of books.

Off to the side of the oval room was a small addition with several desks and bookcases. The room felt small, closed in.

"We need to find out just how proficient in the mages tongue you are. Sit down and let's get going."

He read through book after book, each more advanced in language. About an hour into things, Master Ernie placed before him a thick bound book that squirmed around on the table. Kyler had to keep one hand on the top corner to keep the words steady.

As soon as he started reading, he knew this book was different. The words were in mages tongue, but they seemed to pulse on the pages. A couple of pages in, he began to picture the words he read.

"Cold wind," Kyler read. The image in his head was a gust of snow-filled air blowing over the frozen grass. He did not even have to think about it. The image came at the same time he spoke the word. Within seconds, his neck prickled, and a surge of chilled air blew through his hair.

Kyler sat back. He hadn't tried to work magic. It had worked itself through him. "What happened?" he asked.

"The book your reading is a spell book. The mage who wrote it bespelled the words with images. There is no need to read and focus at the same time. The book does it for you."

"Wow. That's amazing."

"In some ways it is. The truth is that it only does a person good in a library. If you were out in the real world, you wouldn't have time to flip through pages reading words to throw at your enemy. We use it in the school to gauge the amount of power you have behind your words."

"How'd I do?"

"Rub your hand through your hair."

Kyler did as asked and then laughed as his fingers combed through little icicles.

"There's a lot of power in you. The fact that you froze your own hair and didn't put any willpower behind the words says great things. You remind me of your father."

Kyler felt pride well up inside his chest. They spent the next hour going through the book. This time Kyler carefully spoke each word, but even so, he discovered why there were scorch marks on the ceiling.

He also discovered a side effect of using magic. Just as in his early trials of trying to light candles, he began to feel his strength diminish. When he finished reading the book, he was dismayed to find himself sitting in the chair like a limp rag doll. *Maybe I'm not as good as I thought.*

However, Master Ernie smiled. "Amazing. Most students don't get a quarter of the way through that book without needing a nap. You have a well of power inside you. Now we just need to show you how to use it."

DARCY

Her room in the healer's wing was getting old. Kyler spent every evening there having dinner with her and Henry, but the room was so plain, so boring. She wanted to poke her eyes out.

Tonight was no exception. Propped up by pillows, Darcy sipped her noddle soup and tried not to scream out in frustration. Henry had not shown up yet, but he never missed food. Kyler held a piece of bread and butter in front of his mouth. "I don't think I could stand it if I had to be laid up here longer than a couple days."

"Oh, poor you," said Darcy. "You took twenty-four hours to heal up. I'm the one stuck in here."

Kyler's cheeks turned rosy. "Sorry, I didn't mean it in a bad way."

"Yeah, yeah."

"Well, you're almost all better. They said they would send you back to your own room tomorrow."

Darcy threw her arms up above her head and waved them around. "Hallelujah!"

Just then Henry rushed into the room, slapping the door frame as he passed.

"You guys are never going to believe what just happened!"

"What?" asked Darcy. "Tell me before Kyler kills me with his wit."

Henry just laughed and slapped Kyler on the back. With a running jump, he smacked down on Darcy's bed.

"Today was the best day of my life."

"I thought the day we killed the Griffin was," said Kyler.

"That was. Now it isn't. Now it's today."

Darcy began laughing. "Dork, what happened?"

Henry jumped off the bed, his energy engulfing the room. "I passed my journeyman test!"

"Yes!" yelled Kyler. He ran over to Henry, and together they both began jumping up and down like excited kids. Darcy had to throw a pillow at them to stop the ruckus.

"Congrats, Henry!" said Darcy. "Was it as supersecret as they said it would be?"

Henry gave Kyler a shove and then jumped into a clear space by the window. There, he posed with a hand in the air for dramatic effect. "It was amazing. Everyone is invited into the recital hall to hear the senior masterpiece. That's how we know what's happening."

Henry spread his arms out wide, gesturing with a slow movement as if he were bowing. "Me? I just got a note inviting me to meet Headmaster Lex and Lead Bard Young in the archives. I had no clue what was going on. Thought I was in trouble or something."

"What did they want?" asked Kyler.

"Turns out I was to be given a private exam for my final." Henry thrust his hands on his hips in mock outrage. "I had a whole song planned out about our victory over the Griffin. Told all the other students how they would love my piece. Anyway, I had to perform for just the two masters. When I finished, instead of clapping, they turned and nodded at each other. I was like, huh?"

"Then they invited me into an inner room in the bards' archives. It was just an empty room with three doors at the opposite end." Henry nailed Kyler with a smirk. "This is where things get weird. Bard Young told me that when a senior passes their oral performance test, they go to that room. There they have to sing their composition and wait for the room to decide their fate. Then he shut up and wouldn't tell me any more. Totally frustrating.

"So, I sang, and the acoustics were great. When I finished, it felt as if the room were holding its breath. Then slowly the third door cracked open with a loud squeak of its hinges. When I looked back at the teachers, they were patting each other on the back, as if they'd done something grand."

Henry strutted across Darcy's room and stood next to Kyler. "Do you know why?"

Kyler shrugged his shoulders.

"They told me the third door hadn't opened for a student in years. Evidently the first door opens if a student will be a vocal bard alone. The second door opens into an instrument room where a bard can choose his main instrument. The third door, well, it opens into something totally different."

"What was behind the third door?" asked Darcy. She sat up completely straight and then leaned toward Henry.

He smiled. "Well, the third door opened into a hallway full of other doors."

"What?" asked Kyler.

"That's what I thought, too, but as soon as I stepped into the hallway, all I could hear was the most amazing music ever. Behind every door, a different instrument played, and together they formed an incredible symphony." Henry looked off into the distance, and Darcy knew he was remembering the sublime event. Kyler cleared his throat, and Darcy watched Henry jolt back into reality.

"Oh yeah. Sorry. I didn't know what to do, so I tried to open the closest door. Wouldn't budge, so I went to the next, and the next, until I found one that opened."

Henry reached down into his shirt and pulled out a small pan flute attached to a leather braid. The pipes were worn and scratched, and the whole instrument looked crudely put together, in Darcy's opinion.

"Inside was this beauty." Henry waved his hand over the pipes, showing off his treasure.

"Um, Henry? What's so special about a beat-up set of pipes?" asked Kyler.

Henry's face flushed. "What did you say?"

Evidently Kyler had hit on a sensitive topic, and Darcy watched him recover. "I mean, what's so special about those cool pipes?"

Henry's color returned to normal, and then he laughed. "You know what? I asked myself the same question. Sorry, I shouldn't have gotten mad. It's just, these pipes are amazing. The instruments behind the third door are all enchanted. The door only opens for certain people because the instruments inside choose their owner. These pipes chose me! Once I touched them, I knew they were mine."

"Wow," said Darcy. "That's amazing. I don't know any bards with enchanted instruments."

"It's very rare. That's why the headmasters were so excited. They read Master Ernie's report on the Griffin slaying, about how I'd made a shield surrounding Ralph and me, so they thought the door might open for me."

"That's awesome," said Kyler.

"Yep. These pipes are over a thousand years old. The person that made them lived in a small village and crafted them by hand. He later went on to become a famous mage bard, thus the enchantment."

Henry looked down at the floor. "The records don't say what his name was."

"What happens when you play them, Henry?" Darcy asked.

"Ah, now that depends. According to Bard Young, they should amplify my magic. I just have to practice. Right now all I can do is make things move a bit." Henry began playing his pipes, and the music flowing from them was sweet and clear. At first nothing happened, but then Darcy's pillow floated up off the floor and flew over to her bed.

"That is so cool, Henry," said Kyler.

"I know!" Henry beamed. "This is the start of something big."

KYLER

The next day Darcy was allowed back into her own room. The day after that, she joined Kyler for advanced weapons practice. Kyler watched her walk into the arena with a smile engulfing her entire face. He knew this was her dream come true.

Together they worked their forms. Darcy went slow, needing to rebuild her strength, but all things considered, Kyler thought she was close to top form. A couple days after that, Darcy was able to spar with him. They crashed their weapons together, the force knocking them both backward. From then on it was game time, and neither held back.

In the afternoons, Kyler practiced with Master Ernie. Now that he had read through the books, Ernie was teaching him to focus. The hardest part was saying and picturing a word at the same moment. It was like getting two different parts of his brain to cooperate.

About midweek, Master Ernie drew him aside. "Kyler, I've got something I want to show you. Several of the council members are against this, but with our journey looming, I don't care."

They walked out of the training room and down the hallway. At the very end were two large wooden doors with metal hinges and large bolts. "Nowadays," began Master Ernie, "students learn to fight with swords. In fact, it's a rare time that you even see a master mage with a staff. Mine was passed down from my father. I'm not sure when they went out of style."

They stopped before the doors, and Master Ernie looked Kyler in the eyes. "Behind this doorway is the armory. Not just a regular one, but a mages armory. In the past, mages used to enchant their weapons to aid in battle. After the Great War and several hundred years of peace, mages just stopped doing it, and the skill was lost. Now, all the enchanted weapons that are left are behind these doors."

Master Ernie gave the doors two taps with his staff. They silently slid open as if floating on air. Kyler expected a grand room full of marvelous weapons. Instead, he saw a handful of staffs, swords, knives and bows. Most of the shelves were bare and dusty, and the air smelled stale.

"Where is everything?" he asked.

"These are all we've been able to save. Over the years, things went missing, and many became legends. Every now and then we find something in an attic somewhere, but for the most part, these weapons are all that's left of the great battle mages."

Kyler wandered into the room. He ran his fingers over various weapons, pausing occasionally to pick one up. He by-passed the swords altogether. The weapons were all clean and shiny, though the room itself reeked of dust and the passage of time. He finally made his way over to a rack with three staffs leaning against it. All three hummed as Kyler approached.

The hum grew louder until Kyler stopped before them, and then the staffs began to quiver.

"Just like the books in the mages library, these weapons contain a bit of the essence of the original mage that created them. They yearn to be used. It's why they were created. However, over the last century we've rarely found a candidate with a hint of potential." Master Ernie looked at Kyler across the room. "You're the first in a very long time, Kyler."

Something about Master Ernie's words made Kyler feel excited and sad in the same breath. He turned back to the staffs, looking at their intricate carvings and woodwork. The last one on the rack called to him. Not in a voice, but with an overwhelming feeling that Kyler needed to react to. He reached out his hand and brushed his fingers against the staff. At this touch, the other two staffs fell silent. He grasped his chosen staff and felt a warmth flare up under his palm. In seconds, the staff felt as if it were a part of him, a third limb.

"Wow."

"Seems you've made your choice," said Master Ernie. "Now let's go practice with it. I'll have you throwing lightning bolts in no time."

Holding the staff reverently, Kyler followed the teacher outside the room. The doors closed on their own behind them with a loud thunk. Kyler thought about the battle with the Griffin and how Master Ernie had flung energy bolts at the monster. A feeling of responsibility welled up inside him, and the staff hummed in response.

The next morning for weapons practice, Kyler was surprised to see Master Ernie standing side by side with Master Dirk. As he walked over to the masters, he noticed the frown on Ernie's face.

"Kyler, where is your staff?" asked Master Ernie.

"Uh, in my room."

"Why in the world would you leave your weapon in your room? The staff should be by your side at all times."

"I thought I should use it only during mage classes."

"Daft! Go to your room and get it right now."

Kyler glanced at the weapons master for permission, but Master Dirk didn't say a word, nor did he shift his stance. So Kyler booked it out of there fast. On his way through the door, he passed Darcy entering. She gave him a quizzical look, but kept jogging.

By the time he got back, Darcy was already done with the first two forms. Kyler jumped into the ring and took the next stance. He stole a look at Master Ernie, but he was involved in a deep conversation with Master Dirk. Kyler wondered what they were planning.

He found out twenty minutes later, when a flying disc whizzed by his head and bashed into the rock wall behind him.

"The object is to shoot the disc out of the sky using your staff, not duck like a chicken," yelled the weapons master.

Master Ernie sent another his way, and Kyler tried to produce a lightning bolt. In the end, he batted the disc away with the tip of his staff.

"Creative, but not what I'm looking for," yelled Master Ernie.

It was worse than sword training had ever been. Kyler just couldn't seem to put all three actions together. Sometimes he'd produce the lightning, but he'd hit nothing. Other times he'd concentrate so hard on the image that he forgot to move his body, and then there were times when nothing happened, just as at first. Darcy spent half of the time laughing at his mistakes.

"Kyler, when you're in battle, you can't stand still to cast your spell. The enemy will kill you. You need to cast on the run," said the weapons master.

So Kyler began sprint drills. He'd run forty meters one way, turn and race back. At any given time, Master Ernie would send discs his way, and he had to hit them, or they would smack him in the gut. Missing was no longer a pain-free option.

By the end of class, Kyler was covered in large bruises, and he had to limp out of the arena. He'd only managed to hit 20 percent of the discs. Darcy caught up to him.

"I'll bring a bucket of ice up to your room."

"Har, har," said Kyler. Then after a pause, "That would be great."

"Don't forget magic practice this afternoon," called Master Ernie.

"Ugh. Kill me now."

"Nah, you've got plenty more stuffin' to get beat out of you," said Darcy.

Soon the days flowed together, and Kyler grew skilled at knocking the discs away, but the entire time he trained, he itched to be moving out and begin the search for his aunt. When that day finally came, he felt like throwing a party.

KYLER

They set out for the king's castle on a crisp and clear morning. Their supplies were in a wooden wagon led by Master Ernie. He was going along to search the castle's archives for clues. Kyler, Henry, and Darcy each had their own horse, but from the way Kyler's shifted back and forth, he began to wish he were walking. Walter took the lead, alert for any danger.

On the third day, they came upon the castle, its tall stone towers a stark contrast to the surrounding hills. It rose from the ground as if created by nature. The town around the castle sang with the voices of merchants and soldiers, and the smells of unwashed humans mixed and fried foods. Kyler's home village did not compare to what lay before him. To alert the castle of their arrival, Darcy sent a scout ahead. As they approached the main gates, a small party rode out to greet them. As they entered the castle grounds, Kyler looked around in awe. The castle looked tall enough to touch the clouds.

"What took you slowpokes so long?" asked Leroy, who was waiting for them in the royal stables.

Darcy laughed and let her brother help her down.

"You might want to change your clothes before Mom sees you."

"Why are Mom and Dad still here? Shouldn't they be back at the estate?"

"They should be, but after William's death they aren't leaving my side. Dad accompanies me on all outings beyond the castle grounds."

Darcy gave her brother a fierce hug. "Poor you, the overprotected heir."

"Ha!" said Leroy. Then he turned to Master Ernie and helped him down from the wagon.

"Darcy's note was brief. She didn't explain the entourage," said Leroy.

"I have some work to do in the archives. The others are here to support Darcy."

"Support her doing what?" Leroy asked.

"Just wait, big brother. You'll find out soon enough."

Kyler and the rest followed behind Leroy and Darcy as he caught her up on the comings and goings of court. As they entered the castle through the side gallery, Kyler had a hard time picturing the Darcy he knew gracing its halls. Servants showed them to separate rooms. Kyler had one right next to Henry's. Then they were left alone to rest and bathe before dinner.

Kyler took his time in the tub, working three days' worth of grit and grime out of his skin. When finished, he found a fancy outfit lying on his bed. It was silk with blue cuffs and a collar. It fit him perfectly, but the collar drove him nuts.

Why do they wear these things?

When he finally left the room, it was to bump into Henry. His friend had his hair combed back into its normal ponytail, but the outfit he wore appeared as fancy as Kyler's. They stood in the hallway with absolutely no idea of where to go. Master Ernie found them both looking puzzled and directionless.

"Well, I guess you'd better follow me then."

"Sounds good to me," said Henry.

"Hey, how come you don't have to wear fancy clothes?" asked Kyler.

"I'm a mage," said Ernie, and left it at that.

The dining room was a grand affair. Kyler looked around at the ornately decorated walls and the long wooden tables spaced evenly apart. At the front of the room was a horizontal table. From the size of the chairs, Kyler guessed that the royals sat there.

A servant showed them to their seats. The table held fruit platters, bread and cheese trays, and wine carafes. The smell of the fresh bread drove him silly, and Kyler couldn't wait to dig in. He nudged Henry in the hip, pointing out the lush spread.

Then movement at the front of the room caught his attention. In walked an older couple, both dressed in regal attire. Following them was a beautiful lady, her red hair swirling down over her back like a cascading waterfall. She was dressed in a lovely teal dress.

"Darcy looks great, eh?" asked Henry.

"Darcy?" It took a second for Henry's words to register, and then Kyler did a double take. Sure enough, the girl he'd been checking out moments before was Darcy! His mind went blank as he tried to reconcile the fact with his earlier thoughts. He missed the entrance of Leroy, the king's horde of daughters, and the king and queen themselves. When his thoughts finally figured things out, the royals were already sitting at the head table.

Dinner was immediately served by an army of servants. Kyler had no idea why there was so much silverware before him, so he just used the same fork for everything. He often found himself staring up at Darcy, and it wasn't until Henry flicked him in the face that he realized how often he was doing it. His cheeks flushed with heat, and he gulped down a glass of water.

Later that evening, the group gathered in Master Ernie's chambers. Darcy arrived late, and Kyler found himself eager to catch sight of her.

"Okay, everyone. We made it," said Master Ernie. "Now the hard work begins."

Darcy nodded. "I'll be keeping a close eye around court. I know it's not the mission, but I am determined to find out more about William's death."

"That shouldn't be a problem," said Walter. "It would probably be suspicious if you didn't."

"Walter, you'll need to eavesdrop on the staff. Find out if word about what's going on out east is making the rounds. The rest of us will head to the archives first thing. We need more information about Mordrake," said Master Ernie.

"Sounds like a plan," said Kyler. "Until then I'm gonna crash in my room."

"Me, too," added Henry. "After three days on the road and then a dinner like that, wow, I could probably sleep for a week."

"Fine. You two go sleep," said Darcy. "I'm going to find out if Leroy has learned anything."

DARCY

Darcy found Leroy in his quarters. He welcomed her with a big hug and then shooed away the lingering servants. "It won't be easy to find alone time after to-night. My schedule is packed," said Leroy. "Sometimes I have to order Chancellor Usborn to let me go to the bathroom."

"I could tell when I left last month that they were closing the net around you."

"No kidding. It's even worse with Dad hanging around."

Darcy relaxed into a lounge chair and threw her gloves onto the ottoman. "Leroy, I wanted to ask you something, and I don't want you to get mad."

"I am not passing a law banning dresses."

Darcy laughed and felt the tension leave her shoulders. "I was wondering if you'd thought any more about what we talked about when I left. About William."

"Darcy, do you still think he was murdered?" Leroy shook his head, a sad frown on his face.

"I do, and I'm going to find out who did it."

Leroy sighed. "Well, I know there is no stopping you when you set your mind to something, but what exactly are you looking for?"

"You've been here over a month. What have you noticed?"

"What do you mean? I'm so busy learning the rules that I don't get time to think on my own."

"Leroy! Anything. Anything at all that you think is odd."

Her brother sat back and crossed his legs. "Honestly, I don't know what you want. Chancellor Usborn arranges everything for me. I go where he tells me."

"What about ill will? Have you heard anything about angry citizens?"

"No, everyone seems fine with Uncle. The people liked William, too."

"Okay," said Darcy. She stood up and paced. "But you will tell me if you notice anything strange, right?"

"Yes, dear sister, I will. Now scoot out of here so I can get some sleep."

"Fine, good night, Leroy. Sweet dreams."

Darcy was back in her room before she remembered she'd left her gloves on the lounge. *Drat, I'll have to go get them tomorrow.* She went to bed with plans of espionage in her head.

The next morning she made sure Master Ernie, Kyler, and Henry had access to the archives. She stood at the doorway as they entered. "I wish you luck. This place is a disaster."

Kyler looked around, and Darcy noticed his eyes grow large as he took in the hapless piles of documents without any type of organization.

"These are what were left after Naterum was destroyed. They were left to rot in the destroyed palace for centuries before someone thought to collect them. There's a lot of water damage," said Darcy.

"I can tell. The place smells like a musty old closet," said Kyler.

"Well, at least the mages back then put a preservation spell on them when they found them in the old castle. They haven't changed a day since they were put in here hundreds of years ago. Imagine the decay if they'd just sat around here."

"If the mages cared enough to preserve them, then why didn't they organize them?" asked Henry.

"I guess they figured they'd get around to it someday. The records were semisafe, so they just decided to let it slide," said Darcy. "Anyway, I'm off to Leroy's room. I left my gloves there last night."

"You didn't smack him with them, did you?" laughed Kyler.

Darcy shot Kyler a very unladylike look before turning to leave.

When she got to her brother's room, the guards let her pass without question, which was funny, because it would have been ten times harder if he'd been inside the room. She shut the door and then paused, thinking about Leroy. Her greatest fear was that some "accident" would happen to him. She made her way over to the lounge by the fireplace and began looking for her gloves. They were not where she'd left them. "Urg. Guess it'll have to be the hard way."

Darcy tucked up her dress and kneeled down upon the rug. She inched her way behind the chair, and had just spied the tip of her gloves poking out from under the backside of the lounge, when she heard the door open. Surprised that her brother would be free so early in the morning, she popped up her head to say hello, but jerked back down when she saw the grim profile of Chancellor Usborn instead. What was he doing here? Darcy peeked one eye out from behind the cushion and watched as the chancellor walked around her brother's bed. He seemed in no hurry, and was very casual about picking things up and putting them back. The chancellor stopped beside the bedside table and picked up Leroy's journal. He flipped through the pages and read the last several entries. Darcy's mouth hung open as she watched. That guy had some nerve!

When finished, he placed the journal back on the table and then left the room. Darcy stayed in position for another minute, afraid to move. Then she made her way over to her brother's bed and picked up the journal. *I hate to do this, but...*

She flipped to the last page. Recorded in her brother's neat handwriting was the conversation they'd had last night and her belief that William had been murdered.

KYLER

"There is way too much stuff in this room," said Kyler. The piles of papers, books, and ledgers stretched out around him like the rays of the sun.

"Just keep looking," said Henry.

Master Ernie looked up from the table and searched the two boys' faces. "You know what? We need to clear out a space in the room where we can put everything we've already searched." He stood and walked over to the far wall. "Let's move this stuff out of here. Then we can pile things into some sort of order."

Kyler groaned. "That just makes more work."

"Well, who better to do it than two strong men?" said Master Ernie. "Move all the piles over to the far book stands. I am going to make some labels to hang on the wall. That way when we finish at least there will be a chronological system."

Kyler didn't mind the work. He'd done much harder things on the farm, and carrying bunches of old papers wasn't any more difficult than carrying bales of hay.

"Great," said Master Ernie once the boys had finished. "Now let's add some order to our search. Instead of reading everything you come across, look to see if you can find when it was written first. That will eliminate a large chunk. Sort it into the decades I've noted on the wall labels."

So, for the entire day, with only a short lunch break, they sorted instead of reading. When they were finally finished, the entire center of the room was clear, but the walls had piles and piles of junk.

"How many years do you think we have here?" asked Kyler.

"From the look of it, I'd say the records span at least seventeen hundred years," said Master Ernie.

"Ugh," said Henry.

"I agree with Henry," said Kyler.

"Well, it's getting dark, and we've gotten a good start today. We'll start reading tomorrow. Let's go to my room and request some dinner."

"I'm all for that," said Henry.

When they got to Master Ernie's chambers, Walter was curled up in front of the door. He looked up as they approached. "Good, I was beginning to wonder if you we're going to skip dinner."

"Not a chance with these two boys," said Master Ernie.

Inside the room, they all relaxed onto different seats, and Walter stretched out by the fire.

"Let me order up something, and then Walter can tell us how his day went," said Master Ernie.

Dinner was brought up quickly, and Kyler suspected that the kitchen staff was eager to end their labors for the night. He licked the chicken grease off of his fingers while listening to Walter.

"I spent the day in the great hall, a lot of staff coming and going. Didn't hear much of anything but gossip though. I think we need to drop a bee in someone's ear to get things started."

Master Ernie nodded. "That's not a bad idea. William's death was over a month ago, and most travelers left around then, too. The castle's been closed off while they're training Leroy."

"Walter, you should hang out by the stables tomorrow. See if the horses or stable hands know something," added Kyler.

"Sure," said Walter. "Let's meet back here every night for dinner and talk about what we've found out. I bet Darcy can sneak in sometimes, too."

Three days passed.

On the fourth day, Kyler and Henry were alone in the archive room while their teacher was off meeting with the royal court on matters of mage business. Chancellor Usborn was the mage council's go-between with the royalty, but Master Ernie had stepped up to tell the king about the true reason for their visit. Convincing the crown to spend resources out east on just the rumor of Mordrake's return was difficult.

"Why do you think Chancellor Usborn is being such a jerk to Master Ernie?" asked Henry.

Kyler laid aside the book he was reading. "It's just like back at school. Half of the council was against what Master Ernie was trying to do."

"Yeah, but shouldn't the king be more worried about mercenaries in the east?"

"That's just it," said Kyler. "There haven't been any reports beyond normal bandit raids coming in from the east."

"There's got to be something. Mordrake is amassing a huge army of Orcs. That can't go unnoticed."

"You'd think so, huh. We'd better find what we need, and fast," said Kyler. "We need more proof."

That night over dinner, Walter had some interesting news.

"A rider came in today. He must have been on the road for days, for when he got off his horse he almost couldn't walk. The stable hands had to help him inside. Instead of being shown to a room, he insisted on being taken directly to the king, said he had missives from back east."

"Finally. This is what we've been waiting for," said Kyler. "It just took longer than we thought."

"There's another royal council meeting tomorrow," said Master Ernie. "The main topic should concern the letters. Whether they believe in Mordrake or not, there is no doubt about the Orcs. I'll report back afterward."

The next day, Kyler and Henry were eager for word on the council meeting, but Master Ernie told them it wouldn't happen until midmorning. While they waited, they kept up their search in the archives.

Kyler was happy to see Darcy join them later in the morning.

"Hello, knuckleheads!"

"Good morning to you, too, Darcy," laughed Kyler. "We haven't seen you in two days. If I'd known you were coming, I would have ordered tea."

Darcy just smiled and gestured for them both to keep working. "I got tired of hanging out with my cousins. I can't sew another stitch without wanting to vomit."

"It can't be that bad," said Henry. "You're in a room full of girls."

"Henry, you don't have a clue," said Darcy. "Besides, my whole plan was to get information about William's death. No one will talk about it. I've brought up the subject a hundred different ways, even with the staff. It's like I'm hitting a brick wall."

"I'm sorry, Darcy," said Kyler. "But we can definitely use your help in here. There are still hoards of records to go through." He went over to pick up a pile of yellow papers and then plopped them down in front of her.

"Gee, thanks."

"No problem," said Kyler.

All three read in silence for more than an hour. Henry broke the silence and Kyler jumped in his seat.

"Hah!" said Henry.

"Dude, some warning," said Kyler.

"I think I found something."

"What?" asked Darcy.

Henry tapped a faded yellow page with his finger. "I found mention of a kid named Mordrake."

"A kid?" asked Kyler.

"I know," said Henry. "Not quite what we're looking for, but how many Mordrakes can there be?"

"That's true," said Darcy. "The name is taboo just because of the old tales."

Kyler rubbed his chin. "What's it say?"

"It's an account of a mages council meeting just over a thousand years ago."

"Wow. I still can't believe these records go back so far," said Darcy.

"No kidding," said Henry. "It's hard to make out, but from what I gather a young kid named Mordrake interrupted the council meeting seeking an acknowledgment of parentage. He claimed a Lord Gainus was his father." Henry looked up from his reading. "Gainus was the nephew of the king and on the mages council."

"No way." Kyler took a step away from the table. "Do you mean Mordrake was a royal bastard?"

Henry looked back over his shoulder. "Don't know. Says here that Gainus denied the claim. The kid threw a huge fit. Said his mother was ill and they needed money. The council basically kicked him out on his butt."

"Anything else?" asked Darcy.

"Nope, but this is a good start, right?"

"Better than anything we've found so far," said Kyler. "Let's divide up Henry's pile and see if there's anything more from that era."

The three teenagers sat in front of their piles, their eyes scanning the papers as quickly as their fingers turned the pages.

"Got something!" shouted Kyler.

Henry and Darcy dropped their readings and hurried to Kyler's side. Kyler waited until they'd stopped shuffling before explaining his discovery. "This one is several years after the first. If it's the same Mordrake, which I think it is, he's probably late teens, early twenties."

"Does it involve Gainus?" asked Darcy.

Kyler nodded, not bothering to look upward. "Mordrake returned to the council and challenged Gainus to a duel."

"Are you kidding? Nobody duels," said Henry.

"They did a thousand years ago," said Kyler. "Whoever took these notes found it amusing. There's a joke about a donkey and a prince."

"At least someone on the council had a sense of humor," said Darcy. "What happened?"

Kyler turned over the page he was reading and scanned the next. "Gainus won, but he spared Mordrake's life."

"Ouch, how embarrassing," said Henry.

"No kidding," said Kyler. "Doesn't say anything else, either. It just moves on to notes about the next meeting."

"Turd," said Henry. "Why can't this be easy?"

Kyler leaned back in his chair, tilting two legs off the floor. With one hand he rubbed his eyes, causing a small tear to leak out. Then he yawned and dropped his weight back onto the floor. "Let's get lunch. I could eat a dog at this point."

KYLER

Lunch in the castle could be compared to a small feast. Every meal, Kyler sat amazed at the amount of food laid upon the tables, and he never left hungry. Darcy lounged at a completely different table, but Kyler could watch her pick at her food from the corners of his eyes. Sometimes he'd forget to put the food in his mouth, and Henry would bump him on the elbow to get him moving again.

Today, Kyler looked at the boiled ham sliced on the platter before him and stabbed a piece randomly. He rolled a few potatoes onto his plate but passed up the turnips. "We're so close."

Henry was busy chewing on a radish but nodded his head in agreement. Before finishing he added, "Totally," and spit radish pieces all over the table.

"Dude, watch it!" said Kyler.

Henry swallowed down a gulp of milk before a grin spread across his face. "My bad."

Kyler threw his napkin at him. "You are so hopeless."

"At least I'm not hung up over a certain someone."

Kyler felt his cheeks grow hot. "Not."

They took their time eating, hoping to hear news from Master Ernie, but their mentor never appeared. With determination they returned to the archives, signaling to Darcy to follow.

By midafternoon they had worked their way through seven more piles. There were no further mentions of Mordrake. Then Henry spoke up. "Got something."

Darcy and Kyler made their way over to stand behind Henry. "I think they're notes from a mages war council during the time of High King Markus Kingborn. That puts it in the right period. Only problem is, after the heading it's written in mages tongue. Why would they do that unless they wanted things kept supersecret?"

"Let me give it a shot," said Kyler. Henry passed him the pages and Kyler began to read. "Wow, this is amazing."

"What does it say?" asked Darcy.

"Well, this is definitely what we're looking for. Henry, see if there are any other similar pages in your pile. This one looks like the second part of something."

"Tell me what it says while he's looking," demanded Darcy, leaning over Kyler's shoulder.

A shiver ran down Kyler's back when Darcy's words brushed by his ear. He took a second to breathe.

"Well?" asked Darcy.

"Um, it's, wow...This part starts off after Mordrake was bound into a deep slumber. Even asleep, his powers kept his body from injury, and they could not kill him. So the council of mages buried him and the Griffin deep within the earth. Then, using their powers, they stood around the area in a circle and linked their magic. It says the mages sacrificed themselves and were turned into stone guardians. As long as they stand, Mordrake is trapped within their confines."

"Jeez, I can't believe they gave up their own lives," said Darcy.

"Hey," said Henry, "I think I found the first part." He passed a parchment over to Kyler. Kyler scanned the document quickly before speaking.

"Yep, this is it. Mordrake and his forces had overwhelmed the capital, slaying any member of the royal family within his reach. Eww, he had a thing for decapitation. Wow, he really hated them."

"Makes sense if Gainus let his mother die," said Darcy.

"Yeah, but come on. This is like blowing up the farm to kill a single cow."

"Guess he has a temper," said Henry.

"How'd they finally stop him?" wondered Darcy.

"Seems they used a plant called a blushroot to make a sleeping draught. Then they infused it with magic and, by trickery, had it served to Mordrake." Kyler sat back. "I've never heard of a blushroot plant before."

"Is there more?" asked Henry.

"Nope, that's it," said Kyler.

"Well, let's head back to Master Ernie's rooms. He should finally be done with the council, and he might know something about the plant," said Henry.

"Beat you there," urged Kyler. He ran past Darcy as she shook her head.

What the trio didn't expect to find was Master Ernie pacing up and down in his room, his face as red as a beet.

"What happened?" asked Darcy.

Master Ernie turned at the sound of her voice, and gestured for everyone to enter the room.

"Didn't they believe the messenger?" asked Henry.

"That's just it," said Master Ernie. "The messenger was never mentioned. I waited the entire meeting, and not one word was said."

"How is that possible?" asked Kyler. "There's no way news from the east wouldn't be considered important enough to share with the council."

"I don't know, but we need to find out what happened," said Master Ernie. "Henry, go see if you can find Walter. We need to know if there was any more to the rider's story."

"Whoa, wait up. You need to see what we found first," said Kyler.

Master Ernie turned an eager eye. "Did you find something in the archives?"

"We sure did," said Henry.

"Here, take a look at these," said Kyler. He passed his teacher the old documents.

The three friends hovered as he read every word. Kyler wanted to bust into the teacher's thoughts, but focused on keeping his mouth closed.

"This is it. Great job, boys."

"Ahem," said Darcy.

"Oh, you, too, Darcy."

"Is it enough?" asked Kyler.

"Enough to prove something to the mages council?" asked Master Ernie. "Yes. It is a true document from the archives. They will have to believe that Mordrake is more than a legend. The problem will be getting them to agree that he has awakened and that action needs to be taken."

"This is so frustrating," said Darcy. "I can't convince anyone of anything these days. You'd think the word of a princess would count for something."

"Henry, head off and find Walter," said Master Ernie.

While Henry searched, Kyler questioned his teacher. "What about the blushroot plant? I've never heard of it, and I've got a good head for plants."

Master Ernie sighed. "Well, that's just one of our many problems. The blushroot plant is extinct."

"What?" said Kyler and Darcy at the same time.

"It only grew in Naterum in the first place, and when Mordrake burned the city to the ground, he destroyed the plant. All that remained was probably used to make the first potion."

"Just great," said Darcy. "Now what do we do? The battle mages of old couldn't find a way to kill him. How are we going to?"

Master Ernie sat down on his bed, his head hanging low. "I don't know, Darcy."

"I can't accept that," said Kyler. "There has to be something else. He has my aunt Martha."

"I wish I knew what to say," said Master Ernie.

"Well, what more can you tell me about the blushroot plant? Are you sure it's extinct?"

"Very sure," said Master Ernie. "It was rare in its day. If someone found some today, they wouldn't keep it a secret. It would be worth a cartload of gold."

"Drat," said Kyler. "Why was it called blushroot anyway?"

"Oh, that's because it was covered in a fine fuzz, almost like a peach. It also had veins running under its leaves that reminded people of a beating heart," said Master Ernie.

"I haven't seen anything like that in the palace gardens," added Darcy.

Kyler wasn't listening anymore. He was thinking back to when he'd just arrived at school and had gone exploring in the tunnels. He pulled his notebook out of his side pouch and flipped through the pages. His fingers stopped turning when he came to a page with a dried sprig in the spine. "I found this in the tunnels near the mages library. It's dry now, but when I found it, I remember it being fuzzy."

Master Ernie took the plant from Kyler's fingers. "Nobody is supposed to be down in the tunnels. All the mages know they're closed off because of the danger of cave-ins."

"Well, I didn't know."

"I suppose you didn't, or you wouldn't have found the library to begin with. What did you notice about the plant?"

Kyler examined his notebook. "The plant was fuzzy with a throbbing pulse rising through its stem. I also mentioned here that it made me sleepy just to touch it."

"That's incredible," said Master Ernie, rushing across the room and grabbing Kyler's notebook right out of his hands.

"Can you remember where in the tunnels you found it? If I can get word to Master Avery, he might be able to search."

"I think so. It was growing out of a crack in the floor. I only pulled off a shoot, so the rest should still be there."

As Master Ernie wrote a note, Walter and Henry returned to the room.

"What is it?" asked Walter. "What's so urgent? This cur wouldn't say a word."

"I didn't want the wrong people to hear," stated Henry.

"You did just right, Henry," said Master Ernie. "Walter, we've got a lot of ground to cover, but first, is there anything else you can tell us about the messenger that came in yesterday?"

"Not that I can remember. The stable hands took him straight to Chancellor Usborn. That was the last I saw of him."

Darcy jumped up at the mention of the chancellor. "They didn't take him directly to the king?"

"No, from what I hear all reports go through Chancellor Usborn first. What is the difference? The chancellor is the king's right hand man," said Walter.

"The difference," said Darcy, "is that the other day I found the chancellor snooping around Leroy's bedroom. I thought it was weird, but if he's also keeping information from the king, maybe there's more to it than I thought. Hey, that also might be why I haven't been able to see Leroy. My schedule keeps putting me in the solar with my cousins."

"I can't believe the chancellor would have anything to do with keeping information from the king. He's a loyal member of the mages council," said Master Ernie. "Plus, he has been at the king's side for the last ten years."

"Maybe that's why he's so against investigating things out in the East. Maybe he already knows what's going on," said Kyler.

Master Ernie began pacing the room again, "Walter, first things first. Read this note, and then repeat it to Master Avery back at the school. I was going to send it by pouch, but now I don't know whom to trust. Return with the plant as soon as possible."

"What plant?" asked Walter.

"Oh, we forgot to tell you that part of the story," said Kyler. He began to fill in the blanks.

"I'll travel as fast as I can," said Walter.

"Before you go, drink this. It will increase your stamina."
Master Ernie pulled a small stoppered bottle from his bags.
With his knife, he cut open the wax seal and helped Walter
drink it. "Godspeed. The rest of you, we need a plan."

KYLER

The throne room was cold and empty, a strange place to hold a meeting. Walter had left two nights ago, and tonight was the night their plan went into effect. They'd hoped to move on it sooner, but Darcy had been unable to approach the chancellor until that very afternoon.

"Darcy, are you sure he said the throne room?" asked Kyler.

"Yes. I told him I needed to talk to him in private, and he picked the time and place. Thanks for coming with me. I've got a bad feeling about this."

"Well, I hope it's enough time for Master Ernie to search the chancellor's room."

The two of them hovered by the king's large throne. Aside from the throne and the seats for the king's council, the room was just a big meeting hall. Red velvet curtains hung from dowels along the walls, and sconces kept the room lit in a soft glow. Outside it was dark, so no light came in through the large glass windows.

At the far end of the room, the two heavy oak doors swung open. In came Chancellor Usborn, his royal robes draping his body. Kyler noticed that he was carrying a staff in one hand, something he'd never done before. In fact, Kyler hadn't even known the chancellor owned a mage's staff. Uneasy thoughts dashed through the teenager's mind, and he inwardly cursed that he'd left his own staff in his chambers. He wasn't supposed to carry a weapon around the castle, but he wished he'd made an exception this time.

"Ah, young princess Darcy, and who is this? Tyler?"

Kyler stepped forward. "It's Kyler."

The chancellor continued his walk down the long red carpet that led directly to the king's throne. The smile on his face seemed pasted in place. "I thought this was to be a private meeting?"

"It was," said Darcy. "Kyler is my friend. He offered to come."

"I see. Well, it can't be helped." The chancellor stopped at the base of the dais, and with a flick of his wrist he turned and pointed at the throne room doors. They closed with a whisper.

"There, now it's private. What was so urgent that you needed to see me? Is all well with your family?" The chancellor gestured for Darcy to come closer.

Kyler remained standing in front of the throne. As Darcy approached the chancellor, she leaned in to kiss his cheek, as was customary. The chancellor smiled and bent over so she could reach him.

"I wish to speak of some things concerning my brother," said Darcy.

"Yes, I've heard that you have been questioning the servants about William's accident."

"It wasn't an accident," said Darcy. "I believe it to have been much more."

"Dearest Darcy, I already led an investigation into the matter. All evidence pointed to a tragic accident."

"Were you the only one to investigate?" asked Darcy.

From the steps above, Kyler noticed a flush cover the chancellor's neck.

"Why? Is my word not good enough for you?"

Darcy took a step backward, putting distance between herself and the chancellor. Kyler could tell she was considering her next words carefully. "I just feel that something was overlooked."

"I was afraid it might come to this," said the chancellor. Quicker than a snake, he pointed his finger at Darcy and spoke. Without a sound, she collapsed in a pile at his feet. Kyler surged forward, his lips curled back in anger. The chancellor took one look at Kyler and sent a surge of power to fling him backward. He flew through the air, stopping only when he smacked violently into the throne.

Moaning, Kyler stood. He faced the approaching traitor and sent a ball of ice at his head. The chancellor laughed, deflecting the blow.

Kyler began another spell, but the chancellor cut him off by casting first. His whole body felt as if it were on fire, and he stumbled backward onto the throne. Within seconds, his limbs had locked up, and he sat on the throne like a statue. The only thing he was able to move were his eyes.

"Ah, you thought to stop me," said the chancellor. "Well, you did manage to get something out, or you'd be at my feet just like the princess. That should make you proud."

Kyler could only watch as the chancellor picked up Darcy and carried her over to the side of the room, near a window. "Nobody will be surprised that she jumped to her own death.

She's been asking so many questions about William, and everybody knows how depressed she is."

"Mmm."

"Don't try to speak. It will just frustrate you to no end." The chancellor turned toward Kyler. "The problem, of course, is what to do with you. I did not expect an audience."

The chancellor walked toward Kyler with venom in his step. "After all my planning, hmm, I'm going to have to be creative with this one. William was easy. He loved to hunt." The chancellor stopped at the bottom of the steps. "Leroy won't be a problem. He is young and malleable, and with Mordrake on the way, the king will soon be at war. Perhaps you should just disappear. I could say you no longer wanted to wait to search for your aunt and headed off into the night."

Kyler's heart picked up speed, and he struggled to move, even just a finger. The chancellor laughed, and his voice's eerie tremble echoed through the throne room. All Kyler could do was close his eyes and wish for a miracle.

That miracle came when the throne room doors burst open, and Master Ernie sprinted inside. "Usborn, unhand that boy!"

The chancellor turned slowly, without fear, but Kyler noticed he leveled his staff toward the doorway, and it slammed shut.

"Ernie, what a pleasant surprise? It'll be like killing two birds with one stone. You've been causing me no end of problems."

"Stop right there. Don't even touch that boy."

"I wasn't planning on it." The chancellor's evil laughter burst forth again. "I don't need to be anywhere near him to do what needs to be done."

Master Ernie drew closer but kept his staff at the ready. "I know what you did. There's still time to come clean."

"And why would I want to do that? Everything is going as planned."

Master Ernie dropped an old leather-bound book onto the floor and kicked it toward the chancellor. "I found that in your room. Your ancestor was one of the original battle mages that brought Mordrake down. How can you dishonor your family this way?"

"It won't be a dishonor when I rule the land. Mordrake has promised the entire kingdom to me. Leroy will be my puppet."

"You're twisted, Usborn."

Kyler's eyes grew large as he listened to Master Ernie and the chancellor. *What kind of man would sacrifice the world just to own a piece of it?*

Usborn crooned, "It was easy to find where they'd buried Mordrake. All the details were in the journal. The only thing I can't do is break the circle of guardians, but Mordrake has that well in hand."

"One of those guardians is your own blood! He gave his life to keep us safe from Mordrake."

"Too bad for him," said the chancellor.

"You won't confess to the king?"

"Now why would I do that?"

Kyler saw the determined look that came over Master Ernie's face. In the blink of an eye, the teacher leveled his staff at the chancellor, and a bolt of lightning flew from its tip.

However, the chancellor was ready, and a glimmering shield surrounded his body an instant before the energy bolt hit.

All Kyler could do was sit and watch as the battle waged.

Energy bolts flew across the room, scorching the walls. The two were evenly matched, and able to deflect the projectiles. Soon fireballs entered the mix. The room was large and empty, offering no place to retreat for safety.

Master Ernie rushed the chancellor. Kyler could tell Usborn was not ready for weapon-to-weapon combat. Master Ernie slashed his staff against the chancellor's temple, causing the traitor to lose his footing. He fell backward, but not before releasing a gust of air that pushed Master Ernie backward.

From the other end of the room, Kyler heard a loud banging commence on the oak doors. Someone must have heard the commotion and was trying to enter! However, the doors did not budge, and Kyler could only guess that the chancellor had somehow spelled them shut this time.

The battle continued, growing fiercer as the combatants grew tired. Kyler noticed that their aims were off, and they were taking longer to recover after each spell, but their desperation made them both more violent.

Soon the air within the throne room became the vortex of a tornado. The winds rushed angrily around, ripping hangings off the walls and sucking them into the maelstrom. Kyler glanced over at Darcy, worried she'd been harmed, but she lay close enough to a wall that the wind was finding no purchase.

The tornado crackled with energy, and soon random bolts of lightning were shooting off on their own accord. Kyler tried to shrink into himself, but he still could not move. Then Master Ernie shot off a bout of hot steam that rammed into the chancellor. Usborn's face turned red and welted under the heat. He screamed and shot off a blast of energy. The bolt wrapped around one of the flying red window hangings, and the thing hovered midair. Kyler watched in horror as the material rushed at Master Ernie and wrapped him up like a crepe.

Kyler was afraid this was the end. Master Ernie struggled to unwind himself, turning and twisting, but without any luck. However, the chancellor was having just as many problems and was holding his scalded face in his hands, tearing at his eyes and screaming.

The banging against the throne room door grew louder, and Kyler knew that reinforcements had been called. He glanced back and forth between the two combatants, worried that the chancellor would recover first.

Then Master Ernie burst from his wrapped cocoon and staggered to his feet. Kyler tried to cheer.

"Mmm." *Dang*, he thought.

Master Ernie advanced on the writhing chancellor. With a fierce look, he thrust out his staff and shouted, but the chancellor wasn't done yet. He blocked the spell with a shield and then scooted back against the far wall. Ernie advanced again. The chancellor sent off a fireball, but with his eyes scalded by the steam, the fire flew haywire and surged at Kyler. The hanging behind the throne burst into flames, and Kyler could only watch as it came spilling down off of its hooks directly over his head.

Without the ability to move, he could only stare at Master Ernie. Just as the engulfed fabric landed over his head, a gush of air sent it back up into the air and across the room. Kyler felt a burning sensation on his head and the smell of singed hair filled his nose.

He watched as the chancellor sent another fireball at Master Ernie, this time right on target. However, Master Ernie was focused on Kyler and was sending a spell to dampen the fire. Just as Kyler's hair stopped burning, the chancellor's fireball hit Master Ernie squarely in the chest, engulfing him in flames.

A silent scream tore through Kyler's body. His teacher staggered to his knees, the flames eating through his clothing. He crawled forward, determined to reach the chancellor, but only made it a few feet. A horrific shriek tore through his lips and Master Ernie collapsed onto the floor. Kyler could smell his teacher's cooking flesh on the air and bile ran up his throat.

With the last of his strength, Master Ernie cast one more spell. The chancellor was not prepared for the lightning bolt that struck him in the chest and sent him flying backward toward the far end of the room. The chancellor's neck cracked when he smacked into the far stone wall, then his body slumped to the floor.

With the chancellor dead, the spell holding Kyler immobile was broken, and he dashed across the floor, falling upon his knees at his teacher's side. He cast a spell to draw liquid from the air and sent it raining down on Master Ernie. In the background, Kyler heard the doors crash open and voices flood the room, but he paid no attention. The water put out the fire, but black charcoal covered his teacher. Tears fell from Kyler's eyes, and sobs racked his chest.

With a sigh of pain, Master Ernie opened his eyes and stared into Kyler's. "You're safe," he whispered.

"Don't leave me," begged Kyler. Master Ernie strained to reach his charred hand up to Kyler's face. A sob caught in his throat as his tears continued to fall. "Please don't leave me."

His teacher's hand went limp and then fell to the floor. Wide, yet empty eyes stared up at Kyler.

Kyler doubled over, unable to hold himself upright. A hand came to rest on his shoulder, and somebody joined him on the floor. A part of his mind recognized Darcy's fingers wrapping around his own, but in his grief his thoughts were so jumbled that he couldn't fight his way to the surface.

WALTER

Frigid air buffeted Walter as he charged through the forest surrounding the magic school. He was dog tired. So much so, that he didn't have the strength to laugh at his own joke. His paws pounded up the front stairs, and then he burst into the entry room. The room was dark, but his presence ignited several sconces around the room. He hurried over to a side table where a long tasseled rope hung above it. With a leap, he jumped into the air, catching the rope in his mouth and yanking. An alarm blared, loud enough to awaken all the council members.

It wasn't long before several old men and women in sleeping robes hurried into the room. Master Lex charged in last.

"What's this?" he yelled. "What's all the ruckus about?"

All of the mages in the room looked around for the bell ringer. Only Master Avery spotted Walter curled up on a couch.

"Walter, what news have you?" asked Avery as he ran to the wolf's side.

"There's trouble. Master Ernie sent me back to warn the council. We recovered the records involving Mordrake. There is no doubt that he actually existed."

The mages in the room began speaking among themselves, their voices rising in dispute. Master Lex's voice hushed them all. "Even so, how do we know he has awakened?"

"What more proof do you need? A body? By then it will be too late," said Walter.

"I am too tired to speak of this coherently," said Master Lex. "Let those among us who are council members meet together at first light." The matter decided, the headmaster turned a cold shoulder and left the room.

The other mages followed behind in little groups, whispering among one another. Walter doubted many would sleep that night. Only Master Avery remained by Walter's side, and when they had all left, Walter sighed.

"It was as we thought. Oh well, my real message is for you."

"What would you have of me?" asked Master Avery.

"In the castle archives a sleeping spell was discovered that could put Mordrake back to sleep. The main ingredient is the blushroot plant, and Master Ernie asks that you make this potion."

Master Avery shook his head. "There's a small problem. The blushroot plant is extinct."

"Kyler believes he found the plant in the ruins of Naterum. I have his directions."

"Then let's not waste time. Lead the way."

KYLER

Kyler huddled under his covers, intent on ignoring the world. He heard soft footsteps pad into his room, but did not turn over.

"The king wants to see you," said Darcy.

Kyler simply pulled a pillow over his head.

"Okay, maybe later," she said.

He heard her footsteps retreat and knew he was alone. The wall before him was whitewashed and blank, the perfect thing to stare at without having to use his brain. His thoughts caused him piercing pain, and he felt it better to become a void, an empty shell.

He remained tucked into a little ball in the center of his bed until dinner. He only got up then because his stomach wouldn't be ignored. In the hallway, Kyler noticed Henry in his room with the chamber door open. He crossed over and hovered in the door frame.

"Hey," he said.

Henry looked up from his work and frowned. "How are you feeling?"

"I'll let you know next week. How about we go get some food right now?"

"You know I never say no to food," said Henry.

Servants stared at the two boys as they walked the castle halls. Several gave Kyler the evil eye. He felt like the main attraction at the fair.

"Why is everybody looking at me?"

"You're the boy with all the secrets," said Henry. "Darcy was unconscious during the whole thing, and both Master Ernie and Chancellor Usborn are dead. Plus, you haven't been to see the king, and it's been almost an entire day."

"Oh, I guess if you put it that way."

"You know you'll have to see him after we eat. In fact, I wouldn't be surprised if an armed escort came our way."

They were lucky, and no soldiers arrived. Even so, they both ate their meal in a hurry, an impending feeling of doom hanging over their heads.

Later that evening, Kyler walked to the king's private council chambers. It was a medium-size room with large chairs arranged in a circle. The king himself sat in the grandest chair, with several plump cushions piled up around his hips.

"Young man, I am sorry for your loss," said the king as Kyler entered.

A guard pointed to the chair nearest to the king. When Kyler sat, several members of the court took their places. He wondered if this would be more of a trial than a questioning.

"Will you tell us what happened?" asked the king.

"Where should I start? What did Darcy mention?" asked Kyler.

"Never mind my niece. We want to hear your version of things."

Kyler nodded and then launched into everything. He started all the way back with his aunt Martha and the Griffin footprint. His intention was to restate everything he hoped Master Ernie had already told the king during council meetings, but this time the teenager yearned that they'd listen to it not as a story, but a fact.

When he came to the part where Darcy had expressed her suspicions about William's death, the council chambers took on a chilling air. Several councilors sat up straight, crossing their arms across their chests and then leaning back. Kyler got the feeling that this was the part they had been waiting for.

"We came up with a plan, wanting to find out about the chancellor. Darcy asked him to meet with her privately, and while that happened, Master Ernie checked the chancellor's room."

"What was he looking for?" asked the king.

"Well, we weren't sure. It's just seemed odd that word wasn't getting to you about the problems in the East. Master Ernie suspected that Chancellor Usborn was neglecting his duty, but even he wasn't ready for the truth."

"And what truth was that?" asked the king. All the eyes in the room bore into Kyler, waiting for his response.

"He was involved in more than just William's death. He also awakened Mordrake."

Voices broke out in the chambers, and the noise level skyrocketed. Several councilors began arguing with one another, taking sides about the validity of Kyler's words.

"What proof do you have of this?" asked a councilor.

"Proof? Isn't Master Ernie's death enough proof?" said Kyler.

"Only if you'd have us believe that it was the chancellor and not Master Ernie that razed the throne room."

Kyler stomped on the floor. "I was there. I saw and heard everything that happened."

"How convenient," replied a councilor.

"Enough," spoke the king. "Kyler, please continue."

Kyler turned his back on the councilor, determined to explain things only to the king. "Chancellor Usborn asked Darcy to meet him in the throne room. I went along for protection."

A snort came from somewhere behind Kyler.

"The first thing the chancellor did was cast a spell on Darcy. When I saw it happen, I tried to cast my own, but I was too slow, and I was frozen into place." Kyler stared over the king's shoulder while recalling his struggle. "He dragged Darcy over to a window. Said he was going to toss her out and make it look like suicide." Again the noise level in the room rose, but Kyler paid no attention.

"When he came toward me, he said he'd make me disappear and make everyone think I'd gone after my aunt Martha. He said he'd killed William and that Leroy was just as malleable as he'd hoped." At these words, the room became silent.

"Did he say what he planned to do with Leroy?" asked the king.

"No, but after Master Ernie came into the room, I figured it out," said Kyler.

"Go on."

"Master Ernie burst through the doors just when the chancellor was going to kill me. He had an old book in his hands that he confronted the chancellor with."

The king gestured to one of his servants. A second later a charred book landed in his hands. "Was this the book?" asked the king.

"I guess so," said Kyler. "I never saw it up close."

"Most of the pages are burned, and we've only been able to make out a few sections. Did your teacher mention anything specific?"

"Yes. He said it was an old family journal, and that the chancellor had betrayed his own ancestors by using it to awaken Mordrake. One of the chancellor's predecessors had given his very life to entrap the monster."

The king nodded, and became pensive.

Kyler went on to explain the documents they'd found in the archives. He finished with the process used to drug Mordrake and then bind him into eternal slumber. "The chancellor must have done something to the standing stones, and it woke up Mordrake and the Griffin."

"This is a very interesting story," said the king.

"It's more than a story. It's the truth. Chancellor Usborn was keeping events back east quiet so that Mordrake's armies could get close. The deal was that he would be left alone if you were killed. Then he would set Leroy up to reign while controlling his every move."

Again the voices in the room rose, cresting like a wave. The king's flesh was pale, and his eyes had grown weary. "Thank you, Kyler. If you'd please return to your chambers, I have a lot to discuss with my council."

Kyler stood up to leave, but turned back. "Master Ernie was a great man. He believed in me when no one else would. He believed that we could stop Mordrake, and I think we can, too. We just need your support." Kyler nodded at the king and then left.

KYLER

The next morning a messenger arrived early with a note asking Kyler to come to the king's private chambers. He trudged through the hallways, worry nagging his mind. When he arrived he could hear Darcy's raised voice in the room, and didn't want to enter. That girl had a fine temper. He remembered her axe throwing all too well. However, the guard who'd escorted him to the room left no other option but forward.

He took a side step once inside the doorway and watched the confrontation with interest. His odds were on Darcy. The king was already pacing.

"I can't let you go," said the king.

Darcy crossed her arms. "I am going to see this through. I battled the Griffin, and I will defend this land."

"You're a member of the royal family. I wasn't there when you foolishly followed the Griffin into the woods, but I am here now, and you will not be going."

Darcy stepped forward. "Then you'll have to seal me in the solar because I will find a way out of here. This is my choice. My path."

The king pointed his finger at her face. "Darcy, you are a sixteen-year-old royal princess, not a soldier or privateer."

Darcy wasn't about to back down. "What I am is ready. I've fought for this. I've trained for this, and I will do this!"

Kyler couldn't help the grin from spreading across his face. That was the Darcy he knew.

"Darcy." The king lowered his finger, but continued to stare into her eyes.

"No! Kyler and Henry are my friends. We will see this through together. My life is no more important than theirs, and don't you dare tell me I can't go because I'm a girl."

The king sighed and then returned to his seat. "I can see you're set on this course."

"I am."

"Your father won't be happy. He just lost William."

"I just lost William, too, and this is me doing something about it."

The king nodded but then turned his gaze toward Kyler.

"Kyler, what say you in this matter?"

Darcy whipped around and nailed Kyler with a look that would melt iron, but he didn't need the warning, "Your Highness, I wouldn't want anyone else by my side. Darcy is the best."

"So be it. I have consulted with my councilors, and though some disagree, I am prone to support this crazy endeavor."

Kyler saw Darcy take a deep breath and relax her shoulders.

"There are, however," said the king, "some conditions."

Kyler stepped forward. "Your Highness, we will accept any conditions you have, but I beg you, let us wait no longer. The solstice is nigh, and my aunt is in danger."

"Kyler, I know the situation well, but I cannot let a trio of children"—the king shot Darcy a look—"no matter whom they are, go about this quest alone. I will be sending a squad of soldiers with you. I have also requested that the mages council send a new advisor and look through their ranks for those who are battle ready. You defeated the Griffin, but this situation is dire. I believe more help will be needed."

"Yes, Your Majesty," responded Kyler. He could live with those options. "Walter will be back anytime now. I ask your permission to leave soon after."

"Granted. I will send more soldiers, and whatever mages that arrive."

"Thank you, Uncle," added Darcy.

"There is one more thing," said the king. He nodded to a guard near the rear of the room. The guard stood at attention and then marched forward carrying an encrusted gold chest. "The treasures of the royal house are vast, and there are many things from times long ago that rest on the shelves unknown and forgotten. This is one of those things."

The guard stopped before the king and held out the box. The king extended his hand and snapped open the lid. Kyler leaned forward to see what treasure the box held. On a bed of velvet rested a circlet of gold. Connected by silver threads, a large opal rested in the middle of the gold. It reminded Kyler of a planet with rings.

"Last night I sent my historians into the vault." The king lifted the ornament from the box and held it in the air, where it sparkled like fire. "This was found on a shelf beside a faded plaque. The plaque named this piece the 'Lifeblood of the Orcs.' We have no clue what it is beyond that description. However, the date on the plaque corresponds to the year Naterum was razed, and the kingship moved."

Kyler looked at the object in awe. He could feel a slight vibration emanating from the piece and knew that it contained power.

"I want you to take this with you. My hope is that it will aid you in battle, or at the very least be a valuable trade to prevent war."

Kyler bowed. When he looked up, the king held the box out, waiting for Kyler to take it up. "It is my honor, Your Majesty." The box felt heavy in Kyler's hands, but the object inside continued to buzz with energy. Kyler realized the Orcan relic recognized that someone with magic was holding it.

MARTHA

She'd been in the camp for weeks, but Martha didn't know the exact number of days. Her memory was fuzzy, and her mind cloudy. She knew they were drugging either her food or water, but it didn't matter because she needed to eat and drink.

When she'd first arrived at the Orc camp, she and Donald had been thrust into a large canvas tent full of people slumped on mats. She'd screamed for help, but the people in the tent were unresponsive. Now she knew they were in a drug-induced funk.

The tent was large, with nine other men and women held prisoner. When she'd realized that they were drugging her, she'd stopped eating and drinking, but she'd only lasted forty-eight hours before her thirst drove her crazy. Now there was no need to keep her bound because she could function only to eat, drink, sleep, and go to the bathroom.

Today was different from all the rest. An Orc whom she called One-eye had come into the tent before breakfast and pulled Martha to her feet. She told herself to struggle as he led her out of the tent and into the sunlight, but her body refused to listen. Instead, she stumbled and swayed and leaned on the Orc for support. Spread out before her was an entire army camped in rows. It wasn't just Orcs, either. She saw dark elves, Imps, and reptilian creatures. They sat around campfires sharing breakfast.

The smell of the bacon made her stomach rumble and her saliva kick into overdrive. She was starving for more than mush. The Orc finally brought her to a small pavilion covered in silk. He shoved her into a chair and then walked over to a table. She watched as he poured a glass of clear water from a pitcher and held it out for her to drink.

She wanted to deny him the pleasure of her obedience, but the water looked so fresh, and she suspected it wasn't drugged. Martha grasped the glass in shaky hands and gulped the water. It felt cool going down her throat, and she reveled in the sweet feeling. She placed the empty glass into One-eye's hands.

He nodded and then brought her a platter of fruit and cheese.

"Eat."

"Yees," she mumbled. *Why is he feeding me?* But, she didn't care at the moment and ate the crisp fruit and soft cheeses.

When she finished, she sat back in her chair and looked at the Orc. He stood before the entrance with his sword resting in his arms. Martha's head cleared enough to process deeper thoughts. One-eye noticed, and bound her hands. Then he pulled on the ropes and forced her to stand. At once, she began thinking of a spell, but as she pictured the images in her mind, the words wouldn't come out of her mouth. Instead, a mouthful of unlinked sounds emerged.

The Orc laughed. "Lady no speak. Head clear, not mouth." He led her out of the pavilion and deeper into the army camp.

Up ahead she spotted huge, monolithic stones rising from the ground. The stone circle spanned fifty yards, and as they drew closer, she counted twelve stones, but one was cracked and lay half on the ground. Inside the stone ring was a single tent, but it was gigantic. Beside it rose a ten-foot pole that pointed into the sky. Impaled at the top was a head, the dead flesh peeling back over bleached bones. Bugs swarmed in and out of the mouth and nose, causing the leftover flesh to move. Martha dug her feet into the ground, and began pushing backward, but One-eye was twice her weight and shoved her into the circle.

The Orc nodded toward the decapitated head. "Good thing we wait to bring you. Master got mad at last mage. Made him pay for death of Griffin."

Martha knew she was about to meet evil itself: Mordrake.

The Orc led her around a ragged hole in the ground. Martha glanced into its depths and marveled at its scale. Darkness pooled within the hole, and Martha could not make out the interior. The Orc pushed her toward the tent. She struggled with all her might, flinging her elbows out and kicking in every direction.

The Orc picked her up and carried her like a baby.

Inside the tent, the area shined with lamplight and was covered in rugs and cushions. Several tables lined one side of the space, and Martha could see maps sprawled upon them. Then she saw a tall man step out of the shadows, and her heart all but stopped.

"Greetings, mage. Welcome to my resting place," said the man. He walked forward, examining every inch of her from top to bottom. Martha instinctively reached up a hand to smooth her ratted hair, but stopped in mid lift and frowned. The man ceased a mere foot in front of her face.

Martha held very still, but her mind was churning with defensive spells.

"Those won't be necessary." The man raised his hand and cupped the side of her face, staring deep into her eyes. "My name is Mordrake, and you are perfect."

Martha felt his mind push into hers and then take stock of her power. "I needed you to be clearheaded enough for me to read."

He was tall and handsome with long brown hair and blue eyes. He wore leather pants, a tunic, and a broadsword strapped to his hip. Martha could see his trim physique and knew he would make a deadly foe in battle. It was his perfect face that confused her. *This is Mordrake the monster?*

"Mmm."

"No need to speak. Not that you could."

Martha gathered her strength and then thrust Mordrake out of her mind.

"Yes, you will do." He walked around her, taking in her age and appearance. "Seems you've let yourself go, but no matter, it's your magic I need, not your body."

"Grrr."

Mordrake laughed at Martha. "You know this all wouldn't have been possible without a little help from one of your friends."

Now he had her attention.

"Two years ago I was awoken from a very deep sleep. The man went to a lot of trouble to find me. I was buried deep, and he had to break one of the guardian stones to reach me. He's a member of your own mages council."

Martha's eyes grew wide in disbelief. She didn't know anyone that would wake Mordrake.

"Yes, he's a determined man. Wishes to rule his own kingdom and thought I might help take out the present high king. He's a fool. I will take out the high king, but for me, not for him. It took me a year to recover my strength, and then I sent out a call and my army began to arrive." Mordrake motioned at Martha to follow, and then he left the tent. Outside he stood within the circle of stones with his arms spread out like a falcon's wings. "The only things that keep me in place are these stones, and come the solstice they won't be a problem any longer." He looked at Martha, "That's what you and your fellow mages are going to do for me. I will take your powers and break the stones!" He flung his arms down to his sides, and a maniacal grin covered his face.

Martha shook her head in defiance. She would never let him take her powers.

"You won't even have a choice," said Mordrake. He turned to One-eye. "Take her back to the tent with the others."

The Orc dragged Martha back to her original tent, but this time she was clear enough to look around and judge her fellow captives. She recognized all of the men and women, having met them when she'd been on the mages council. As One-eye pushed her down and rolled her onto her side, she gasped. One of the men looked so familiar that she thought she must be mistaken. Her brother, Kyler's father, lay on a far mat. Of Kyler's mother, there was no sign.

KYLER

Walter returned two days later with a pouch containing the sleeping draught. He went directly to Kyler's room, where Darcy and Henry were already present.

"Walter, we are so happy to see you," said Darcy, rushing to hug him.

"What a fine greeting." He licked her face.

"Does the pouch contain the potion?" asked Kyler.

"Yes, Master Avery made it himself. In fact, he follows a few days behind with a group of mages loyal to the cause."

"So you received the king's missive?" asked Kyler.

Walter turned his head to the side. "No, I left immediately with the potion. Master Avery stayed behind to gather allies for battle."

Kyler hung his head. "Then you haven't heard."

"Heard what?"

"Master Ernie. He's…he's dead."

Walter's lips pulled back from his sharp teeth, and a tremendous growl erupted from his belly. "What! Who has done this? Lead me to them and I will tear them to shreds."

"There is nothing you can do Walter," said Henry. "The chancellor died, too."

"I think you'd better tell me what happened," demanded the wolf.

As the story unfolded, Walter's fur stood on edge. "Traitor. He betrayed his own kind, his own blood." If a wolf could spit, he would have.

"The king's message asked for mages to come fight," said Darcy.

"They come," said Walter. "And without a demand from the king. They come because of you, Kyler."

"Me? I am humbled, but that's a lot of pressure."

"Pressure makes diamonds," said Henry.

Kyler shoved Henry. "We need to prepare," said Kyler. "Darcy, tell your uncle we leave in the morning. Whatever soldiers he wishes to send should meet us at the front gate."

They rode out in the bright morning sunshine with a squadron of soldiers at their backs. They planned to follow Walter's guidance and find the site of the caravan remains. After that, Kyler hoped they'd find some tracks because the East was a lot of ground to cover.

Three days passed, and the travel was easy. On the fourth day, they found the busted wagons of the caravan and the bloated bodies scattered across the ground. The smell of rotten meat and decay swam thickly in the air, and everyone had to put cloths in front of their faces to fight off the scent. Kyler used his staff to look around, and discovered a single set of wagon tracks heading back west.

"Dorothy's wagon is gone," said Walter.

"That's good," said Kyler. "Hopefully she and her son both escaped."

The soldiers broke up into pairs and dissected the area in a grid-like pattern searching for clues. Several of the bodies belonging to Orcs had large blast holes in their chests. Kyler attributed the wounds to Martha and was glad she'd got in some good blows before her capture.

Darcy wandered over to Kyler. "We should do something about the bodies. The birds and wolves have already gotten to them."

"You're right, but honestly, the thought of touching them makes my skin crawl. They've been here for weeks. Notice nothing ate the Orcs though."

"Yeah, guess they're nasty no matter what. How about using some magic?" asked Darcy.

Kyler looked over the battlefield and at all the corpses. "I think I can manage something, but I don't think we'll have the time to bury them all."

"What if we burn them? It would set them at peace and keep the animals away."

"I'll go talk to the captain," said Kyler. "When they're done with their investigating, I'll see what I can do."

An hour later, Kyler stood at the edge of the field using his staff to raise each body into the air and place it into a pile. The work was tedious, and he often had to go back for fallen body parts, but in the end, he'd put the poor caravaners together. He left the Orcs were they'd fallen. The soldiers stood back and removed their helmets while Kyler took up position beside the corpses. Then with a mumbled word, Kyler pointed at the pile and the bodies burst into flames.

The group left quickly afterward, hastening away from the smell of scorched human flesh. They followed a large trail of flattened grass and wheel marks that headed east. As they traveled, there were no signs of fellow travelers. The once busy trade route was deserted.

The silence began to weigh on them all and an overwhelming depression beat against the group. They trudged on, following in one another's footsteps. Kyler didn't even look around at the scenery. He just stared at the back of the boots in front of him. Soon the clops of the horse's hooves were the only noises filling the air. Then Kyler heard something beautiful, the sound of sweet musical notes. He turned back to see Henry playing his flute, a look of bliss on his friend's face. The mood lifted and the soldiers began talking among themselves. Henry continued to play, often just small background trills, but enough to lend an undercurrent of hope.

That night they camped in a copse of trees that sheltered them from searching eyes. Walter scouted ahead, but with no sign of people, let alone Orcs, the captain felt it was safe to build several fires. Kyler, Darcy, Henry and Walter sat around one allowing the heat to work its way inside their bones. The journey was more difficult than before, and the kids moaned about their long travels on horseback. Walter was the only one who had it easy, but he was constantly searching ahead of the main party, wary about attack.

"Henry, that music was a brilliant idea," said Darcy.

"Thanks. I just felt so down, and the next thing I knew I was reaching for the flute."

"Well it worked like a miracle," said Kyler. He reached out his hand to stroke Walter's fur. "Walter, how much longer until the solstice?"

"Not much time. I'd say just over a week."

Kyler threw a stick into the fire and watched the sparks fly into the air like little lightning bugs. "We're running out of time."

Darcy reached over and grabbed his hand. "We're going to make it."

"Yeah," said Henry. "There is no way Mordrake's going to win."

"I really hope so," said Kyler. He reached into his side pouch and pulled out the Orc treasure. He'd been studying it every evening, trying to understand its powers. So far he didn't have a clue.

"I wonder if this thing will help or if it's just a pretty toy?" he asked.

"It was in the vaults for a reason," said Darcy. "It must have a purpose."

"If it does, I can't figure it out."

"I thought you said it was magic," said Henry.

"It is," said Walter. "I can feel the zing from here."

"Just because its magic doesn't mean it'll help us, especially if I can't figure out how to use it." Over the last week, Kyler had tried every way he could think to tap into the circlet's power, but the only thing that happened was an amplification of an internal humming sound. He couldn't siphon any power away or cause any behavior differences. With a sigh, he stuffed it back into his satchel beside the well-wrapped container of Master Avery's potion.

As the night grew deeper, people rolled out their sleeping blankets and snuggled in deep. Kyler and his group were not asked to keep watch, and he didn't mind one bit. He had the worst time getting to sleep every night. The hard ground and the cold air were a combination he couldn't ignore. Last night one of the soldiers had shown him a trick using rocks heated up in the fire pit to keep the blankets warm. He'd slept semi-well for the first time.

Tonight, he'd forgotten to get any before heading to bed, and now that he was well wrapped and fairly snug, he couldn't decide if it was worth the effort to emerge into the cold air and get stones from the fire. As tired as he was, he drifted in and out of sleep, the debate cloudy in his mind.

The hoot of an owl in the distance brought Kyler out of his funk. By now the air was so cold that he could see his breath in the night. He rolled over and looked at the fire pit. The embers were still glowing, so the rocks would still be warm. He gathered up his courage and unrolled a layer of blanket. He wrapped the rest around his shoulders and hopped over to the fire pit.

As he gathered a bunch of nice warm stones into his arms, he looked around at the sleeping camp. Most of the soldiers slept huddled together for warmth and the horses stood in a close group sheltering one another. He looked out at the starry night and took in a breath of crisp air. The night seemed alive, even though everyone slept. He hopped back to his place next to Henry and began stuffing the rocks into his blankets. Before lying down he looked around the camp. The feeling that he was forgetting something nagged at him, but the rocks were spreading delicious warmth, and soon he couldn't ignore the urge to hunker down and doze.

KYLER

He was somewhere in that place where a person is half-asleep, but a part of the brain is working on the problems of the day. Suddenly, he sat straight up in his blankets and shuddered as reality hit him smack in the head. He shook Henry, but kept one finger over his friend's mouth to keep him quiet. Henry's eyes sprang open, and he looked ready to jump.

"Shh," whispered Kyler.

Henry stopped struggling and then focused. "What's wrong?" he mouthed.

"The guards," said Kyler, leaning over near Henry's ear. "They're not walking around camp. All I see are people sleeping."

"Where are they?"

"I don't know. Roll over and tap Walter and Darcy. I think something's up."

All four of them sat in the cold darkness of the night. Kyler communicated in hand gestures to keep things silent. Walter was the first of them to move. He got up and padded through the sleeping soldiers, looking for the guards. Soon he wandered into the trees, and Kyler lost sight of him.

Not knowing what else to do, Kyler grabbed his boots and began pulling them on. Henry and Darcy did the same. With his staff in hand, he hurried over to the closest soldier and shook him awake. The soldier went from sleep to consciousness in a blink, and Kyler jumped back as a knife lashed out. Trained well, the man stopped the knife and looked around, alert but silent. With a nod to Kyler, the soldier leaned over to wake up the man beside him.

A loud snarl ripped through the air, and the growls of a wolf echoed into the night. A symphony of battle screams rushed at Kyler through the trees, and the shadows of Orcs flooded through the moonlight. Henry and Darcy were by his side in moments. Only a few of the soldiers had arisen previous to the attack, and they rushed into battle to give their awakening comrades time to arm themselves.

Into the circle of camp staggered an Orc with a furry shape clinging to its back. Kyler could make out Walter's jaws clamped onto the back of the Orc's neck. The Orc stumbled around, until with a vicious snap, Walter dug out a chunk of the spine, and the Orc fell.

With a roar, Kyler flung himself into the battle. All around him swords rang out, and grunts and moans filled his ears. He pointed his staff at an Orc and sent a bolt of electricity flying. The Orc sailed backward, a scorch mark on its chest. Henry brought out his sword, and back-to-back they fought. Darcy fought nearby, her style and form fierce.

Kyler didn't know how much time passed, but the cries of soldiers became more frequent and he found himself backed into a small circle with those closest to him. The

Orcs pounded on them, cudgels swinging and swords slashing bellies. Their enemy was so strong that it took several soldiers to take one down.

Tiredness washed over him, and he found himself stumbling as he moved. Guts and gore covered his body, and a nasty cut over his eyebrow left a stream of blood running into his right eye. The fresh smell of death hung in the air. The Orcs were too close to fire lightning at, so he began using his staff as a weapon, thrusting and jabbing.

The roars of the vicious Orcs echoed in his ears, and he blindly hit anything that came his way. He saw Walter out of the corner of his eye. He was snarling at three Orcs that surrounded him. Kyler felt his strength leaving as his hope dimmed. His little group was forced backward, and he struggled not to trip.

Walter jumped over one of his kills and dashed to Kyler's side. Their small group was all that remained. A large group of Orcs encircled them, jeering and laughing. Kyler knew there was little hope, but then he heard the sound of Henry's flute and a small glimmer of faith ignited.

As Henry's music grew in strength, a golden shimmer dropped like a dome over the little group. With a shield in place, the Orcs could no longer reach them, but Kyler knew they would never leave, and the enemy had only to wait for Henry to tire.

As the music flowed through the night, the little group of survivors slumped together, their breaths ragged and heavy. The Orcs threw rocks, and even though they bounced off the shield, each one that struck caused every member of the group to jump. Kyler leaned on his staff, trying to draw strength into his body and soul.

"What do we do?" panted Darcy.

By now, all the surviving Orcs surrounded them, and by Kyler's count there were at least twenty in the first row. "I don't know."

"We can't give up," said Darcy. "Henry is giving us time. Let's use it."

"We should drop the shield and charge," said one of the two remaining soldiers with the group. "If we can cut out a path, the princess might escape."

"I'm not running like a scared chicken," said Darcy.

"Give me a minute to think," said Kyler. "Ugh, if only Master Ernie was here."

Rocks and sticks continued to sail their way, but the group was quiet, waiting for Kyler. When the idea to use the Orc treasure first came to him, he pushed it away as a long shot, but the longer it took him to regain even a small amount of power, the more his mind dwelt on the artifact.

He pulled the golden circlet from his bag and looked down at it. Now what? It was then that he noticed the Orc directly in front of him stood still, a look of awe plastered on its face. With a thrust of courage, Kyler held the circlet high above his head, turning in a small circle so all the Orcs could see his treasure.

Like dominoes, the Orcs froze in place one after another.

"What are you doing?" asked Darcy.

"I don't have a clue," said Kyler. "They seem to be reacting to the very presence of it."

"Well, do some magic or something," said Walter.

As Henry continued his music, Kyler focused on the circlet as he would his staff. He tried to send out an onslaught of wind to knock over all the Orcs, but nothing happened. "It isn't working."

"Try something else," said Darcy.

The Orcs were no longer frozen in shock, but they stood at attention, fully focused on Kyler.

Kyler did the only thing he could think of: he yelled out the wish of his heart. "Go away and don't come back!" He knew it was a silly thing to do, but he was at the end of his rope.

First one Orc and then another turned and walked away. Kyler's mouth fell open, but he remembered to hold the circlet high up in the air. Henry kept the shield up until each and every Orc had left. When he stopped playing, there was not an Orc within fifty yards of them.

"Wow. What happened?" asked Darcy.

Kyler brought the circlet down and looked at it in the moonlight. "I think it controlled them somehow. I just don't know why?"

"Who cares why?" said Henry. "That thing saved our butts."

"Do you think they'll come back?" she asked.

"Not if they're really following what I asked," said Kyler.

"We need to check for wounded," said one of the soldiers. So they all spread out, going body to body checking for wounds and pulses. Every soul was dead.

Their group gathered what they could find of supplies and repacked their bags. A couple of them had bloody wounds that needed tending, but in their hurry all they could do was wrap the gashes in rags.

All of the horses had scattered, leaving the group to go forward on foot. Darcy had wanted to burn the bodies, but

Kyler worried fire would bring more Orcs. Without time to bury the soldiers, and with his magic on low, Kyler helped the others drag the bodies into a pile. They then placed pine fronds over the bodies to camouflage them from the sky.

They left just as dawn broke the horizon, a group of battered and bruised survivors.

KYLER

They traveled east, their way slow as they stayed within the tree line. The threat of another Orc attacked loomed over their heads, and without knowing exactly how the Orc artifact worked, Kyler was hesitant to trust in its powers. They were all worn and tired, and come midafternoon; they found a sheltered grove where they could rest.

"Not having horses is a big downer," said Henry.

Kyler heard his friend, but he was so tired that he mumbled and rolled over into his blanket. The use of his powers last night had left him significantly more depleted than his companions.

The soldiers allowed the party to rest for two hours, and then Walter traded watch with the soldiers so that they were able to recover.

Finally the group trudged on, soon entering a six-foot-tall field of grass. They moved through the stalks single file, one of the soldiers in the front scouting the way. To Kyler the monotony of the landscape was hypnotizing. Everywhere he looked he saw pale green grass struggling to reach the sky. When he looked upward, the cloudless blue sky ran on into eternity. He found himself staring at his mud-encrusted boots.

"Do you think the party of mages will find us?" asked Darcy.

"They might," said Kyler. "I just don't know if it will be in time."

"We could use their help," said Henry.

"They'd be here if they could," added Walter.

"Maybe there's a transportation spell?" wondered Henry.

Kyler laughed. "I've never heard of one, but wouldn't that be awesome?"

The lead soldier looked back toward them, "Would you lot be quiet. Our enemy might not be able to see us, but they can sure hear us."

Duly reprimanded, Kyler went back to studying his boots. He had no idea how the soldier was navigating their path, and truly hoped they weren't going in circles. Time passed, but the terrain remained the same and Kyler followed blindly. Then he bumped into Henry's back.

"What?" whispered Kyler.

Henry held up a finger to his mouth and pointed in front of them. The field of tall grass had ended, and a large expanse of tilled cropland reached outward. The lead soldier crouched down, making his way into the field for a better look. The rest of the group spread out, each watching the scout's progress. The soldier was cautious, but Kyler could see no place where he could cross undetected. The farmland ran on for acres, as far as his eyes could see. There would be no going around.

Their scout stopped and then straightened, trying to see ahead. He turned his head both directions, his hand over his eyes to block out the sunshine. It happened in a split second.

If Kyler had blinked, he would have missed it. Out of the mud rose small gnarled figures, their bodies camouflaged in ragged clothes. As one unit they placed blowguns to their lips, and Kyler watched as the soldier was turned into a porcupine.

At first the scout stood still, and then he reached down and pulled a small sliver of wood from his arm. He then began pulling them out like thorns.

"I know what these things are," whispered Walter. "Martha and I ran into the Imps on the first journey. They're not so bad. The projectiles should make him numb."

"Um," said Darcy, "I don't think so."

As the group watched, the captured soldier began to grasp at his throat, pulling at the skin. His face turned blue and then the sites where the slivers had hit began to swell to the size of chicken eggs. The man fell to his knees, his hand reaching out toward the Imps.

When his body began to thrash, Kyler turned away. Death was not a spectator sport.

"Holy moly," said Henry. "What happened?"

"They used poison," said Walter. "Nobody move a muscle. If you drop to the ground, they'll notice the movement."

The Imps walked to the body of the soldier and examined his crumpled form. Then one of them let out a whistle, and several more Imps unearthed themselves. These Imps took off in an arc, heading toward the tall grass, hunters looking for prey.

"Don't move," reminded Walter.

Kyler itched to drop down onto the ground and curl up out of sight. As the scouting Imps grew closer, beads of sweat broke out on his upper lip. He almost reached up to wipe the drops away, but caught himself at the last second. The

Imps stopped twenty feet out and were surveying the grass. They stood as still as statues, their every sense focused. Kyler closed his eyes and took deep breaths. The urge to scream was building up within him.

A whistle from the central Imps caused the hunters to return to their brethren. Once there they gathered up the body of the soldier, and then they made their way across the churned-up earth and off into the distance.

"Do you think they're gone?" asked Kyler.

"It's impossible to tell," whispered Walter. "We need to find out though."

"I can scout things out," said the remaining soldier.

"And what? End up dead just like him?" said Darcy. "By the way, what is your name? I can't just keep calling you 'soldier.'"

"It's Borris, Your Highness. Sergeant Borris."

Henry nodded. "We need a better plan."

"First, let's sit down and drink some water," said Kyler, "I don't know about you guys, but my legs are trembling from standing still."

"I'll keep an eye on the field," said Walter. "See if they come back or if there is any new movement."

"I don't think I'd mind staying here for a long time," said Kyler. "That poor guy."

"It was a bad way to go," said Darcy. "He was brave."

The remaining soldier nodded.

"How are we going to get across that field?" asked Henry. "It's wide-open for ambush."

"We could try a distraction," said Darcy. "See if we can draw them out."

Kyler leaned back and rested his head against his pack. "I don't think any of us should go out there. It's foolish."

"Do you have a better plan?" asked Darcy.

Kyler stayed quiet, thinking.

"I could play my flute, see if they react to the music," said Henry.

"That's not bad," said Darcy. "But if they are still there, they'd know exactly where we are hiding."

"We need to think of something," said Borris. "Sooner or later they will come back. This is obviously an ambush site."

Kyler raised his hand into the air, watching as the sunshine filtered onto his flesh. He closed one eye, moved his hand, and then opened his eye. "What about an illusion?"

"Can you do that?" asked Darcy.

"I don't know, but it's worth a try. If they're still out there, it should force them into view."

"Let's try it," said Henry.

Darcy reached over and grabbed Kyler's hand. "Are you sure you're up to it? That battle last night drained you."

Kyler felt the warmth of Darcy's hand wrapped around his own. A pleasant tingly feeling fluttered in his chest, and he knew he'd make this work, no matter the cost. "No problem, Darcy. I've got skills." *Was that lame? Ugh!* He risked a glance at Darcy's face, but she was looking at Walter.

Kyler stood and made his way to the edge of the grass. "Okay, everybody, keep your eyes open." He had never attempted anything of this magnitude before, and doubt began to creep into this thoughts. He looked at Darcy. Her face was full of confidence, confidence in him.

Focusing his thoughts, Kyler pictured an image of himself crawling out into the field. He spoke the words and the image appeared. It took every ounce of his willpower, and he realized that a stable illusion was massively easier to create than a moving one. His alter image crept over the tilled ground, and soon he reached and passed the spot where the soldier had been killed.

He held the illusion for another ten feet and then let it go. "I think we're safe, but we'd better hurry. No telling when they'll be back."

The group hurried over the acres of land, all hunched low. They made it across the clearing without an Imp popping up anywhere.

"Lets head opposite from the direction the Imps went," said Darcy.

"No kidding," said Kyler. The group dashed into welcome tree line coverage and kept going.

KYLER

They didn't dare stop for the next several hours, and by then it was nightfall. The group made camp in a cove of trees, but with the fear of Imps still with them, they didn't light a fire and slept in a huddled tangle.

The next day they arose early, stiff from the cold ground. Kyler heated up a pot of water with his magic to avoid a campfire and smoke. They ate oatmeal and dry bread for breakfast, but Kyler's stomach grumbled, wanting more. The size of their undertaking was beginning to weigh on his shoulders. They'd lost so many people already, and Kyler felt fear growing within his gut that he might lose another friend.

When they set out, Walter took the lead, scouting and talking to the animals to get a good sense of what waited ahead. They traveled in near silence, the sounds of snapping twigs the only sign of their passing. As the afternoon shifted to evening, Walter appeared and signaled a stop.

"There's a river up ahead, but strange creatures guard it. I don't think they're friendly."

"Well, we'd better check it out," said Kyler. "Lead the way."

The sound of rushing water grew stronger as the group followed Walter. He led them to the edge of the trees and then waited for them to take in the scene.

Kyler focused first on the creatures. They looked like alligators but walked upright with human arms and legs. He had no idea what they were and really didn't want to find out. A squadron of them guarded the only bridge across the raging river.

"What are they?" asked Darcy.

"I can't believe it," said Sergeant Borris. "We're taught about all the enemies of the kingdom when we train for the royal guard, but I never thought I'd actually see one of them."

"All sorts of funky creatures are popping up these days," said Henry. "So, what are they?"

"They're called Torics. They live down south, past the mountains and along the shore, at least a month-long journey. We've had a truce with their kingdom for over five hundred years. They aren't supposed to cross our borders."

"Looks as if things have changed," said Walter. "Any ideas?"

"What about another bridge?" asked Darcy.

"There are others, both north and south, but they're at least another day out of our way," said the soldier. "Plus, we don't know if there are more Torics at those passes."

"We can't afford that much of a delay," said Kyler. "The solstice is close."

"What if we went down a ways and swam across?" asked Henry.

Walter shook his snout. "I'm a good swimmer, but even I wouldn't stand a chance against those currents."

"What about you Kyler?" asked Darcy. "Any ideas?"

Kyler tapped his staff against the ground. "Against a group that large? I don't know. I could send some energy blasts their way, but I have no idea if it will have any affect against their reptile scales. Plus, then they'll attack."

"Could you use another decoy?" asked Darcy.

He shook his head. "That took a lot of effort, and even if I did, we'd only draw out a few Torics. I bet the rest would stay with the bridge."

"As I see it," said Walter. "The bridge is our only option."

Henry raised his arm into the air as if asking a question.

Darcy laughed. "Henry, we're not in school."

"I know. I just wasn't sure if I wanted to throw this out there."

"What were you thinking?" asked Kyler.

"Well, I haven't done a lot of experimenting with my flute. I mean a shield is real cool, but what if I could do something else?"

"Like what?" asked Darcy.

"It's a long shot." Henry looked down at his boots. "But what if I tried to put them all to sleep?"

"Do you think you could?" asked Kyler.

"Honestly? Don't know, but I'd like to give it a try."

"I don't see why he shouldn't," said Walter. "Sounds as if he might be on to something."

"The rest of you guys go hide in the trees. If there's trouble I don't want them to find all of us," said Henry.

Kyler patted Henry on the back, and then the group left him alone. From where Kyler hid, he had a good view of both the Torics and Henry. He watched as Henry pulled out the pan flute from inside his shirt and then closed his eyes. After several seconds, he opened his eyes, brought the pipes to his lips, and began to play.

At first the music was subtle, but as it built it grew stronger in both sound and resonance. Kyler looked toward the Torics.

Many of them had their heads cocked to the side. A small group of Torics huddled together, pointing into the woods in Henry's direction. They each grabbed a spear from a weapons pile and began to advance.

Henry's music grew more intense, and Kyler felt something in the air shift. One by one the Torics stopped in their tracks, cocked their heads, and listened. Soon all the Torics began swaying in place to the rhythm of the music. Then they sat down and fell asleep. It didn't matter where they were. They feel asleep in the spot they sat down.

As he continued to play, Henry began walking forward, toward the river. He stopped near the closest Toric and gave it a once-over, and then he turned back toward the trees and signaled with a nod of his head for the rest of the group to follow.

They skirted around the sleeping bodies and stepped over fallen spears. Walter was the first to cross the bridge, followed by Darcy and the soldier. As Kyler started across, he signaled at Henry to follow. His friend walked toward the bridge while his fingers flew over the pipes. Already across, Kyler turned to watch Henry's progress.

All was well until Henry tripped over a Toric's leg. He'd been looking across the bridge at the group and misstepped. He fell flat on his stomach, with his arms flung out to either side. His flute flew from his hands and bounced farther down the bridge.

Kyler froze. Henry struggled to sit up, but it was obvious that all the air had rushed from his lungs at impact. He looked around for his pipe and began crawling toward it. Behind him, the Torics began to stir.

"Henry! Go faster," said Kyler.

The Torics stood, looking around, baffled. When one spotted Henry on the bridge, it shouted out, trying to focus all the Torics on the infringement.

"Run!" shouted Kyler.

Henry scooped up his pipes and sprinted, but the Torics were quick to grab their spears and rush the bridge. Kyler had one thought. *Stop the Torics.* He leveled his staff at the mid-bridge and flung out a bolt of energy.

Henry crossed the last plank just as the bridge let out a large creak and split in two. The Torics on the bridge fell straight into the rapids and were carried away. The others stood on the embankment and howled. A first spear was thrown but landed in the water. Others followed suit, the Torics' anger spurring them on.

Henry's companions stood on the far shore, hugging him. "Great job!" said Darcy. "You did it!"

"Not so great," said Henry. "I let you guys down halfway across." He hung his head.

Kyler wouldn't let it pass. He bumped Henry in the shoulder. "Henry, we're all in this together. You got us across. I just blasted the bridge."

Henry looked up at Kyler with a smirk. "Yeah, that sleeping thing was very cool."

"Hey, guys," said Darcy. "We'd better keep moving."

"Yes," said Walter. "The Torics will have to travel a day up or down the river to alert any other groups. Let's not waste the advantage."

Kyler threw his arm around Henry's shoulders. "That was way cool."

DARCY

She knew they were getting closer to Mordrake's camp when the smell of hundreds of unwashed bodies filled the air for miles. It was also necessary to dodge the several Orc and Imp patrols that guarded the perimeter.

"We've made it. Now what?" asked Henry.

"We need to gather information," said Darcy. "Walter and I should scout ahead and get the lay of the camp."

Kyler turned her way, worry in his eyes. "Why you? Shouldn't Sergeant Borris be the one to scout?"

"I didn't come along to sit on the sidelines," said Darcy.

"Princess…" said Borris.

She pointed her sword at the soldier. "Don't you dare 'Princess' me. I'm small and I can fight. I can get to places you guys can't."

"You know, when she's made up her mind there's nothing to be done," said Walter.

"I don't like it," said Kyler.

"Deal with it," responded Darcy. She turned to Walter. "Let's get going. You head east, and I'll go west. The rest of you make camp and stay out of sight."

Henry saluted. "Yes, ma'am."

Darcy headed off, but not before she shot Henry a withering glance. She traveled low to the ground, conscious of enemy patrols. It looked as if the camp was a basic circle. It spanned a couple miles, but she felt confident she could skirt around the edges and take note of soldier numbers and positions.

The going was slow, but the information was worth the caution. Several tent cities dotted the camp. Darcy assumed from the layout that the Orcs, Imps, and Torics had shown up in random groups and staked out spots to sleep. Mordrake's army must have been growing for a couple of years. Just thinking about the sheer knowledge and preparation of the enemy left her stomach in knots.

She continued around the perimeter, stopping occasionally to take in conversations. The vast majority of the enemy army were Orcs, but from their talk it seemed that a lot of them didn't want to be there. She overheard one small group whose talk indicated they'd rather be back underground in the tunnels of the North.

Why were they here if they didn't want to be?

She kept the question in the back of her mind as she continued spying.

KYLER

The group found space to shelter in a gnarly patch of trees. Kyler and Henry reposed on the ground while Sergeant Borris stood watch, unwilling to rest so close to enemy territory. Kyler was wary, but he also knew that Walter and Darcy would be gone for a while, and now would be the best time to get some rest. From the look of Mordrake's forces, Kyler and his friends were in for a long haul.

As time passed, he grew more uneasy about Darcy being out there on her own. "Henry, do you think she'll be okay?"

"Well, she can kick my butt, so she's fully capable of taking care of herself."

"I know she's good, but Orcs? Man, they're huge."

"I'm sure she'll be careful. It's not like she's going to charge a whole squadron. She's probably scoping things out from a distance."

Kyler fell silent, but his worry grew. He knew that Darcy would be mad if she knew what he was thinking, but the thoughts kept coming anyway. Soon it was all he could think about, and he couldn't sit still any longer. He surged to his feet and began walking in circles.

"Dude, the way you're crunching on twigs is gonna bring the whole army our way," said Henry.

"I'm going after her."

"What? That is so not a good idea," said Henry.

"Probably not, but sitting here feeling like I'm going to pull my hair out isn't getting me anywhere."

"You'd better come up with a good reason. If you tell her you were worried about her, she'll knock your head off."

"I'll think about it as I go. You hang out here and wait for Walter."

"Not a problem. I'm happy to stay in one place for a while."

Kyler headed out in the same direction Darcy had taken. She'd had several hours' head start, but if she were scouting, her progress would be slow. He stayed in the tree line, far from the camp, but close enough to feel the hum of activity. As the sun dropped lower in the sky, he began to wonder if he'd passed her in hiding.

He decided to turn back and search deeper into the tree line. At first there was nothing, but then a sound caught his attention. The faraway ding of metal on metal rang out from deeper in the woods. Kyler advanced, wary of what awaited him. He didn't want to run into a squad of Orcs at sword practice.

What he found when he passed into a clearing made his jaw drop: Darcy fighting a young Orc. From the sweat dripping from her face, the fight had been going on for some time. He felt the need to level his staff and blow the Orc to bits, but restrained the urge, allowing Darcy her time. He would be there if she needed him.

The two opponents circled each other, weapons hanging low in their grasps. Kyler could hear the rasps of deep breathing and knew the fight was close to finishing. Neither fighter had the strength to continue longer. He watched Darcy's face and realized she'd also taken in the situation. She drew in a long, steadying breath and narrowed her eyes. On the next pass, she brought her sword in low. Instead of a killing swipe, she'd opted for a debilitating blow, twisting her body around and bringing the edge of her sword behind the Orc and slicing into the back of its knee.

One moment the Orc was standing, the next it was on the ground, its hands wrapped around its leg, trying to stop the bleeding. The creature's deep moans filled the clearing. Darcy walked over to the enemy and leveled her sword at its neck. Battle rage filled her eyes, and the Orc knew her adrenaline was pumping. Kyler wondered if she'd deliver the killing blow.

Instead, he watched as Darcy pricked the Orc's neck and a thin line of blood dribbled down its chest. Then she stepped backward. Her sword still ready, but her fury dispelled. "Do you yield?"

The Orc snarled. Frustration leaked out as it ground its teeth.

Darcy dug the tip of her blade farther into the enemy's neck, toward the jugular. The Orc howled and then cursed.

"I yield."

"Good," said Darcy. She pulled a cloth from her pocket and tossed it at her captive. "Bind your wound."

Kyler advanced toward the scene, careful to make noise so as not to startle Darcy. She looked at him and nodded, completely at ease with his presence.

"Good timing," she said. "Grab some rope and tie it up."

When Kyler was finished, he turned to Darcy. "What happened?"

"What makes you think something happened?" Darcy was wiping down her sword, paying close attention to the streaks of blood.

"I assumed you got caught by a patrol."

Darcy laughed and then shook her head. "Jeez. You didn't think that perhaps I led it into a trap?"

"Uh…"

"Didn't think so." She gave Kyler a quizzical look. "What brings you out here? You're supposed to be with Henry."

He'd been thinking of something smart to tell her the entire time he'd searched for her, but now he stumbled. "Just wanted to see that things were okay." As soon as the words left his mouth, he knew it was exactly the wrong thing to say.

"Okay?" Darcy advanced on him. "Did Henry go check on Walter? You know, just to make sure he was okay, too?"

"Um, no."

Darcy stopped in front of his face. "I am perfectly capable of looking after myself, you big dolt. I can't believe you didn't trust me."

"It wasn't that. It's just that—"

"Shut up, Kyler!" Darcy sheathed her sword and then crossed her arms over her chest. Then, with a very unladylike sound, she spit at his feet, before turning her back and stomping over to her prisoner.

Kyler decided to stay put. Anger showed in every muscle of Darcy's body, and when she reached the Orc, she kicked it in the bad leg.

"I have some questions, and you're going to answer them," she growled.

In response, the Orc stretched out its lips and showed its pointy teeth. Its nose puckered up like a pig's snout.

Darcy paid it no heed. "Why are the Orcs here? Why are you fighting for Mordrake?"

Kyler wondered at her question. He assumed that the Orcs were evil, and fighting was what they liked to do.

The Orc stared at Darcy, but stayed silent.

"Let's try this one," said Darcy. "What do you know about Mordrake's plan for the solstice?"

With a swirl of phlegm deep in its throat, the Orc spit a wad of goo at the ground.

Darcy stepped closer, her hand resting on the hilt of her sword. "Why are you collecting mages?"

The Orc hissed, and Darcy backhanded it across its face. "You will tell me what you know," she yelled.

As her questioning continued, Kyler advanced on the pair, eager to get some answers himself. He stopped before the Orc and kneeled down so that they were eye-to-eye. He pulled a dagger from his boot and leveled it at the creature. "The lady asked you a question. I think you'd best be answering."

Silence was the monster's response.

Kyler moved, switching his stance for better balance. He unslung his bag and let it slide to the ground with a thump. In front of him, the Orc's eyes went wide, and his whole visage changed from defiance to awe.

"Kyler," said Darcy. "Your bag."

He looked down at his side and saw that his satchel had opened, and the Orc artifact had rolled halfway out onto the ground. The Orc watched it, mesmerized. Kyler picked it up in his hands, turning it around. "You like this?"

"Where? How?" the Orc asked.

Kyler looked up at Darcy. "Now we're getting somewhere."

"Ask him about your aunt," she asked.

He held the orb out so the Orc could see it clearly. "Do you know where my aunt Martha is?"

"I don't know any Aunt Martha," said the Orc.

A sigh left Kyler's lips. "The mages," he said. "What do you know about the mages?"

This time the Orc nodded. "Them fools kept in the tent?" it asked. "They're to be killed by Mordrake at the solstice."

"Why?" asked Kyler.

"Don't know. Not my business."

Kyler felt like bashing their captive over the head with the relic, but Darcy stepped in to take up the challenge.

"I heard different Orcs in different camps say they want to go back home, back up north. What's stopping them?"

"Mordrake," said the Orc. "He holds some power over us. He calls to our blood and brings us south, and then we can't leave. He commands us."

"And you let him?"

"Yes. Most of the tribes think he is their salvation, the way back into the world. Some of the ancients disagree. They want to go."

"What do you want?" asked Kyler.

"I want glory and honor."

"You call this honor? You're killing innocent people," said Darcy.

"I am proving myself a warrior."

"That's disgusting," said Darcy. She leaned back. "Wait a second. Why are you suddenly answering all my questions?"

The Orc pointed at Kyler and the relic. "He holds the heart of the kings."

"What?" asked Kyler.

"Back in the time before—the time before we lived underground—Orcs ruled the land and our kings led us in victory."

Darcy snorted. "Well, that's debatable."

The Orc snarled, but continued. "The heart of the kings was passed down from king to king, a symbol of power, of obedience. He who holds it must be obeyed."

"Even now?" asked Kyler.

"Always."

Kyler turned to Darcy. "That must be the magic I feel swirling around inside it." He eyed the prisoner. "What happened to it?"

"It was lost during the Great War. Some believe a human slew the mighty Orc king and then took it as a plunder of war. I think a cowardly human stole it."

"So, whatever I tell you, you'll do it?"

"No!" said the Orc. "The heart represents the will of the people. It cannot be used to harm us or make us harm one another."

"Then what good is it?" wondered Darcy.

"Don't you see," said Kyler. "This isn't meant to be a weapon. It's meant to be a tool of leadership. It commands the Orcs, but doesn't endanger them. That's why during the fight they listened when I told them to leave. It wasn't an order that would harm them or go against their well-being."

"So we can use it to get them to do things, not to fight them."

"Exactly." He turned to the Orc. "Is the power of the heart greater than that of Mordrake?"

The Orc struggled against its bonds, but the words were forced through its lips, "Yes."

Kyler nodded, his thoughts churning.

"Is there any more about Mordrake's plan that you can tell us?"

The Orc shook its head.

"In that case, I want you to head north, back to your home. Do not tell a soul that you have seen us or that we have the heart of the kings." Kyler sliced the prisoner's bonds with his dagger and then stepped away.

The Orc rose to its feet and stumbled sideways. It traveled slowly, favoring its one good knee.

"I think we just caught a break," said Kyler.

"Let's head back to the others. I want to know what Walter discovered," said Darcy.

WALTER

When Walter left his friends, he had headed quickly to the rim of the encampment, eager to look for Martha. At first he kept to the tree line, but soon he realized that the camp's inhabitants paid a lone wolf no attention. He began to wander among the tents, listening to snippets of conversation.

The camp itself was huge, and most of the conversations he caught involved regular army affairs such as cooking, laundry and patrol schedules. If he heard a juicy bit of information, he would lie down by the fire pit and pretend to doze. As he spied, Orcs would pet his hide and throw him scraps from their plates.

He learned that the last few raids the Orcs had conducted were for capturing mages in far-off towns and hamlets. The Orcs had been thorough and rooted out every human within leagues. At the fire, they complained about the long travels just to bag a skinny old human who lay drugged for weeks, even months. Walter's ears perked up at the mention of drugs, and he realized that wherever Martha was, she would be incapable of helping herself.

After a time, Walter got up and shook his fur. He continued deeper into the camp. He learned to avoid the Imps, for they thought him a fun animal to ride upon, and after his first horsey ride he was not in a good mood.

Luck was with him when he found one of the supply tents. From within he heard the telltale sign of pesky invaders. Wherever there was food, there would always be mice.

"Psst," he whispered. The mice ignored him, and Walter realized he'd have to take a more direct approach.

"Hey, mice! Over here."

A pink twitching nose poked out from under the canvas tent flap. A small head followed the nose and then the rest of a small body. "Who is it? Who's there?"

Walter leveled himself flat onto the ground. "It's me, a friend."

The mouse eyed him warily. "A wolf? I'm no fool, and you are no friend." The creature began scooting backward.

"Wait!" called Walter. "I am Walter of the woods. Surely you've heard of me? The mage that protects all animals."

The mouse stopped his retreat but didn't move forward. "How do I know it's really you?"

"Do you know any other wolves that can talk to mice?"

"You make a valid point. What do you want?"

"I have some questions, and I know that a smart mouse like you will know the answers."

The mouse sat on his haunches and swiped at his whiskers. "That's right. I know everything."

"Good. You see, I am looking for a group of mages. It may be that they are drugged or unconscious."

The mouse bobbed its head. "Well, I don't know if they're mages, but there is a tent full of sleeping people. It's a good place to sneak inside. They leave crumbs everywhere."

"Where is this tent located?"

"I wouldn't know how to tell you, but I can show you."

Walter sat up eagerly. "Wonderful. I'll follow."

The mouse dashed off, leaving Walter to sprint behind. They scurried past several campsites and went deeper toward the middle of the army. Finally, the mouse stopped outside a large pavilion tent surrounded by guards. It squeaked and nodded at the tent.

Walter shook his muzzle in thanks and then began to scout the area. He had waited some time before someone emerged from within the tent. A guard immediately escorted a person to what Walter judged to be a latrine pit. When the prisoner came back, the guard lifted the flap, and Walter was able to see inside.

On the floor rested a group of people on mats, all stretched out on their backs. Walter sniffed the air, and though one single scent was hard to make out among a score of unwashed bodies, he picked up the familiar odor of Martha. His joy almost made him howl into the air, but he caught himself and snapped his jaws shut. He lingered by the tent, waiting to sneak inside, but the guards did their duties well, and the chance never arose. However, he was able to listen as the Orcs spoke to one another with no hesitations or worries. He focused in on two Orcs, one with a spear and the other with a cudgel.

"This is the last night of this mess," said the Orc with the spear.

"It will be good to join our brothers at the fire tomorrow."

"It will be good to drink!"

"Ha!" laughed the Orc with the cudgel. "Is guard duty hampering your appetites?"

"Mordrake would kill us if we drink on duty."

"He'd do more than just kill us." The Orc's weapon shook in its hands. "I do not think about such things."

"What about tomorrow? Do you think we will get to watch?"

The other Orc swung its cudgel in a circle. "What a treat that would be!"

"Rumor says he will kill them all. Suck their powers out one by one and break the stones."

Walter crept closer, eager to hear of Mordrake's designs.

"At last he will be able to walk among us."

"Quiet!" yelled another Orc. "You're on guard duty. This is not a party."

They hushed. Their words ran through Walter's mind. *The stones must be the watchers, the mages turned to stone.* He needed to check them out. He made his way back into the busy camp and skulked along, head hung low. He had wandered for a while before he heard screaming. Following the sounds, he found what he knew to be the standing stone circle. Inside the circle rested a large pavilion, and the screaming came from inside it. Walter heard loud laughter. A figure burst from inside the tent, a young human girl running for her life. She hadn't gotten more than two feet when an arm reached out and grabbed her tunic, yanking her back inside.

A growl rose from deep within Walter's belly. His muscles quivered as he fought the urge to dash inside the tent and rip everyone to shreds. He had to force himself to step away, one paw at a time. He allowed his thoughts to focus on each step and nothing else until he was out of range.

The sky was inky black now, and Walter decided to make his way back to the tree line. He needed to share his bleak thoughts with the others.

KYLER

The group gathered within the ring of shrubbery where Henry now stood guard. Kyler and Darcy sat upon a pile of leaves, waiting for Walter's return.

"Do you think the relic will help in the battle?" asked the soldier.

"We can't use it against them, but if we get creative I bet we can cause a lot of havoc."

"At least we have an edge now," said Darcy. "We might be able to use it to sneak past the tents."

"It only works on Orcs," said Kyler. "We'd be in big trouble if we ran into Torics or those nasty Imps, and they're everywhere."

Kyler leaned back against a tree while Darcy continued to spout ideas. As the sky grew darker, a rustling in the bushes alerted the group to someone or something approaching.

Henry took up a place outside their perimeter, waiting for the unknown intruder. He didn't have long to wait before Walter breezed into the circle, his ears perked and alert.

"Welcome back, Walter," said Henry while lowering his sword.

"Yeah, we were getting worried," said Kyler.

"I wasn't," said Darcy. "Walter can take care of himself." She shot Kyler a nasty look from the corner of her eyes.

Walter sat in the middle of the group and looked each member in the eye before beginning. "I found her."

"What! Where? Is she okay?" yelled Kyler.

"She's among a group of other mages. They're drugged, but they're alive."

"How well are they guarded?" asked Darcy.

"The whole tent is surrounded by Orcs. They never leave their posts."

"Dang it! Why can't it be easy for once?" said Kyler.

"There's more," continued Walter. "From what I over-heard, Mordrake is planning to kill them on the solstice and use their powers to free himself from the stone circle."

Kyler hung his head on his chest and sighed. "We're out of time. We need to get in there tomorrow."

"We need a plan," said Henry.

Walter looked over toward Darcy. "Did you find anything on your side?"

With a nod, Darcy explained about the Orc and the relic.

"There's a way we can use it to our advantage," said Walter. "I just need time to think."

Everyone began tossing out ideas, but the soldier and Walter shot most of them down. "Look," said Walter, "I know you kids are eager to rush in and save Martha, but we need to be careful. I want us to come out alive."

As Walter spoke the sound of a bird cawed from above. They looked up into the dark sky, trying to spot the creature.

They didn't have to search long. A raven flew into their midst and landed on Kyler's shoulder.

"Well, that's new," said Kyler. The bird cawed and then pecked Kyler's ear. "Hey!"

The bird paid no attention and hopped onto the ground. It waddled around, looking for an empty spot, and then stood still. Kyler felt a tingling in the air and reached for his staff, but before he could grab it, the raven transformed into a black-cloaked man.

"Howard!" clapped Walter. "Well met!"

"You also," said the man. Then he turned to Kyler and held out his hand. "I am Master Howard. We haven't met yet."

Kyler reached out and shook the mage's hand. "How did you find us?"

The mage laughed. "I just aimed for the big horde of enemies with a billion glowing campfires. I spotted Walter a while back and followed him to your camp."

"That's great," said Kyler. "Another mage will help."

"Well, on that aspect I'm just like Walter—a shape-shifter. I was sent ahead to find you by Master Avery. He and my fellow mages are two days behind. The king's army travels with them."

Kyler closed his eyes and slumped. "Two days? They might as well be two months."

Master Howard shook out his robes and reached within a deep pocket. He pulled out a gold chain with a large blue gemstone. "We know. That's why I brought you this." He held the pendant out to Kyler.

"What is it?" asked Kyler. He took hold of the pendant and studied the deep blue gem.

"It's a conductor," said Master Howard.

"A what?" asked Darcy.

"Those are very rare," added Walter.

"Indeed," said Howard. "We brought it with us from the school archives in case there were a need, and there is."

"I still don't get it," said Darcy.

"A conductor is a source for power," explained Walter.

Master Howard gently took the pendant from Kyler's hands and slipped it around the youth's neck. "Master Avery knew we would not make it in time, so he sent me ahead. Tomorrow night, the night of the solstice, all the mages with him will form a circle and focus their powers. They'll focus on that gemstone." He pointed to Kyler's neck.

"Wow," said Henry.

"They will not be here physically, but you will be able to use their powers to fight Mordrake."

The weight of the pendant was heavy on Kyler's chest. "Holy moly," he whispered.

Darcy reached out and grabbed Kyler's hand. "Will it be enough?"

"It has to be." Kyler looked at his group of trusted companions. "Now we really need a plan."

"I think I have one," said Walter. "At least how to get us to Martha. After that, it's up to you, Kyler."

KYLER

The evening of the solstice approached slowly. As dusk neared, Kyler urged his group forward, straight into the devil's camp. They'd entered near an encampment of Orcs, and Kyler walked with the Orc relic in front of his chest, in full view. Master Howard flew overhead, scouting a path around any Imps or reptilians. Walter's job was to keep an eye on the bird and lead Kyler in the correct direction.

As Kyler walked he spoke softly, a hum above the normal camp din. "You will let us pass and raise no alarm. Just keep doing what you are doing."

They wound their way deeper into the camp until the bird flew down and perched on top of the tent that Walter had specified. Sergeant Borris took the lead, approaching the unguarded tent.

"Where are the guards?" whispered Darcy.

The soldier lifted the tent flap and went inside but returned moments later. "They're gone."

Just then a roll of thunder trembled through the sky, causing all to look upward. When the rumble did not end,

Kyler realized it was actually the sound of hundreds of drums banging in unison. The small group headed toward the noise.

They hid behind a wooden wagon, looking toward the ring of stones. Row upon row of the enemy soldiers lined up before Mordrake's tent as if preparing for battle, but it was not a battle they witnessed. It was a slaughter.

Before his pavilion, Mordrake stood facing ten slumped figures propped up by pillows. They kneeled in a line with an Orc guard standing on each end. The eleventh figure lay splayed out on his rug. His eyes looked burned out, only black sockets remaining. Kyler knew he was dead.

Within the stone perimeter, Mordrake paced the ground. His dressy silk robes swishing as he walked. Four Orcs stood off to the side, each in full military adornment. Outside the circle, the ranks of soldiers watched as Mordrake continued his ceremony.

He walked over to the second person in the row, grabbed his face, and looked into the man's eyes. The mage tried to struggle, but his drug-induced stasis was strong and he could barely wiggle. The drumbeats in the background sounded like a giant's heartbeat. Darcy reached out and grabbed Kyler's hand.

"What's he doing?" she asked.

"I don't think we want to know," Kyler said.

Kyler glanced down the line of prisoners, his eyes searching for Aunt Martha. There she was! Last in line, her body slumped over as all the rest, but he knew it was her from her dirty patchwork dress.

Mordrake stood up and walked behind his target, then with a roar of primal lust, he placed his hands on the man's head and spoke. Kyler was too far away to hear anything, but it was obvious what was happening. The man screamed like an animal while his body arched into a bent pretzel. A golden light streamed from the top of his head and into Mordrake's hands. The man struggled, fighting for his life, but Mordrake continued to suck out his life force and absorb his powers. Two twin flashes of light exploded from the mage's eyeballs, and then his body fell over, depleted. The corpse lay on its side, its blackened eye sockets facing Kyler.

"Holy crap," whispered Henry.

"We have to stop him," said Darcy.

"Yeah, but how?" asked Kyler.

"Hush," said Walter. "This man's death will not be in vain if we can figure out a way to attack."

"I need to head back and tell Master Avery what is happening," said Master Howard. He changed shape and flew off silently into the night.

Mordrake turned toward a stone guardian, by its side two other pillars lay cracked and broken. He raised his arms into the air and then shouted. Golden light flew from his fingertips and burrowed into the upright stone monolith. Minutes passed. The light continued to surge into the stone while Mordrake stood in a trance.

"He's going to kill each of the mages to break the stone guardians," said Darcy.

"But look," said Walter. "Mordrake is oblivious to events around him. He is consumed by the effort of breaking the stone and controlling the powers flowing from within himself."

"Do you think it is enough of a weakness?" asked Kyler.

"It might be the best we have," said Walter.

The golden rays of light from Mordrake's fingers began to thin, and after a minute they extinguished completely. A loud crack split the air, and the stone pillar cracked in half. One side tumbled to the ground with a thunk and lifted a cloud of dirt. The enemy soldiers cheered. Mordrake dropped to his knees, shaking and exhausted. An Orc rushed over to his side, offering a goblet of wine, which Mordrake downed greedily. He remained in that position as more food and wine arrived. Minutes passed as the monster king recovered.

The line of mages slowly began to stir as awareness returned to their minds. Several lifted their heads and looked around but were unable to move. Their eyes grew wide in fear as they watched Mordrake and saw their fallen companions. Kyler focused on his aunt. She alone was not looking at Mordrake but was looking around for a weakness. Walter stepped out from behind the wagon and sat on his haunches. As Martha swiveled her gaze, she found Walter's profile. For a few brief seconds, she gazed their way, but then turned toward Mordrake as if nothing had happened.

Walter slunk back to the group. "She saw me."

"How can you tell?" asked Henry.

"I just know," said Walter.

Kyler turned back to his aunt and then looked down the row of mages, searching for other familiar faces, wondering if any of his teachers were in the mix. Halfway through the line, a bowed head with long blond hair caught his attention. Something about the man seemed familiar. When the man looked up at Mordrake, Kyler got a good look at the mage's face. With a cry, Kyler began to scuttle out from under the wagon. Darcy grabbed his ankle, pulling him back. Soon Henry joined the effort, and Kyler slid back.

"Let me go," Kyler pleaded.

"What's wrong with you, kid?" asked Sergeant Borris. "You want to get us all caught?"

"Don't you see him?" said Kyler. His body trembled in shock. "Don't you know who that is?"

"Kyler, take a deep breath and tell us what's happening," said Darcy.

Walter walked over and gave Kyler one big, slimy lick. Kyler settled down and wiped the slobber off his face.

"The man in the middle. It's my dad!" said Kyler.

"What?" said Walter. The wolf peeked around the wagon and then returned to the little group.

"He's right. I'd know George anywhere," said Walter.

"Kyler, calm down," said Darcy. "We'll think of something."

"Yeah," added Henry. "We're here to save them, remember."

"We need to think of something fast," said Kyler. "When Mordrake recovers he'll start on the third mage."

KYLER

"Well, what do we know?" asked Walter.

"We know that only a handful of Orcs are inside the circle with him," said Henry.

"Great. What else?" asked the wolf.

"When he releases all that power, he goes into some sort of trance," added Darcy.

Kyler nodded. "And when he's done, he's left totally drained. It's been...what? Twenty minutes."

"So we need to get to him when he's sending power at the stones," said Walter.

"But that means we have to let another mage die. I'm not good with that," said Kyler.

Darcy reached over and wrapped an arm around Kyler's shoulders. "Ky, I don't think we have a choice. Mordrake is more powerful than any number of us combined. We need to attack him when he's at his weakest."

Kyler sighed, hanging his head in defeat. "I know, but it just doesn't feel right."

Darcy hugged him tightly.

"How are we going to rush Mordrake with a whole army protecting him?" asked Sergeant Borris.

"There are only six Orcs within the ring," said Henry.

"Yeah, but what's to stop the rest of them from running in?" asked the soldier.

"Henry will," said Kyler.

"What?" said Henry.

Kyler looked up at his best friend. "We need a shield, buddy, and it's got to be the biggest dome you've ever made, big enough to encircle a fifty-yard circumference of standing stones with us inside."

"But...but," Henry stammered. "I've never done one that big."

"Henry, what we're about to attempt will take everything each of us has," said Darcy. "I know you can do this. It's why the flute chose you. You're special."

"Crap," said Henry. He pulled out the flute and held it cupped within his palms.

"Henry, you'll need to put the shield up after we've all gotten inside," said Walter. "Kyler and I will take out Mordrake." The wolf looked at Kyler. "You've got the sleeping potion ready?"

Kyler patted his side pouch. He pulled out the stoppered bottle and used his knife to loosen the wax seal. "Ready."

Walter turned toward Darcy and Sergeant Borris. "You two will focus on the Orcs."

"Then what?" asked Kyler. "Where do we go from there? The four of us can't drag eight drugged mages out through a camp of Orcs and things."

"We'll figure it out if we succeed," said Walter. "Chances are we won't even make it that far."

The group of five held hands and paws, drawing strength from one another. The drums began to grow louder again, their beat shaking the ground.

"I think Mordrake's recovered," said Henry, as they eased their way around the wagon.

Mordrake stood on his feet, a smile on his face. He approached the next mage eagerly.

"Be ready," said Walter.

It was hard for Kyler to watch the mage being drained of life. He focused instead on his dad, taking in the welcome sight of him after all these years.

"Go," shouted Walter.

Kyler sprang to his feet, already running. The entire army was focused on Mordrake as he turned to the next pillar and shot a beam of intense power at it. The group made it within the ring of stones without being noticed.

Henry began playing his pipes with a vengeance. It was hard to hear over the beat of the drums, but he didn't need people to hear his music for it to work. In fact, it was probably best if no one noticed him at all.

A shimmer appeared in the air and then dropped to the ground, sealing off the circle of guardian stones. Within his trance, Mordrake noticed nothing, but the six remaining Orcs turned, looking at the approaching five. The Orcs bellowed in rage and attacked.

Henry stopped and took cover behind a pole while Darcy and the soldier took the lead. They engaged the Orcs, the clangs of steel echoing in the air. The drums had stopped beating, and a host of enemy soldiers pounded against Henry's barrier. Kyler watched as Henry closed his eyes, his focus on his music. As Walter and Kyler rushed by the bard's side, they dodged the Orcs attacking Darcy and the soldier and narrowed in on Mordrake. Kyler blasted an Orc out of their way, not even pausing a step.

Walter cruised ahead of Kyler, his paws flying over the ground. The wolf leapt into the air with his claws extended and landed on Mordrake's back. The stream of power shut off, and Mordrake locked his eyes on Walter. Kyler saw him struggle to push Walter off of him, but he was weak, just as they'd hoped.

In seconds, Kyler reached the scene. He flipped Mordrake over while Walter held the monster king down. Kyler's hands easily found the bottle of potion, and he popped the top with his thumb. He straddled Mordrake's head, forcing the man's mouth open with one hand. Mordrake bucked and rolled, but Walter's weight held him in place. The thick, dark liquid oozed from the bottle and fell into Mordrake's mouth. He closed his lips, but not before the draught flowed into his throat. Kyler placed his hands over Mordrake's mouth, forcing him to swallow.

Mordrake's thrashing grew less fierce, and soon his body went limp. Kyler rolled off of his supine figure and watched as Mordrake's eyes closed. Walter stayed on his chest until deep breathing issued forth from the villain's chest.

"Get some rope and tie him up," said Walter.

Kyler didn't need to be told twice. He untied the ropes from around one of the mages and used it to hog-tie Mordrake. They left him there and ran to join the fight against the Orcs. Darcy and the soldier had made a good accounting, but there were still three Orcs left. Walter sprang into action, flying through the air and taking one down. Kyler leveled a lightning bolt at the one attacking Darcy and blew a hole through its chest. Together, Darcy and the soldier turned on the last Orc, their blades slashing it to pieces.

Standing by the pole, Henry played on, oblivious. Kyler walked to his side and then whispered in his ear, "Don't stop. But we did it. We got them."

Henry opened his eyes, taking in the victorious scene. His fingers never paused, but his music slowed into a more comfortable rhythm.

"Let's get the mages free!" said Kyler.

They rushed over to the remaining eight mages, who were now fighting their bonds. Kyler didn't know whom to run to first, but when he looked at Aunt Martha she was nodding in the direction of his father.

Kyler untied his father's bonds and then held his body as it slumped.

KYLER

When all of the mages were untied, Darcy ran back into Mordrake's tent for food and wine. The mages were starving, and they devoured the refreshment. Kyler could not stop staring at his dad. He was older looking, and streaks of gray worked their way through his blond hair. Kyler helped his father eat and drink.

Martha, with the help of Darcy, made her way over to Kyler. She seemed more aware than the rest of the group.

"I couldn't believe it when I saw him either," said Martha.

Kyler looked up, tears in his eyes. "Aunt Martha, I'm so glad you're safe."

His aunt leaned over and hugged both Kyler and his dad.

"How come you're talking, and these guys are so out of it?" asked Kyler.

"I was a recent capture. Some of these people have been drugged for over a year. I can't imagine what that did to them."

"Martha," a thin voice croaked out of Kyler's father's lips.

"Dad!" said Kyler.

"Son, how...what?" he mumbled.

"Rest for a second," said Martha. "We all need to gather our strength."

Donald was the next to fully recover. He gave Martha a welcome hug and then made his way to Kyler's side to introduce himself. "I can take over for the young boy playing the flute."

"You can?"

"Yes, it's a different type of magic, but the dome is already there. I'll just reinforce it. The poor kid looks as if he needs a break."

"Are you sure you can handle it?"

"It won't take too much. He's already done all the work."

They walked over to Henry. His face was flushed, and he leaned heavily against the pole. Donald sat on the ground, and a look of concentration broke out over his face. When Kyler was sure that Donald had everything in hand, he tapped Henry on the shoulder.

Henry blinked back into reality with a start.

"Henry, you did a great job!" said Kyler. "You can stop playing now. Donald's giving you a rest."

Henry pulled the flute from his lips and sighed. "Thank goodness. That was the hardest thing I've ever had to do."

"And you did it great," said Kyler. "Come on. Let me introduce you to my father."

The weary group of victors and survivors sat around in a circle with pillows and blankets spread out between them. Outside the dome, the enemy frantically beat their weapons trying to break inside.

"Kyler," said his father. "Your mom..." He shook his head.

Tears flowed from Kyler's eyes, and he knew that his mother was dead.

"What happened?" asked Martha.

"We were studying the Torics down south. We'd been with them for a year, and she was getting itchy to go get Kyler. We were already late collecting him, and she was ready to leave."

His father looked him in the eyes, "We were going to get you and bring you with us. Then the strangeness began. Whole villages of Torics disappeared. Nobody knew why, and the other Torics began to panic. Their chief asked us to investigate, and even though we wanted to come get you, Kyler, we knew we had to help."

Kyler nodded his head. He understood their problem.

"It continued happening off and on for months," continued his dad. "Your mom and I searched every village and questioned all the neighbors. We learned nothing. Then one night it happened to the village where we lived. We noticed a commotion outside, and got up to investigate. All of the Torics, from the chief to the children, were walking out of the village and heading north. We tried to stop them, ask them what was happening, but they shook us off, mumbling that they had to move north."

"I think I know what was happening," said Walter. "We ran into some Imps with the same problem."

"Well, we didn't," said Kyler's dad. "We were clueless, but we packed our bags and followed. They walked for a solid day without stopping, and then all at once they lay down and went to sleep. It was the creepiest thing we'd ever seen."

"Did you figure it out?" asked Kyler.

"Not at first. But when the Torics awoke, they were fully conscious and able to speak. We found the chief and questioned him. Turns out they were being led north by an unknown force. They had all their wits about them, but were unable to break the force controlling them to move. We continued with them for two months. It was then that the Orcs appeared. At first the Torics wished to fight, but something stopped them in their tracks, and they couldn't lift a weapon.

"Your mother and I did our best, but between the two of us it wasn't even a fight. When the Orcs found out I was a mage, they tied me up and put me in a supply wagon. I could see your mother struggling to reach me." Kyler's dad cried in loud sobs, his memories overwhelming him.

"I watched them behead her."

Kyler felt as if the ground would open up and swallow him whole. "No!"

His dad couldn't continue, and his cries filled the night. Kyler and Martha joined him, sobbing.

Nobody spoke. Darcy made her way over to Kyler and wrapped him in her arms. He ducked his chin inside her neck and let the tears continue to flow. She rocked him back and forth, stroking his hair.

Time passed, and their sobs grew silent. Darcy continued to hold on to Kyler, and he held her back tightly. Henry broke the silence.

"What's burning?" he asked.

An evil laugh flooded the night, sending chills down everyone's spine.

KYLER

"That would be me!" a dark voice shouted.

Everyone looked up, startled. Mordrake was no longer asleep and bound. He was now standing with his arms spread out and his ropes burned apart.

"Did you think it would be so easy? Did you think I'd let the same thing happen to me again?" he roared.

Kyler, Darcy, Henry, and Walter sprang into defensive positions before the group of recovering mages. The sergeant began herding them away, toward Donald and the tent.

"What now?" whispered Henry.

Mordrake laughed, enjoying the terror he'd produced. He pointed an arm at the group.

"Move it," yelled Kyler. A bolt of lightning landed where they'd been standing. The group had scattered, but with nowhere to go they were sitting targets.

Kyler knew he was the group's only real defense, so after the others cleared the area he turned and planted himself in Mordrake's path. The monster king roared a challenge and sent a bolt of pure fire at Kyler. There was no time to think, only to react. Kyler pointed his staff and screamed out, causing the air before him to form a barrier. The fire hit the solid mass of air and then dispersed. Wasting no time, Kyler shot an energy bolt, aiming for Mordrake's heart. The bolt hit Mordrake, and he flew backward. Surprised, Kyler failed to follow up with another attack, but just stood there with his mouth hanging open.

Mordrake regained his footing and roared. Kyler braced himself for another attack, but Mordrake lowered his arms and shouted, "Finally, a worthy opponent! I challenge you to a mages duel following all the rules and accords of the mages council."

"Huh?" said Kyler. He turned to look at his friends now grouped around the pole with Donald. Darcy shrugged her shoulders, but Martha stepped forward, followed closely by Walter.

"Kyler, a word," Martha called.

Wary about turning his back on Mordrake, Kyler walked backward, using small steps so as not to bump into anything. The entire time he kept his eyes trained on the enemy. Finally, he felt Martha's hand on his shoulder, halting his path. He turned slightly so he could keep both of them in his sight.

"Is he kidding?" asked Kyler.

"Its old history," said Walter. "There hasn't been a mage duel in centuries."

"Yes, but back in his day and age they were common," said Martha.

"I know. But what exactly does it involve?" asked Kyler.

"It is a competition between two mages to prove who is the most powerful. The fight doesn't end until one of them is dead," said Martha.

"Not cool!" said Kyler.

"There are rules," said Walter. "You each take turns on the offensive. So, you both can't fire at the same time. The turns go back and forth until victory is declared."

"You mean until I'm dead!"

Martha turned to Walter. "I'm not liking this. Does Kyler even know how to use magic? I never taught him?"

"Yeah, about that," said Kyler. "A big thanks for dropping me off at a school of magic without telling me a thing about it! I felt like an idiot."

"That wasn't my intention. I was teaching you so that you'd be ready for your father to train you. I never expected him not to show up, or for the Griffin to emerge."

Darcy came up behind Martha. "Now is not the time to argue. We've got more important things to deal with."

"There is no way that I am fighting to the death against Mordrake! Even the mages a thousand years ago couldn't defeat him," said Kyler.

"But he's weak," said Darcy. "Didn't you see him stumble? He's unstable from the draining."

"Don't forget you have the amulet," added Walter. "You will not be fighting him alone. You will have a score of mages funneling you their magic."

Kyler scuffed his shoe against the ground while gripping the amulet. "It was always going to turn out this way, wasn't it?"

Walter nodded. "From the very beginning, it's been you, Kyler. There was no one else who believed enough to face him."

"Kyler, I'm sorry this has landed on your shoulders," said Martha. "It is a horrible thing for a young boy to face, but, Kyler, you are stronger than you know. I've been training you since you were a baby, and your power is vast. You know all that you need to know. Never has a mage been trained so young in the mages tongue as you were. You are stronger than your own father was at your age. I'd help if I could, but my powers are so low, all of our powers are low."

"I understand." Resigned to his fate, Kyler leaned forward and hugged his aunt. "I love you, Aunt Martha."

"And I you," she said.

Kyler turned to Darcy. "If this all goes downhill, I just want you to know that you are the most amazing girl I've ever met. You're strong and beautiful, and you have a heart of gold." He reached out and pulled her into his arms. Darcy clung to Kyler, sobbing.

When they broke apart, he noticed others had lined up for good-byes, including his father and Henry. "Don't forget to relieve Donald," he reminded Henry. Kyler's friend patted him on the back and then grabbed him by the head and rubbed a knuckle into his scalp. With a yelp, Kyler pulled away.

"Something to remember me by," said Henry. "If you want revenge, you'll have to live." A small grin lifted the corners of Kyler's lips.

His father stood before him next. "Be careful, my son. I don't want to lose you after finally finding you." Before turning to face the battle, Kyler looked at Walter. "Any advice?"

"Actually, yes. Get him to agree to your conditions. Tell him that the prisoners are to go free, no matter the winner."

Kyler nodded and then turned his back on his stalwart supporters and went to face Mordrake.

"Your decision?" asked Mordrake.

"I have a condition first," yelled Kyler. "If I agree to this duel, I want you to promise that the prisoners will go free."

Mordrake placed his hands on his hips and studied Kyler before speaking. "What you ask is impossible. They are my key to escaping this hellhole. The best I can offer you is that your friends involved in the rescue will be allowed to live."

Kyler knew the deal had been a long shot. His only real option was to defeat Mordrake and free both his friends and the prisoners. "I agree."

"Good! This will be the most fun I've had in ages," bellowed Mordrake. "In fact, I will let you have the first go."

Kyler stepped back, trying to prepare himself. His breath was coming in fast gasps, and his heart was rampaging like a runaway train. He rubbed his hand up and down his staff, hoping to calm his mind. When all was ready, he sent out the first volley, a blast of air.

Unfortunately, Mordrake had only to wave his hand to send the air off in a different direction, and then it was his turn. A bolt of lightning flew at Kyler so fast that he only had time to jump sideways. The bolt singed his shirt and left a burn mark on his arm. Stumbling to his feet, Kyler rubbed his arm, the burn throbbing like it had a pulse.

Next, Kyler sent a bolt of his own lightning, but he was slow and Mordrake had only to step aside.

A fireball flew at Kyler's head. This time he deflected the fire with his staff and threw it toward the dome. He was beginning to realize this duel was about endurance just as much as it was about power. Cleverness would win the battle, and Kyler had only seconds to think.

He reached deep down into his soul and remembered all the things his aunt Martha had taught him, all the words he knew by heart. If he could only let his instincts out, then his fear would take a backseat. The amulet burned on his chest, and Kyler knew that all he needed to do was act. He narrowed his eyes and looked at Mordrake. With the breath of a word, he sent a stone zinging at the monster king's head.

Mordrake deflected the stone, but Kyler was ready. As soon as Mordrake sent off his next attack, Kyler deflected it and immediately sent back an arrow of frozen air. From then on Kyler didn't think. He reacted quickly and precisely. The power of the amulet kept him from tiring, and shot after shot was sent. Soon the battle flashed between the two contenders with amazing speed.

Kyler would not back down, but neither would Mordrake. Their battle raged on for hours. Eventually the combatants were spending longer periods of time recovering between each attack, and Kyler knew that Mordrake was struggling. The power flowing into Kyler was less, but he still hadn't tapped into his own resources.

From the sidelines, Kyler could hear his friends cheering him on, but he pushed their voices to the back of his mind. His sole focus was on Mordrake. They continued their battle, each staggering around within the circle of stones between attacks. Mordrake threw out a bolt of energy, but this time instead of deflecting the energy, Kyler sent his own bolt to impede the other. Power flowed between the two, pushing first one way and then the other. Kyler continued blasting Mordrake while advancing. Soon, he was within six feet of the man. With a scream, he threw everything he had into a stream of energy.

His beam punched through Mordrake's defenses and nailed him in the chest. Kyler didn't hesitate. It was his turn to attack. He rushed forward, jabbing with his staff. He rained blows down on his enemy one after the other. Mordrake turned the tables by tackling Kyler at the waist and sending him into the air. They rolled on the ground, bashing each other with hands and feet.

Kyler realized his mistake too late. He was no match in strength for Mordrake. The man was squeezing Kyler's ribs tightly enough to break them. They rolled over one more time, and Kyler felt the world drop out from under him.

DARCY

"Kyler!" Darcy screamed. Horror filled her stomach as she watched Kyler and Mordrake both tumble over the edges of the pit at the side of the circle. She ran, blowing past Henry and falling to her knees by the rim.

"Kyler! Kyler, can you hear me?" she yelled.

Walter ran up behind her and sniffed the air. "It's the pit where Mordrake was held prisoner. Who knows how deep it goes? Even with my eyesight I cannot see the bottom."

Darcy continued leaning over the side, screaming Kyler's name.

Henry arrived and grabbed Darcy from behind. "Be careful, or you'll go in, too."

"What do we do?" sobbed Darcy.

"We wait," said Walter. "Henry, head back to Mordrake's tent and see if you can find some rope. Maybe we can lower someone down."

As Henry sprinted away, Darcy looked up at the sky, surprised to see the rosy pink of dawn glistening around the clouds. She looked over at the dome, wondering about the Orcs outside. They no longer faced the battle, but were fanned out among their campsites.

"Walter, something is going on out in the camp," said Darcy.

Walter turned to look. He then loped over to the edge of the dome to peer through the barrier. When he returned to Darcy, she could see that his weary eyes were now bright and shiny.

"They're gathering for battle," said Walter.

"What? Are they going to attack the dome after all this time? They must know it's pointless," said Darcy.

"I don't think that's the plan. They are gathering together for a serious onslaught. I think maybe the king's army has arrived."

"Yes!" shouted Darcy. "Finally."

Henry returned with a small coil of rope. "I don't think it is nearly long enough to reach down into the pit. Maybe if we tie all the ropes together that were used to bind the mages, but even then, we don't know if it'll reach. Plus, it would take a while."

"Darn!" said Darcy.

"Kyler's just going to have to fend for himself for a bit," said Walter. "We'll set some of the mages to tying the ropes, but the rest of us have something else to do."

"More important than rescuing Kyler?" asked Darcy.

"Darcy," said Walter. "We are doing everything we can, but right now we need to get outside the dome and find out what's happening."

"Is that possible?" Darcy asked Henry.

"I honestly don't have a clue," he said. "I'm a newbie here. Let's ask the mages."

Within Mordrake's pavilion, the remaining mages were resting, except for Donald, who was again taking a turn powering the dome. They sprawled out on clumps of pillows and fuzzy carpets, all relaxing for the first time in ages. Martha noticed Darcy and the other's return first.

"Did you find Kyler?" she asked.

"No, there's no response from down in the pit. We need some of you guys to start tying ropes together. It's our only shot of getting down to help him," said Darcy.

Martha nodded and then nudged a couple of the mages reclining nearest to her. "I'll get them started."

"There's something else," added Walter. "Mordrake's army is on the move. We think that the king's army has reached the outskirts of the camp. If we're lucky, they are already engaged."

"We need to get outside the dome and check on things," said Darcy.

"That might be possible, but I don't think we should remove the dome completely," said Martha. "We need to keep it up over the pit and the pavilion. Most of my fellow mages are not in fighting shape."

"Is it possible?" asked Henry. "I've only ever put one up or down."

"Hmm," said Martha. "I think that if you and Donald work together you can shrink the size of the dome down and allow a few people out."

The other mages were now fully aware of the conversation. Several offered up ideas, but nothing seemed as easy as just shrinking the dome.

"So who is going outside the dome?" asked Kyler's dad.

"I am," said Darcy. "Walter, too."

"Don't forget me," said Sergeant Borris.

"I'm coming, too," said Martha. "I've still got a little power up my sleeve."

"Great, then let's begin," said Darcy.

It took them a mere ten minutes to put their plan into action. Once outside the dome, Darcy led the others to a nearby tent to hide. Most of the enemy had left the area, and only a few stragglers remained.

"I think some guerrilla tactics are called for," said Darcy.

"You want to hit them from behind?" asked the soldier. "There're only four of us."

"Let's find out what's happening first," said Walter. "Then we can make a decision."

Information was easy to gather. One of the remaining Orcs walked right into their hiding place. Darcy leveled her sword at it while the sergeant took out the beast's knees.

The Orc snarled and spit, but with the four of them surrounding it, there was nothing it could do.

"What's going on?" asked Darcy.

"King's army is here," the Orc growled.

"Perfect," said Darcy. She hit the Orc over the head with the hilt of her sword and then watched as it sank to the ground. "Let's tie it up and then create some havoc."

None of them could pass for Orcs or Torics, so they carefully advanced on the enemy. From far back, Martha would trip up fighters with her magic and send others into chaos. Darcy, Walter, and the soldier took out individual fighters, hunting like ghosts in the night. It wasn't enough to defeat an army, but it was enough to cause trouble in the ranks.

KYLER

Why is it so dark? was the first thought that Kyler's fuzzy brain registered. Then it quit working as wave upon wave of pain broke over his form. He could not move, not even to turn his head. Everything in every place hurt. Looking up he could see a sliver of dim daylight, but that was all. He took several deep breaths, hoping to ease his suffering. The air smelled damp, yet musty, and everything was dead silent.

It was then that his memory returned. Flashes of his battle with Mordrake sparked to life, and he remembered the horrible plunge into darkness. Where was Mordrake?

Kyler went about taking stock of his body. As time passed, he was able to control his muscle movements, but the pain tearing up his left leg almost made him pass out. Slowly he sat up in the darkness, reaching for his injured leg. His fingers felt a wet slickness and then a sharp bony extrusion. He needed light.

With a hushed word and thought, he called his staff to him, hoping it did not lie broken in some corner of the hole.

He felt the reassuring thunk as it flew into his fingers, and tears rolled from his eyes. He was alone, injured, scared, and surrounded by darkness. His sobs grew, and grew, until they shook his entire body.

He needed to take control. He sent his thoughts into his staff, and lights appeared in the air around him, illuminating a small area. It was enough to see the bone sticking out of his leg, and the blood oozing from the ripped flesh, and enough to see the pool of vomit that he then sprayed out next to himself.

He managed to remove his shirt, and gently wrapped it around his leg. It wasn't a good splint, but at least he couldn't see his bright white bone shining through his own blood anymore.

Using his staff for leverage, he pulled himself into a sitting position and backed up against the rock wall. He needed to know where he was, so he sent the lights out in several directions.

Close by was a stone container, roughly human-size. A lid lay beside it, cracked and askew. To its left was a pile of old and discolored hay. It reminded Kyler of a giant bird's nest. It was then that it hit him. He was deep inside the pit where Mordrake and the Griffin had slept for a thousand years. Shaking his head in wonder, he scanned the rest of the cave.

Several yards away he could see Mordrake's body, sprawled over a stone. From the way he had landed, it looked as if his back was bent in two, his head looking up toward the distant sky. *Is he dead?*

Kyler needed to know for sure. Despite the agony of movement, he struggled to stand. He used his staff as a crutch and limped over toward the monster king. When he drew close, he could hear Mordrake's ragged breathing. Then a gust of air whipped Kyler around and threw him back down.

"I may not be able to move, but I can still kill you," hissed Mordrake.

Sprawled on the rocky ground, Kyler struggled to breathe. The landing had jarred his broken leg, and now spikes of pain were shooting up his spine. Moaning, he tried to roll over and scoot away, but he found himself against the rock wall.

Before him, Mordrake's body began to rise into the air, like a broken doll held by a child. Fear blossomed again in Kyler's chest, and his breathing picked up like a steam engine.

"What? Did you think a little fall would kill me?" laughed Mordrake.

Kyler shrank away from the grotesque figure floating before him, its head lolling to one side and its back clearly broken. Its arms and legs hung limply, unable to move, but it was Mordrake's eyes that pinned Kyler into place. The darkness, the evil that swirled within them was a deep void.

This was the endgame. Kyler knew that only one of them would leave the pit. He leveled his staff and gathered his powers. He reached down to hold on to the amulet, but found a broken piece of jewelry instead. He would have no outside help. It was all up to him. His anger built, replacing his fear. With a scream, he let a bolt of lightning free. It arced across the space between them, striking Mordrake square in the chest. Kyler didn't let up his attack. This was no longer a duel, and he sent bolt after bolt into his enemy.

Mordrake roared back in fury, and Kyler braced himself. Suddenly the pressure in the chamber grew, and Kyler felt as if his head might explode. The feeling of being squeezed like an orange would not let up, and soon Kyler's chest buckled inward.

With the last of his strength, he threw his staff like a javelin toward Mordrake. Things grew black, but Kyler watched as his staff began to glow and then pierced Mordrake's chest, impaling his heart. The pressure stopped instantly. Kyler lay on the ground, sucking in the air and holding his ribs together. Mordrake's body shuddered, and he crumpled to the ground in a lifeless pile.

DARCY

On the battlefield, Darcy wove back and forth between tents, taking down one enemy at a time. It had begun to feel like a game of cat and mouse. Then the strangest thing happened. Before her eyes, the enemy, all of them, from the Imps to the Orcs, stopped moving and looked around at one another.

The Imps were the first to move. They simply stepped out of the battle and headed west, forming into small groups as they walked. The Torics were the next to react. They let out cries of fury, but instead of reengaging, they rushed toward one another, hugging and slapping one another on the back.

Darcy watched all this in wonder. Then it dawned on her. Mordrake's hold had been broken! That meant Kyler had won! He'd done it! She turned to run back toward the ring of stones, but was stopped by an Orc. Anger filled the Orc's eyes and it screamed, raising its war hammer above its head.

With little time to react, Darcy brought her sword slicing through the air, eviscerating the Orc's bowels. He dropped where he stood. She looked around more closely. The battleground was in disarray. The Torics were talking among themselves, but many of the Orcs were still fighting, attacking the king's men.

Darcy sprinted forward, encountering Henry and Martha as she headed back toward the stone circle.

"He did it," shouted Martha.

"I knew he could," yelled Walter.

They passed the sergeant on the ground, a sword still in his hand. They slowed, and he looked up at them with blood-shot eyes. "I'm okay. Send someone back when you can."

Darcy nodded and then picked up her pace. They made it to the dome but could not break through. It was pointless to bang on the shield, but they tried anyway.

"They don't know what's happened?" shouted Darcy.

Just then a figure came running at them from inside the dome. Darcy could make out Henry's form as he turned around and began waving his hands to alert the people in the pavilion. The shield fell as silently as it had gone up. Darcy rushed over and grabbed Henry in a tight hug.

"What happened?" asked Henry. "What's going on out here?"

"He did it," cried Darcy. "Mordrake's power isn't controlling people anymore."

"Did you finish the rope?" asked Walter.

"Yes, some of the mages were heading over to the pit. Let's go," said Henry.

They ran, out of breath, but filled with hope. Darcy watched as two mages pushed the rope over the edge of the pit and began lowering it. She held her breath as she waited, but there was no movement of the rope. Her group moved closer, right to the edge.

"Someone needs to go down there," said Martha.

"I will," said Darcy.

"No," said Henry. "You've been out there fighting. I've still got all my strength. I'll go get him."

He was right, and Darcy knew it, but still she wanted to get to Kyler as fast as possible. She bit her lip as Henry swung himself over the edge and began climbing down. The mages held on to the rope, looping it around their waists to hold Henry's weight.

They waited, and Darcy paced. Then a distance voice floated up through the cracked ground. "I found him. He's alive."

Cheers went up around her, but Darcy couldn't speak.

"I'm going to need more than a rope to get him up there. Someone make a stretcher."

Darcy didn't need to be asked twice, and she headed straight to the pavilion for supplies.

When they finally pulled Kyler to the surface, she took in his pale face and bloody clothes. He looked like death, but she didn't care, and ran to his side and grabbed his hand in hers. "You made it."

He smiled up at her. "Was there ever any doubt?"

Darcy began to laugh, and then everyone in the group did. Their laughter rang out into the air like happy music. Then they heard a scream. Over at the pavilion, Orcs were attacking. The mages were weak but able to shot off a few energy bolts. Darcy and Walter took off running while Henry and Martha stayed at Kyler's side.

KYLER

From where he lay, Kyler had a perfect view of the fight. Darcy and Walter leapt into the fight with gusto, their earlier weariness traded for a second burst of energy.

Martha leaned into his view. "I'm going to try to stitch your leg bone back together."

Kyler nodded and squeezed her hand. He watched as she removed his bloody wrapping and exposed his wound. Henry turned away with a gulp.

"This is going to hurt," said Martha.

Kyler was about to speak when Martha reached down and snapped the bone back into place. The scream that tore through his body was louder than the noise from the battle waging just a short ways off. Then Martha began mumbling, and Kyler's leg began to burn as if she had lit his skin on fire. His shrieking filled the air, and Henry reached down to hold Kyler in place. When Martha finally sat back, Kyler stopped flailing and then sank into Henry.

Darcy ran up to Kyler's side, her face covered in blood. He hoped it was from an Orc and not her own.

"Kyler! Are you okay?" she panted.

"He's fine," said Martha.

"Well all right then, 'cause we have work to do," said Darcy.

"What's happening?" squeaked Kyler.

"It's the Orcs," said Darcy. "When you killed Mordrake, the Imps and Torics stopped fighting, but the Orcs are still at it. Right now they're engaged with the king's army, but a few are returning, and we're an open target."

"Get me up," said Kyler. "I know what to do." Resting on Henry and Martha, he looked around within the circle. "Where's my bag? I dropped it somewhere?"

Understanding dawned in Darcy's eyes. "Everyone spread out and find that bag!"

The hunt was quick, and soon Kyler held his satchel. He flipped the pouch open and pulled out the Orc relic. "Get me to the fighting!" he demanded.

With the help of the mages, they carried Kyler on their shoulders, like a hero returning from war. Kyler held the heart of the kings high in the air, capturing the attention of every Orc they passed. Soon a large Orc following trailed behind Kyler's small group. Then they were into the king's territory. All fighting stopped as the Orcs turned to Kyler, and the king's soldiers followed their gazes.

"Hear me now!" shouted Kyler.

"Let me help," said Martha. She pointed at Kyler's mouth and spoke a few words.

"Hear me now!" This time Kyler's voice spread across the battlefield like a wave of water. Fighting in the farthest corners ceased.

"This battle is over. There will be no more bloodshed," yelled Kyler.

Across the battlefield, the king's soldiers shook their heads at the audacity of the young mage—but the Orcs weren't laughing.

Before Kyler, a path opened up, and the king rode in astride a monstrous war stallion. His personal guards circled around him, alert for danger. He approached Kyler, his eyes dancing at the sight of his niece Darcy.

"Young Kyler," said the king, "it does my heart good to see thee well."

"And I you," said Kyler. "This battle needs to stop."

"It looks as if you have a plan," suggested the king.

"I do. Will you trust me?"

The king looked at Kyler, taking in his haggard appearance and bloodstained clothes. Then he nodded.

Kyler continued, his voice echoing over the battlefield. "I propose a new treaty with the Orcs. One to be worked out between the king and the Orc leaders. In return, and as an act of good faith, I will return this relic to where it rightfully belongs."

The Orcs bowed their heads. "Lay down your weapons and then return north. In six weeks' time, send a delegation to the king's castle, where a treaty will be drawn up and the artifact returned. There will no longer be fighting between us."

First one, and then another, and then entire groups of Orcs laid down their weapons and retreated back to camp. Kyler watched as they gathered their supplies and treated their wounded.

"Do you think it is wise to return the relic to the Orcs?" questioned Darcy. "Shouldn't we keep it to control them?"

"I don't think it is anyone's right to control another," said Kyler. "We should not hold that power."

The king nodded his head. "You are wise for one of your years. A new treaty will be made."

Kyler was set down onto the ground and refused to move. Everyone would just have to walk around him. "Can someone bring me some water?" he called.

"And by someone do you mean me?" asked Darcy.

Kyler winked at her. "I would never ask a princess to bring me a glass of water."

Darcy bopped him on the head. "Maybe just this once."

And so the battle ended. The Orcs headed north with the king's soldiers watching them warily, ready to jump once more into battle. However, the Orcs never wavered in their path.

Kyler's dad found him sitting on the ground and plopped down beside him. "I think it's about time I got to know my son. He's not the same child I left."

"No, I'm not, but I sure wouldn't mind my old bed."

As the king's army arranged for their departure, father and son were finally free to share their joys and sorrows.

Thank You
To my family. I love you.
To ANWA and the SCBWI for your great support.
To Skyrocket Press.

ABOUT THE AUTHOR

Dorine White graduated from Brigham Young University, Utah, with a BA in humanities and art history. She began writing at a young age, producing books for her family. Today she spends her time writing children's books, mostly fantasy. Currently, she lives in the beautiful yet rainy Northwest with her husband, Trevor, and six children. You can find her online at www.dorinewhite.com.

Made in the USA
Charleston, SC
06 December 2014